SNAKE BITE

SNAKE BITE

ANDREW LANE

MACMILLAN CHILDREN'S BOOKS

First published 2012 by Macmillan Children's Books
a division of Macmillan Publishers Limited
20 New Wharf Road, London N1 9RR
Basingstoke and Oxford
Associated companies throughout the world
www.panmacmillan.com

ISBN 978-0-230-75886-5 (HB)
ISBN 978-0-230-76300-5 (TPB)

1 3 5 7 9 8 6 4 2

A CIP catalogue record for this book is available from
the British Library.

Printed and bound by CPI Group (UK) Ltd, Croydon CR0 4YY

Dedicated to Mike Elliott, Keith Garland, Derek Rothwell, Angus Martin, Lynn Martinez (or Lynn Furby, as she was then), Paula Fountain and (most especially) Sonia Morrish – the people who helped me survive the years 1982 to 1985 with some modicum of sanity. Thanks for being there.

Dedicated also to Steven Moffat, Mark Gatiss and Guy Ritchie, for keeping the legend alive on the big and small screens.

And with grateful acknowledgements to the skill and diplomacy of Sally Oliphant, who has worked above and beyond the call of duty to keep me sane and focused through bad times, and Polly Nolan, who managed to cut 12,000 words out of my first draft (including several hundred needless uses of the word 'just') and improved it immeasurably.

PROLOGUE

The corridors and rooms of the Diogenes Club are, perhaps, the quietest places in the whole of London. Nobody who enters is allowed to speak – except within the Strangers' Room, and only then when the door is firmly closed. The staff who work there – the footmen and the waiters – have padded cloth attached to the soles of their shoes so that they can move silently, and the newspapers which the club members read are printed specially for the Diogenes on a paper that does not rustle when it is folded. Any member who clears his throat or blows his nose more than three times in a month is given a written warning. Three written warnings lead to expulsion from the club.

The members of the Diogenes Club value their silence.

When Amyus Crowe pushed past the footman in the lobby and strode through the club's maze of corridors and reading rooms to where Mycroft Holmes waited for him, he didn't say a word, but there was something about him that made everyone look up in disapproval, and then look away suddenly when he met their gaze. Although he was silent, although his clothes barely whispered as he moved, although the leather soles of his boots made little more than a scuffing noise against the floor tiles, he appeared to radiate an energy that crackled fiercely and loudly. He seemed to be broadcasting audible fury from every pore in his body.

He slammed the door of the Strangers' Room behind him so hard that even the special pneumatic hinges failed to stop the *bang!*

'What have you heard?' he demanded.

Mycroft Holmes was standing to one side of the main table. He winced.

'My agents have confirmed that Sherlock was kidnapped in Farnham and transported in a drugged state to London. There he was loaded on to a ship named the *Gloria Scott*.'

'An' what you are doin' about rescuing your brother and my student?'

'I am doing all I can,' Mycroft said. 'Which is not very much, I am afraid. The ship has sailed for China. I am attempting to track down a manifest so that I can anticipate when and where the ship will dock for supplies along the way, but that is proving problematic. The ship's voyages are organized at the behest of its captain, who is notoriously eccentric, according to my agents. His starting and finishing points are fixed – London and Shanghai – but he might stop anywhere in between.'

'An' –' Crowe paused – 'and you are sure that Sherlock is *alive*?'

'Why drug and kidnap him if the intention is to kill him? Why go to the trouble of transporting him to a ship when he could just be buried in the woods somewhere? No, logic tells me that he *is* still alive.'

'Then what is the point of taking him?'

Mycroft paused for a moment. His face grew, if anything, more serious. 'The answer to that question depends on who it was that took him.'

'Ah think we both know the answer to that,' Crowe growled.

Mycroft nodded. 'Reluctant as I am to come to conclusions in the absence of evidence, I cannot think of any other possibility. The Paradol Chamber have him.'

'There is some evidence,' Crowe pointed out. 'On his way up to Edinburgh he swore he saw that man Kyte, who turned out to be an agent of the Paradol Chamber, on a station platform at Newcastle. He mentioned it to Rufus Stone, an' Stone mentioned it to me. We both suspected that the Paradol Chamber were keeping an eye on him, but we didn't think they'd actually take any *action*.'

Mycroft nodded again. 'And that explains your anger, which is not directed at me but at yourself. You are angry

3

that you did not anticipate the danger that Sherlock was in.'

Crowe glanced away from Mycroft, his eyes glaring from beneath bushy white eyebrows. 'You said that if we knew who'd taken him then we'd know why he was taken. So – we know it's the Paradol Chamber. What do they *want*?'

'The Paradol Chamber are – forgive me, would you care for a small dry sherry? No? Well, you don't mind if I help myself then? Yes, as you already know, the Paradol Chamber are a group of politically motivated agitators who wish to change governments in order to achieve their own ends, which I presume are to make a great deal of money from dealing in stocks and shares and from armament sales, among other things. I have heard them described as being like a small nation without boundaries, territory or a capital city, which seems as good a description as any. In my limited experience they rarely have one reason for doing anything. Any action of theirs is predicated on that action helping them to progress on a series of fronts. If I were to venture a guess . . .' He broke off, and shook his large head. 'A pastime I find most abhorrent, by the way. But yes, if I were to venture a guess, then I would suggest that their reasons for abducting Sherlock are, firstly to punish him for his involvement in stopping several of their plots,

4

secondly to prevent him from stopping any *more* of their plots, and thirdly to throw you and me into a state of confusion which would hamper our efforts to find out what their other plots actually *are*.'

'But they didn't kill him,' Crowe pointed out. 'Why not?'

'Killing Sherlock would have punished him for a few seconds, after which he would not care one way or the other what they did. Being stuck on a ship, separated from his friends, his family and any possibility of a decent meal – no, that kind of torture lasts for a long while, at no cost to them. And rather than hampering our efforts in discovering their plots, they must know enough about you and me to know that if Sherlock were to die then we would spend every waking moment and every guinea we could lay our hands on in tracking them down and bringing them to justice.'

'Or metin' out some justice of our own,' Crowe rumbled. 'The kind of justice that comes out of the barrel of a gun.'

'For once,' Mycroft conceded quietly, 'I might just agree with you on that one.'

'Can't you send a Royal Navy ship to intercept this *Gloria Scott*?'

Mycroft shook his head. 'I do not have the authority to dispatch a vessel for one boy, even if that boy is my

5

brother. Even if I did, I would not. Those ships have more important duties, guarding our coasts against attack and enforcing the will of the Queen abroad. Against that, the life of one child weighs as nothing.' He sighed, and clenched a fist helplessly. 'All of this discussion leaves us better informed but no better off. We cannot *help* Sherlock. He is on his own.'

'Sherlock on his own has better resources at his disposal than most people surrounded by friends and family.' Crowe's tone was calmer now, and the fierce energy that had appeared to radiate from his body had abated somewhat. 'He's brave, he's strong and he knows his own mind. Oh, and he's handy with his fists as well. Ah think he'll work out that he's got to make the best of it. He knows that the ship is comin' back to London, eventually, an' that gives him a guarantee of returnin' that he doesn't get if he tries to jump ship in mid-voyage and find a ship comin' in the opposite direction. The Captain will be short-handed, because captains always are, and so he'll set the youngster to work. It'll be hard work, but he'll come through it. An' he'll probably come through it stronger an' more self-reliant as well.'

'Hardly the kind of torture that the Paradol Chamber were thinking of,' Mycroft pointed out drily.

Crowe smiled. 'The people in charge of the Paradol Chamber, as far as ah can tell, live comfortable lives with

6

servants tendin' to their every whim. For them, splicin' a mainbrace or haulin' anchor *would* be torture. For young Sherlock it'll be an adventure – if he chooses to make it so.'

'I hope so. I really do hope so.'

'Ah think ah'll take advantage of that sherry now,' Crowe said. 'God knows ah can't see the appeal of it mahself, but ah do feel in the need of some strong liquor.'

Mycroft busied himself with pouring a glass for Crowe from the decanter on the sideboard.

'I will write letters,' he said as he handed the glass across. It was almost lost in Crowe's enormous and weather-beaten hand. 'They can be transmitted by telegraph to various ports along his route. I can ensure that diplomatic staffs are on the lookout for the *Gloria Scott*. They can pass on our messages and report on how he is. He can write to us. There will be ships at every port he stops at which are heading to England. They can bring letters back.'

'He'll only be gone for a year or so,' Crowe pointed out. 'Maybe less, wind an' weather permittin'. You'll see him again.'

Mycroft nodded. 'I know. I just . . . I feel so *responsible*. So helpless.' He took a deep breath, steadying himself against some sudden storm of emotion. 'I shall not tell Mother, of course. Her health would not stand it. And

7

I will not write to Father until I have more news – and perhaps not even then. I will send a note to our aunt and uncle in Farnham, telling them that everything is all right. They do worry about him.'

'And ah'll find some way of tellin' Virginia 'bout what's happened,' Crowe said. 'An', frankly, that conversation scares me more than anythin'. She's really taken a fancy to that brother of yours.'

'And he to her,' Mycroft mused. 'Let's hope that the memories they have of each other are enough to keep them going . . .'

CHAPTER ONE

There was a dark line on the horizon. Sherlock could see it as he gazed out across the ocean. Mostly the sky was a clear blue, but there, in the distance, it shaded down to an unhealthy purple darkness, like an old bruise. He would have assumed that it was land, except that it was off to the west of the ship. The only land nearby was to the east – the southernmost tip of Africa.

He wondered if he should tell the First Mate – Mr Larchmont – about it. Mr Larchmont had taken Sherlock under his protection and given him a place on the crew after Sherlock had woken up to find himself on the ship, already sailing away from England. Perhaps he should tell Captain Tollaway himself, but the Captain was a remote figure, rarely seen on deck. Maybe he should just tell one of the other sailors. Sherlock glanced around, but they were all going about their duties unconcerned – as he should be. He was meant to be swabbing down the deck: clearing off the bits of wood and lengths of old rope that had accumulated over the past few days, along with the fine rime of salt that covered everything thanks to the spray from the ocean and the evaporating heat of the sun.

He shook his head and went back to his mopping. He was the least experienced sailor on board. It wasn't his job to bring things to the attention of the others. They didn't like it.

He dipped his mop into his bucket and swabbed a patch of deck where one of the sailors had bled, earlier that morning. The man had caught his little finger in a coil of rope which had been suddenly whipped away by a movement of the sails, taking his finger with it. The ship's doctor – actually one of Mr Larchmont's assistants, who had some knowledge of medicine – cleaned and bound the wound, and the sailor was now resting in his hammock with a double ration of rum to numb the pain. That left a gap in the duty roster which Sherlock knew he would be expected to fill.

For what felt like the thousandth time, he wondered how he had gone from being a boy living in Hampshire to a sailor on a ship bound for China. There was a gap in his memory between suddenly falling asleep back in his uncle's library in Farnham and waking up on the *Gloria Scott*. The best explanation he could come up with was that he had been drugged, abducted and left on the ship before it sailed, but who would do that to him, and why?

The only answer he could come up with was the criminal organization that called itself the Paradol

Chamber. He had crossed them too many times. Maybe this was their revenge?

For a while Sherlock had planned to jump ship at the first opportunity and try to find his way back home, but logic eventually overcame homesickness. The *Gloria Scott* was a known quantity – he was friendly with the crew, he had a hammock and food, and he knew that the ship would be returning to England eventually. If he were to abandon the ship whenever it docked for supplies he would be alone, in a foreign country. He could fall prey to any number of criminals, and there was no guarantee that any ship he could find heading home would be as comfortable as the *Gloria Scott* – and the *Gloria Scott* was far from comfortable.

Sighing, he pushed the detritus of the deck over to the side. There were gaps in the railing there through which he could push it off and watch it fall towards the water. The sea birds – albatrosses and seagulls – which followed the ship swooped to investigate, in case there was food among the wood and the rope strands. Far below, the detritus hit the water with a splash of white spray.

Sherlock raised his gaze towards the horizon again, to check out that dark line, but his eyes were caught by a movement beneath the water. As he watched, a glistening grey shape broke the surface. It was a fish, but one that seemed to be bigger than he was – as big as his

11

tutor, Amyus Crowe. He gasped in surprise as another five – no, ten or more shapes broke the surface after their leader. They had long, beaky snouts, and flat tails, and their eyes were large and dark.

'Checkin' out the girlies?' someone called from behind him.

Sherlock turned his head and shouted back, 'One of them says she's your wife! She says you promised to send her half your wages, but you never did. She's come to collect!'

There was laughter from the sailors on deck. Sherlock had quickly found that they were always probing each other with personal jokes. It reminded him of dogs – always snapping at each other and play-biting to establish who was in charge. You could either take offence, in which case the jokes would get harsher and more pointed, or you could join in, and in doing so elevate your position. Sherlock had been taking the second option ever since he had joined the crew, and it seemed to be working. They accepted him, and he wasn't at the bottom of the pecking order. He was a long way from the top, but at least he was treated as one of them, not as an outsider.

One of the crew – Jackson, his name was – stood close to Sherlock. He indicated the things in the water with a twist of his thumb. 'Never seen their like before, I warrant.'

'That's true,' Sherlock admitted. 'What are they? Can we eat them?'

Jackson crossed himself. 'They're called porpoises,' he said, 'and it's bad luck to kill one, let alone eat it. They keep the ship company. Some say that if a sailor falls overboard, then the porpoises will circle around and keep him afloat, and fight off any sharks that try to get to him.'

'Sharks?' Sherlock asked.

'The wolves of the sea,' Jackson said. 'Teeth like a band saw. Take your arm off just by brushing their mouths against it.'

'Right. I'll try not to fall in then. Or, if I do, I'll try and do it when there are some porpoises around.' He took the opportunity to nod towards the horizon. 'What's that?' he asked. 'The colour looks . . . strange.'

Jackson lifted his gaze to the horizon, and frowned. 'You've got good eyesight,' he admitted. 'That looks to me like a tropical storm. Mr Larchmont will want to know about it. You want to go and tell him?'

Sherlock shook his head. 'You do it,' he said. He knew that Mr Larchmont kept a mental list of all the sailors, with a little mark against their name to denote how well or how badly he thought of them. Those marks slid up or down depending on whether the sailors were working hard or not, how observant they seemed, how

13

deferential to him and to the Captain they were and how many fights they got into on board the ship. By being the first sailor to draw Mr Larchmont's attention to the storm, Sherlock could get some additional points – if it *was* a storm. But by passing the opportunity to Jackson, Sherlock could make the sailor into more of a friend, and that might prove useful in the future.

'Thanks,' Jackson said, eyeing Sherlock curiously. 'I'll not forget that.'

He turned away and headed towards the raised section at the back of the ship where the wheelhouse was located, and where Mr Larchmont could usually be found.

Sherlock glanced at the horizon again. The dark line was now more pronounced. It stretched as far above the horizon as a couple of fingers held at arm's length, and its edges seemed to be stretching out to either side, like arms seeking to encircle the ship. There was something about the unnatural purple colour of the storm that made him feel sick in the pit of his stomach. He could feel a warm breeze on his face, blowing from the direction of the storm. He noticed that the deck was pitching beneath his feet more heavily than it had been even a few moments before. When he looked at the grey-green mass of the sea he could see that the waves were getting higher, and the white spume on their tops was blowing off like the froth from a pint of beer and floating above the water.

'Ahoy! All hands on deck!' a gruff voice called. Sherlock turned to see Mr Larchmont standing on the raised area to the rear of the ship. Jackson was standing beside him. 'Raise as many sails as possible, and tighten all the ropes,' Larchmont shouted, his voice carrying clearly all the way from one end of the *Gloria Scott* to the other. 'There's a storm coming, boys! There's the mother of all storms coming, and we're going to try to outrun it.' He grabbed Jackson by the shoulder. 'Go and notify the Captain,' he said, more quietly. Sherlock could tell the words from the shapes his mouth made. 'Tell him what's happening.'

'Aye aye, sir,' Jackson responded, and turned away.

The deck of the ship was suddenly a seething mass of activity as sailors ran or climbed in all directions. Larchmont's gaze fell upon Sherlock, who was standing still in the midst of the chaos. 'Avast, young stowaway! Get up that rigging and check the foremast sail ropes for tightness or I'll leave you behind in a rowing boat to face the storm yourself!'

'Aye aye, sir!' Sherlock raced for the nearest web of rigging. It led like a spider's web of rope up towards the stacked sails. The rope was rough against his skin, and he felt his newly developed muscles straining as he pulled himself upward. The ship pitched and tossed as the rough

15

waves pushed against it: for a moment, as it leaned over, Sherlock looked down and saw the sea directly beneath him. The waves almost seemed to be reaching up for him – hundreds of white hands clawing their way up from the water. He shook off the image and kept climbing.

He got to the bottom-most sail and scrambled along the yard, fingers clenching against the rough wood, checking in turn each of the ropes that tied the top of the sail to the yard. They were all tight – no chance of them giving way in the storm unless it was particularly bad. He kept a firm grip on the ropes to prevent himself from falling, and kept an eye out for splinters on the wooden yard. He'd seen what happened to sailors when they got a splinter embedded in their skin: the wound could get infected and swell to twice its usual size, and then it was touch and go whether the injured area would have to be removed. There were a thousand and one ways to get badly hurt on a ship. For once, Sherlock could see Mycroft's point – the safest way to live your life was just to stay at home all the time. But if you did that, you missed out on all the adventure. He smiled to himself. Maybe the best thing to do was to make friends with a doctor – that way you would always have treatment close at hand.

Distracted by his thoughts, his hand slipped on a patch of algae that had somehow gained purchase on a length of rope and he found himself falling. He clenched his legs tight on the yard but the weight of his body dragged him around until he was hanging upside down. The wet canvas of the sail kept slapping against his face as the wind caught it. He couldn't get his bearings. Which way was up? He arched his back and reached out to where he thought the yard was, but his clutching hands kept grabbing at air.

He could feel his legs slipping. Any second now he was going to plummet all the way to the deck – head downward.

His right hand caught hold of something warm. He grabbed frantically at it, and felt himself being pulled upright. His left hand clutched at a rope and he heaved at it desperately. Suddenly he was the right way up again. He glanced over to the face of the person who had saved him. It was a young sailor named Gittens. He stared down at Sherlock from where he crouched clutching on to the mast with his left arm.

'Thanks,' Sherlock gasped.

'Landlubber!' Abruptly he let go of Sherlock's hand and clambered up the mast to the next sail without looking back.

Sherlock manoeuvred himself to the mast and pulled himself upright using a trailing rope. It was like holding on to the top of a tree trunk in the middle of an earthquake. The mast whipped back and forth as the ship was tossed around on the waves. He took a moment to look out towards the distant horizon, and then wished he hadn't. The storm now took up a full quarter of the sky. It was gaining on them.

The other sailors were getting on with their duties, and Sherlock knew that he should be getting on with his. Despite the pounding of his heart, and the terror that he could feel trickling like ice along his nerves, he scrambled past the mast and out along the other side of the yard to checked the ropes there. They were all sound. By the time he got back to the mainmast he was soaked with a mixture of sea spray and sweat, and his muscles ached as if he had run a marathon. Gratefully, but carefully, he clambered down the web of rigging to the deck.

He had never been so happy to feel something firm beneath his feet as he was at that moment.

Mr Larchmont was standing nearby. 'Rigging secure on the foremast, sir,' Sherlock reported.

'Good work, laddie.' The First Mate turned to stare at him. 'You've the makings of a good sailor. If we get through this storm and make Shanghai in one piece, you can stay on. If you want.'

'I'd like that, sir,' Sherlock replied. If only to get back to England, and my friends, he thought.

Larchmont strode away, berating some poor sailor who had let a length of rope run through his fingers too fast, and was now looking at the bloody palms of his hands in shock. 'Get out of the way, you ham-fisted idiot!' Larchmont shouted. 'Let someone who knows what they're doing have a go!' As he grabbed the end of the rope and pushed the man away Larchmont turned to see what was happening across the deck. 'Batten all the hatches!' he yelled. 'Secure every last thing that moves. Oh, and get those goats and sheep below decks before they become shark-food!'

A creak of wood attracted Sherlock's attention. He glanced upward, towards where the masts were swaying and the sails were flapping. The sails were pushed taut by the wind, and the masts almost seemed to be bending forward under the immense pressure. A broad V-shape of foam swept backwards from the bow of the ship, and Sherlock could hear a hissing sound as the ship cut the waves apart. He glanced up again. The pure blue of the equatorial sky had turned a strange metallic shade. Something was missing, and it took him a moment to work out what it was. Birds. The ever-present seabirds had vanished. Knowing there was a storm coming, they had probably taken their chance to get out of the way, riding the precursor winds to a calmer area. Very sensible too, Sherlock thought.

It seemed suddenly a lot colder on deck, and the light had taken on an ominous shade. Glancing back, towards the ship's stern, Sherlock saw that purple clouds were obscuring half the sky now. A smattering of raindrops splashed across his cheeks and forehead – not cold and needle-like, as he would have expected back in England, but fat and warm. Sherlock braced himself with his arm wound through the rigging and looked around, trying to work out if there was anything he could be doing to help. He saw something that made his heart clench in sudden fear. As the front of the boat was twisting one way, the back of the boat was twisting the other. The whole structure of the ship was *flexing* in the grip of the wind and the waves. For Sherlock, who had been thinking of the ship as something solid, it was a revelation, and not a good one. He suddenly realized how fragile was this little structure of wood and cloth that had become his world.

'Sherlock!' a voice called. 'Sherlock! Over here!'

He glanced towards where the voice was coming from. One of the hatches was still unbattened, and a figure was poking out of it, black hair plastered across his face and eyes. It was Wu Chung, the ship's Chinese cook. He was a big, jolly man with a black ponytail, a long moustache that hung down on either side of his mouth and skin that was pockmarked by some disease. He had become the closest thing to a friend Sherlock had on the *Gloria*

Scott, and he was even patiently teaching Sherlock how to speak Cantonese – the language that was spoken in Shanghai, where they were headed.

Sherlock released his grip on the rigging and staggered over to the hatch, trying to anticipate which way the deck was going to pitch as he did so.

The cook caught his arm to stop him from being blown past. 'Need you in the galley,' he shouted against the roaring of the wind. 'My pots and pans, they are all over place. Need to get them secured.'

'All right!' Sherlock shouted, and followed Wu down the hatchway ladder and into the interior of the ship.

The corridors were a flickering mass of shadows, as the pitching and tossing of the *Gloria Scott* caused the lanterns, which were attached to hooks along the walls, to roll back and forth. The light from the candles inside them made everything look yellow and sick. Without the sight of the horizon to keep his sense of balance intact, Sherlock was beginning to feel the same. The smell down there was the usual combination of unwashed humans and candle tallow. Water sloshed across the decks as the ship moved. Usually it was only in the black depths of the hold that water penetrated, but it seemed to be present everywhere.

Sherlock followed Wu to the galley, which was a narrow room at the end of one of the corridors. The stove had

21

already been doused, Sherlock noted, otherwise sparks might spill out and set fire to something. The copper pans which Wu used were supposed to be hanging from hooks on the ceiling, but most of them had fallen off and were rolling around the floor. The few remaining ones were swinging dangerously. A blow from one of them could knock a man out cold. Cupboards and drawers were built into every available nook and cranny, and as the ship lurched from side to side the doors were swinging open and then shut again, and the drawers were sliding out and back. It was as if a malevolent poltergeist was trying to cause chaos. The sound was deafening.

Wu shoved a hand towards Sherlock. 'Take!' he said. Sherlock raised his cupped hands up, and Wu dropped ten or more thin wooden wedges into them. 'Make drawers and doors fast,' he said. 'Do it now!'

Sherlock got the idea. Quickly, avoiding the obstacle course of swinging pans, he wedged all the cupboard doors and drawers shut by thrusting the wooden triangles into any gap he could see and hammering them home with the heel of his hand. Wu, meanwhile, did his best to get the rest of the pans down without them bashing his brains out and shove them into the biggest cupboard.

All around them, Sherlock could hear the wooden beams of the ship creaking, thanks to the stress under which they were being put. Once, in London, he had seen a wooden cart come apart as it tried to take a corner too fast, toppled over and hit the ground. Now here he was, inside a glorified wooden box held together with nothing but nails and tar, too far from the coast to swim for safety if the ship came apart.

Was this what the Paradol Chamber had in mind for him? Was this their punishment?

When all the drawers and doors were secured, he turned to Wu. The creaking and groaning of the ship's beams were too great for him to make himself understood, so he gestured around and raised his shoulders in a shrug as he yelled, 'I want to be on deck!' Actually, he didn't – he just didn't want to be trapped inside the ship if the storm capsized them, but Wu wasn't a sailor. Wu nodded. His pox-scarred, moon-shaped face was serious. He half pushed Sherlock towards the door, steering him left, away from the hatch that led up to the deck. Sherlock resisted. When Wu tried to push him again, Sherlock grabbed at his wrist and shook his head violently.

Wu obviously wanted to be as far from the storm as possible, and if that meant being deep inside the bowels of the ship then that was fine with him.

Wu tried to push Sherlock again, but Sherlock shook his head. 'No!' he yelled. Wu seemed to lip-read what he was saying, because he let go of Sherlock's shoulder and then patted it sadly. It was a goodbye, of sorts. Wu obviously wasn't expecting to see Sherlock again.

Sherlock slid past the Chinese cook and half ran, half stumbled towards the ladder which led up to the hatch.

He turned as he put his foot on the bottom rung, and saw the cook's broad back vanish around a corner. He scuttled up the ladder, hoping that Wu was wrong, and that they would both survive. That they would *all* survive.

Three sailors were attaching the wooden hatch cover when he popped his head over the edge. They were soaked from head to foot, and their faces were haggard with strain and fear. One of them pulled him up while the others fastened the cover down and nailed it on.

Things were worse than before, up on deck. The sky was now a uniform purple from horizon to horizon – or at least, it would have been if the horizon had been visible. As it was, visibility dropped to zero a few hundred yards from the ship. Sherlock spent a second or two taking it all in – the waves, taller than the ship, the spume that covered everything, the sharp tang of salt in the air – and then ran for the nearest rigging where he could wind his arms through the ropes and hang on for dear life. As he was halfway to his goal the ship suddenly lurched to one side and the horizontal deck became a wooden slide down which he skidded, splinters catching in his clothes. He slammed into the railing around the edge of the ship, nearly breaking his legs, and would have gone through one of the gaps and vanished into the churning waters below if he hadn't managed to grab hold of a brass knob that was bolted securely to the wooden rail. He'd often wondered what the knob was for – none of the sailors ever seemed to tie anything to it – but whatever use it had he was thankful that it had been there when he needed it. Carefully he pulled himself back on to the deck and wound first one arm and then the other around the rail, closely followed by his legs.

His heart was hammering in his chest, and he could feel his throat closing up with terror. The storm had overtaken them with frightening speed.

Other sailors were scattered around the deck, each one with his arms wound into the rigging so that a wave wouldn't carry him off the deck and into the heaving sea.

A flash of light suddenly blinded him. Automatically he counted seconds – one . . . two . . . and then a tremendously loud *crash* echoed all around. Sherlock could feel it through the wood of the deck and railings as much as hear it. Two miles. The storm was still two miles away. He knew that because Mycroft had once told him that each second's gap between thunder and lightning meant that the storm was another mile away.

And if this was two miles from the centre of the storm then what was it like in its centre?

Through the rain and the spray, he could see Mr Larchmont standing at the wheelhouse. His legs were braced against the deck and his hands were clamped on a rail hard enough that Sherlock could swear that they were actually embedded in the wood. His hair was whipping around his face. He didn't look scared, or even concerned. He just looked determined. He stared straight down the centreline of the ship as if daring the storm to do its worst. Sherlock saw his lips move and, incredibly, heard the commanding tone of his voice even above the storm.

'*Loosen the sails!*' he yelled. '*Loosen those sails if you ever want to see your mothers and your lovers again!*'

Sherlock glanced up at the sails, and immediately understood. They were pulled tight under the force of the wind – so tight that they might rip from top to bottom if the storm got any worse – and if the *Gloria Scott* was two miles from its centre then it might very well get worse. The ropes that held the sails were also pulled as tight as violin strings. They might break, leaving the canvas to flap about destructively. The wind might also be strong enough to topple the ship over, if it didn't rip the canvas. If the sails were loosened then the crew at least had a chance. They would be adrift and at the mercy of the storm, not knowing where they might end up, but their chances of getting through this would be increased.

26

Incredibly, some of the sailors scrambled from their places of safety across the deck for the points where the sail rigging was attached. Sherlock wasn't sure if they were more scared by Mr Larchmont than they were by the storm, or whether they just knew that they had to risk their very lives in order to save the ship. Whatever the reason, they grabbed for where the ropes were wound around hooks and stanchions and, two or three together, taking the strain, they released the tension in the ropes and reattached them loosely. Immediately the wind caught the sails and pulled the ropes tight, but as the wind shifted the sails flapped loose and the ropes sagged, only to be pulled tight again moments later.

Sherlock glanced out past the railing, and caught his breath. Once, a year or more ago, he had woken up in a bedroom in a château in France belonging to Baron Maupertuis. Thinking he was in Farnham, he had thrown open the curtains, and been shocked speechless by the sight of mountains outside the window. Suddenly he was back there again, staring at mountains in bemusement, but these mountains were made of water, and they were a lot closer. Close enough that he felt he could almost reach out and touch them.

Suddenly the immensity and the grandeur of the world struck him. A feeling of exultation seemed to flood through his body, washing away all the fear and replacing it with wondrous amazement. Farnham was small. London was small. There was so much else out there to see. How could Mycroft bear to stay in his flat and in his club and in his office, scuttling between them in a closed carriage, when there was all this spectacle in the world?

The real storm broke over an hour later, but in Sherlock's mind it had lost its power over his emotions by then. From that moment on he was just a spectator, awestruck at what he was seeing. All physical sensation – fear, tiredness, pain, hunger – all of it faded away in the face of the incredible sights and sounds of nature at play. It didn't matter that the *Gloria Scott* was being tossed around like a leaf on the edge of a waterfall; it didn't matter that lightning struck the mainmast twice, leaving gashes of scorched wood and the smell of burning in its wake; it didn't matter that so much water was sloshing across the deck that the planks were invisible and the battened hatches were obvious only because the water would suddenly break against their edges and spray upward. None of it was important. The ship and the sailors were like ants in the face of something massive and unstoppable and beautiful.

At one stage he slipped somewhere between sleep and a hypnotic state, his eyes open but seeing nothing.

He gradually came to his senses to find that the storm had abated. Sailors were moving across the deck, tightening the lines, unbattening the hatches and sweeping as much water as possible off the deck and back into the sea. The sky was blue again, blue and clear. There were birds flying behind the ship once more, waiting for food to be thrown overboard.

Mr Larchmont was standing a few feet away. He glanced over at Sherlock.

'Enjoy your little sleep?' he asked.

Sherlock knew what he was expected to say. 'Ready for duty, sir!' he snapped, climbing to his feet.

'Glad to hear it,' Larchmont said. He looked up at the foremast. 'I see some loose lines there. I would be much obliged if you would tighten them for me.'

'Aye aye, sir!' Sherlock headed for the rigging, but turned back and looked at Larchmont for a moment. 'How many sailors did we lose, sir?'

Larchmont shook his head. 'Too many,' he said quietly. 'And good men, all of them.'

CHAPTER TWO

Despite the exertions of the previous day, Sherlock awoke early. Lying in his hammock, gently swinging from side to side in the relative darkness of the sleeping area – which was barely more than a widened section of corridor with hooks screwed to either side of the wall where the hammocks could be slung – he listened for a while to the gentle background noise of creaking timbers, waves slapping against the sides of the ship, sailors snoring, snorting or talking in their sleep, and the blundering sounds of men either getting out of their hammocks or getting into them. The business of running the *Gloria Scott* went on all day and all night, of course, and as one shift was rising another was going to sleep. Bells were rung to signal the beginning and end of shifts, and Sherlock's wasn't for a while yet.

Eventually Sherlock slid out of his hammock and dressed in the same clothes he had worn the previous day, and the day before that, and all the days before that leading back to his abduction. The only washing the clothes got was the soaking from the waves which came over the side of the ship. Ducking beneath the line of canvas hammocks that, strangely, almost mimicked the ship's sails in their swollen, occupied state, he made his way to the galley.

Wu Chung was absent. Instead, another sailor – a cadaverous individual named Scorby – was dishing out a mixture of hard biscuits, oat porridge and dried meat. Sherlock took a plateful, sat at a vacant bench and quickly scoffed it down. He wondered what had happened to the Chinese cook. The last time Sherlock had seen him, Wu had been going towards the depths of the ship. Had he survived the storm, or had something happened to him? Perhaps he had accidentally hit his head on a low beam when the *Gloria Scott* had been listing from side to side under the heavy hand of the wind. Or perhaps he had gone down to the bilges – the dark, wet depths of the ship closest to the keel – and somehow fallen over and drowned in the stagnant water that sloshed back and forth down there.

Sherlock pushed his empty plate away and got up. His place was instantly taken by another sailor. Heading back to where Scorby was still serving, he asked, 'Where's Wu?'

'Wu Chung?' Scorby asked, as if there was another Chinese sailor named Wu on board who Sherlock might have been asking after. 'Up on deck, mate. 'E's doin' some kind of strange dance.'

31

Sherlock felt a sense of relief wash over him. Wu wasn't exactly a friend, but he was one of the few sailors to have taken an interest in him. If Wu had died then who else was going to teach Sherlock Cantonese?

He headed up the ladder towards the deck. The bright light made him blink and screw up his eyes. When they had adjusted he looked around, checking for any damage that the storm had left. It was as if nothing had happened. The sails were full, the masts and yards were intact, and the deck was as dry as it ever got. The sailors on shift were moving around normally. Despite the violence of the previous night Sherlock got the impression that tropical storms were something that happened, were dealt with and were then forgotten. Everyone and everything moved on.

Wu Chung was standing in the centre of the deck. He was poised with his weight on his bent right leg. His left leg was extended straight to the deck in front of him. His right arm was raised in a hooked shape, almost cradling the back of his head, and his left arm was extended to match his left leg. The fingers were together and curled, with the palm facing upward, as if he was gesturing someone to approach him. The pose looked as if it was putting significant stress on the muscles of Wu's right leg and back, but he kept as stationary as a statue for a minute or more before moving slowly to another pose.

As Sherlock watched, Wu Chung took a series of statue-like poses interspersed with slow movements. As Scorby had said, it *was* something like a dance, but there was more to it. Sherlock began to detect repeated elements within the poses – blocks and strikes, as if Wu was engaged in a very slow fight with an invisible opponent.

Eventually, he straightened up, letting his arms fall to his sides. He was breathing deeply, but not heavily. He glanced over to where Sherlock was standing.

'You see me practise, ha?' he said in English.

'I did. What is it that you are practising?'

Wu smiled. 'What you think?'

'I think it was like a fight, like boxing but different. I think it was like *shadow*-boxing.'

Wu nodded, and bowed slightly towards Sherlock. 'Very good. Most people say I am dancing badly.'

'I've never seen you do it before.'

'You have never been awake this early before. I do this every morning for one hour.'

'Why?' Sherlock asked simply.

'Ah, that is a good question.' Wu came over to stand beside Sherlock. 'In your country, boxing is something men learn so they can hit other people and make them bleed. In my country, *T'ai chi ch'uan* is something

33

children learn so they can calm their minds and master their bodies.'

'*T'ai chi ch'uan?*' Sherlock asked.

'It means "boundless fist", or maybe "great extremes boxing".'

'Tell me more,' Sherlock asked.

Wu gestured to an empty area of deck over to one side. 'Let us sit. There is much to tell, and I am not as young as I once was.' Once they were both settled, cross-legged on the deck, he started to speak, and Sherlock listened, fascinated. 'I start by telling you that there are two different styles of fighting in China. There is *Shaolinquan*, which is all –' he waved his arms around wildly – 'action and activity, all about the body doing things, and there is *Wudangquan*, which is all about the mind *controlling* the body.' He sniffed derisively. 'Those who practise *Shaolinquan* leap about with strength and force, but people who are not good at this kind of training soon lose their breath and are exhausted. *Wudangquan* is unlike this. We strive for quietness of body, mind and intention. We seek that still point in the centre from which all activity must begin.'

'I don't understand,' Sherlock admitted.

'Good,' Wu said. 'That is a start.' He paused for a moment, gathering his thoughts. 'I have told you a little about China, but you should know more about the

Chinese before you arrive.' He glanced around at the other sailors. 'These men are all fools. They do not care about where they are going. They want everywhere they go to be the same – same food, same language, same kinds of people. They are not interested in difference, only sameness. You, you are different. You look for differences, and are interested in them. You are more intelligent than them.'

'I've always been interested in learning things,' Sherlock admitted.

'In your country, boxing and God and food and nature – they are different, yes?'

'Ye-es,' Sherlock admitted, not sure where Wu was going.

'In China, they are all parts of something. We believe that everything is connected. Changes to one thing affect everything else.' He smiled.

Wu kept talking, and Sherlock listened, but he wasn't sure that he understood much of what was said. It didn't really matter. Wu was obviously passionate about his beliefs, and Sherlock found himself entranced by his friend's eloquence. On a couple of occasions Wu shifted into Cantonese when he didn't know the correct English words, and Sherlock found that he was still following the conversation. What Sherlock did understand was that *T'ai chi ch'uan* was something between a way

35

of meditating and a way of fighting, and that it was a reflection of a deeper religious aspect of Chinese life.

Eventually, when Wu ran out of words, Sherlock asked, 'Could you teach me?'

'I am already teaching you – Cantonese. You want me to teach you cooking now?'

Sherlock smiled. 'No – not cooking. I want you to teach me *T'ai chi ch'uan*.'

Wu stared at him for a long moment. 'You want me to teach you to fight?'

Sherlock recognized the trick in the question.

'No,' he said. 'I want you to teach me how to control my body with my mind.'

'Right answer.' Wu smiled. 'Then I teach you that. The fighting will come with it.'

The weather got hotter as they hooked around the bottom point of Africa – the Cape of Good Hope – and headed back towards the equator. The skies returned to their pure blue, and the sun beat down on the deck and on the sailors, drying the one to the point where the wood began to crack while raising blisters on the backs and shoulders of the other. The sea grew quiet again, and porpoises began to accompany the ship, as they had done before, racing ahead of it like a pack of hunting dogs. Sherlock sometimes caught glimpses of other things paralleling the ship, beneath the waves, dark shapes that seemed as big, if not bigger, than the ship itself, but they never broke the surface. Were they sharks? Or maybe whales? He had read about whales. Or were they some other kind of life that nobody had yet given a name to? He didn't know, but he desperately wanted to.

The days blurred into one another. When he wasn't working or sleeping then Sherlock was practising the violin, learning Cantonese from Wu Chung or following the slow-motion movements of *T'ai chi-ch'uan* that Wu Chung rehearsed on deck every morning. Sherlock was beginning to see that if he took the graceful movements and speeded them up then they really would make an effective form of defensive fighting – blocking punches and then returning blows with either the hands or the feet. He could also see that by practising the movements slowly at first, so slowly that his muscles sometimes began to scream under the strain, he was building up a memory of them. If he ever had the opportunity to use this martial art for real then he could see how his body would automatically follow the movements that it had memorized without him even having to think about it.

Why had something like *T'ai chi ch'uan* never been developed in England? he wondered. The closest thing England had to a martial art was boxing, and this thing that Wu was teaching him was so much more effective than boxing. Were there other types of martial art? he wondered. Did other countries have their own, different versions?

When Sherlock was working he was concentrating so much on his tasks that he could see nothing else around him. But on those occasions when he had some time to himself he sometimes, in the evening or the early morning, noticed the ship's captain, Tollaway, standing on the rear deck making observations of the sky. He used a brass device that looked like a cross between a small telescope and a large set of compasses. He seemed to be observing stars. Sherlock remembered something that he had read once about navigation at sea, and decided that the thing the Captain was using was a sextant.

As the ship ploughed on through the waves, the horizon a line that merely separated one shade of blue from another, it was hard to believe that they were making any progress. Maybe the *Gloria Scott* was sitting stationary on the surface of the ocean, and the sense of movement was an illusion caused by the waves and the feel of the wind on their faces. Only the billowing of the sails indicated that something was actually propelling them forward.

Sherlock found himself joining in more and more with the sing-songs in the evening. After the sailors received their ration of watered-down rum – something for which Sherlock found he was acquiring quite a taste – they would gather together and sing sea shanties. Sherlock's developing skills at the violin were much in demand – so much so that a sailor everyone called Fiddler, who had lent Sherlock his instrument, was relegated to the sidelines. Sherlock's excellent memory meant that he could remember all the words as soon as he heard them, and he discovered to his surprise that he had a fine baritone singing voice.

Sherlock found that there were whole stretches of time – hours, in fact – when he didn't think about home, about Mycroft and about his friends – Amyus Crowe, Matty and Virginia. Was he coming to terms with his situation, he wondered, or was it just some kind of mental self-protection mechanism – his mind avoiding subjects that were too painful to think about?

Sherlock didn't know how long it was after the storm, but one morning Mr Larchmont called everyone to the stern of the ship, where he stood on the raised area of deck and looked down at them.

'It's been a long journey, lads,' he shouted, 'and there're more to go, but the Captain reckons we're just a spit away from Sumatra now. He intends to dock in Sabang Harbour. Sumatra is controlled by the Dutch, of course, which at least means that the food will be edible, they'll take the Queen's coins and we'll be able to make ourselves understood. Some of you have been there

39

before – for those of you that haven't, all I'll say is that Sabang is a rat-hole infested with all kinds of tropical diseases that can rot a man's fingers and toes off within a day, and that you're far better off staying on the ship than going ashore. The only thing worse than Sabang is the jungle that covers the rest of the island. Not that I expect that to stop you from going ashore. We'll be there for two days, picking up a cargo of coffee beans and taking on a Dutchman as a passenger.' He gazed around the crew, who had visibly brightened up at the news they would be hitting land soon. 'That's all. Back to work, all of you, and hold off on dreamin' of those beautiful Sumatran maidens until land is in sight.' He turned back to the wheelhouse, and Sherlock heard him saying, only slightly less loudly than his previous shouting, 'Tack five degrees to starboard and then maintain a steady course.'

The next day, land was sighted. It started as a dark line fractionally above the horizon, much as the storm had done, but instead of running from it Mr Larchmont ordered that a course be struck directly towards it. How did he know that it *was* land? Sherlock wondered. As they got closer, however, it became clear that he was right. Soon the whole crew could see what looked like hills, but which soon resolved themselves into mountains covered with lush green vegetation.

They arrived in Sabang slowly, and accompanied by a great deal of waving from children on the quayside. In comparison with Dakar – their last port of call – Sabang was a bustling mass of people heading in all directions on all kinds of business. Men wore what looked like brightly coloured sheets wrapped around their waists. Some wore jackets to cover their chests, others went bare-chested. The women wore the same kinds of brightly coloured sheets, but wrapped around their whole bodies rather than just from the waist down. All in all, the place was a riot of colour and activity.

After they docked, the first order of business was for the Captain, accompanied by Mr Larchmont, to go in search of their cargo of coffee beans. The crew were allowed to disembark, and within a few moments the *Gloria Scott* was empty apart from the two sailors left behind to guard it, and Wu, who said that he preferred to sleep.

Sherlock walked down the gangplank with some trepidation. As with the arrival at Dakar, he found that making a transition to walking on a surface that wasn't moving up and down was pretty tricky. It took him a good few hours to stop feeling queasy. Looking at the men who passed him on the quayside and in the street, he could tell which ones were sailors who had recently disembarked. They were the ones who were staggering from side to side, anticipating waves that never came.

The quayside was lined with cranes made out of bamboo which had been tied together using some kind of local rope. They looked pretty ramshackle compared with the more substantial cranes that Sherlock had seen in the docks in London and Southampton. He wondered how often they failed, and how many men were injured each time.

In the shadow of the cranes he noticed stalls selling all kinds of food and other goods, like clothes, and knives, and musical instruments, and wooden puppets. Sick and tired of the restricted ship's rations, Sherlock decided to look at what was on offer. Remembering the advice that Mycroft had once given him about never taking the first hansom cab he saw in case it was a trap, Sherlock went past the first few stalls and stopped at one further down the line.

The man running the stall was small, brown-skinned and dark-haired. He smiled at Sherlock with a mouth that seemed to contain too many teeth. He held out a stick on which were some chunks of meat coated in a brown sauce. 'Very nice,' he said. 'You try, yes?'

Sherlock gazed dubiously at the proffered morsel. 'What is it?' he asked.

'*Satay Ponorogo*,' the man replied. 'Is goat. Goat in

42

sauce.' He frowned, and turned to the next-nearest stallholder. They talked in what Sherlock presumed was Sumatran, if there was such a language, for a few moments. The stallholder turned back. 'Is sauce made with peanuts,' he said.

Sherlock shrugged. He'd never eaten goat in England, although as far as he was concerned it was no different from eating lamb or mutton. He had tried peanuts when he was in New York a year or so back and liked them. 'All right,' he said, and handed over a coin. The stallholder passed the stick to him, along with some change.

Sherlock bit into the meat. For a second he could taste the goat and the peanuts, but then his lips started to tingle. He debated whether to spit the meat out or swallow it. In the end he swallowed it, if only so that he didn't offend the stallkeeper. He could feel the burning sensation all the way down his throat.

'Sauce is also made with chilli and lime,' the stallholder added with a big smile. 'You need drink to cool mouth down? Coconut milk do cooling job really good.'

'Thanks,' Sherlock said, 'but no thanks. And I admire your technique for getting customers to buy your drinks as well as your food. Very good. Very clever.'

He walked on, waiting for the burning in his mouth to subside. After a while he felt a prickle on the back of his neck. It felt like someone was watching him. He didn't believe that there was some kind of sixth sense that meant he could tell he was being watched even though his back was turned, but he was prepared to believe that he might have caught a glimpse of a watcher out of the corner of his eye and that part of his brain was trying to alert him to something. He turned, letting his gaze roam across the crowd of sailors, Dutch and English settlers and locals.

One man stood out. He was wearing a grubby linen suit and a straw hat, and his white shirt was creased and sweat-stained, but the most obvious, and strange, thing about him was that his face and hair were completely obscured by a black gauze veil, like the ones worn by beekeepers. The veil was tucked into a silk cravat which was tied loosely around his neck. The cravat was wilting in the heat and the humidity. He was leaning on a cane and seemed to be staring at Sherlock, although the black veil made it difficult to see anything more than the shape of his head.

'Can I help you?' Sherlock called, feeling a shiver run through him. He thought it was just the memories of being watched from afar by the agents of the Paradol Chamber that were making him edgy, but as the man started to walk across to where Sherlock was standing the feeling became more intense.

The man stopped a few feet away. 'Are you from the

44

Gloria Scott?' he asked. His voice was thin and reedy, like the sound of an oboe, or a high note from a church organ.

Sherlock nodded.

'My name is Arrhenius,' he said. 'Jacobus Arrhenius. I will be a passenger on your ship. Please to tell me where the Captain may be found.'

'He . . . he is currently ashore, sorting out our next cargo,' Sherlock said. 'I think he intends to be back soon, if you could wait.'

'Thank you,' Arrhenius said. 'I will wait in the shade by the gangway.' He glanced up at the sky – or, at least, that was the direction his head turned in. The veil made it impossible to tell what he was actually looking at. 'The sun and I do not get on well. Not at all.' He turned away, then looked back so that he could see Sherlock again. 'You know my name, but I do not know yours.'

'Sherlock. My name is Sherlock Holmes.'

'I am pleased to meet you,' Arrhenius said. He extended his right hand, which was encased in a black leather glove which ran up inside his sleeve so that no flesh was visible. Sherlock took the hand gingerly. Beneath the soft leather it felt strange – not like a normal hand.

'I will see you again,' Arrhenius said before moving

off, and Sherlock wasn't sure if that was a promise or a threat.

He watched the veiled man's retreating back, then, when Arrhenius had been swallowed up by the crowd, he moved on.

After a while Sherlock got bored by the stalls. The heat and the humidity were weighing him down. He wondered whether to explore the town further, or to go back to the ship. Eventually he decided to go back: it wasn't as if he was going to be living in Sabang for any length of time, and being back on board would allow him to continue with his violin practice, Cantonese lessons and *T'ai chi ch'uan* in peace for a while.

When he reached the gangway he turned and looked around the bustling quay. He could feel the same tickle on his skin as he had earlier. Somewhere, Arrhenius was watching him again. Eventually he spotted the veiled man in the shadows beneath a palm tree. When he saw that he had been spotted, Arrhenius bowed slightly to Sherlock.

A few minutes later Captain Tollaway and Mr Larchmont returned from their meetings in Sabang, and Sherlock watched from the deck as Mr Arrhenius stepped out of the shade to greet them. Sherlock couldn't hear what they were saying to each other, but neither of the two sailors seemed at all amazed by the black all-encompassing veil or the gloves. Either they had met him before, Sherlock reasoned, or they had been warned in advance.

The three men came up the gangway and disappeared into the depths of the ship. Sherlock presumed they had gone to the Captain's cabin. About half an hour later a cart arrived alongside the ship, pulled by some kind of big-horned cow. When Mr Arrhenius appeared at the side of the ship to watch the contents of the cart being loaded on board Sherlock concluded that it was his luggage.

One box in particular seemed to concern the Dutchman. It was made of wood and had holes drilled in the top. Arrhenius came down the gangway and walked behind the local labourers as they carried it on to the ship. The wind changed direction briefly, blowing towards Sherlock, and he caught a whiff of a strange, musty odour. The box vanished down a hatch and presumably towards Arrhenius's cabin, as did the rest of his luggage, and the strange smell vanished with it.

More carts began to turn up with crates – bigger ones this time. Rather than being carried on board, the crates were attached to the ropes hanging down from the two nearest bamboo cranes and then hoisted up into the air. Mr Larchmont had mentioned coffee beans earlier, and Sherlock assumed that was what these were.

It took the rest of that day and a significant portion of the next for the crates to be lifted on board the *Gloria Scott* and lowered into the hold through the deck hatches. Sherlock watched during the breaks in his violin, *T'ai chi ch'uan* and Cantonese classes. With few sailors on board, and the Captain and Mr Larchmont eating with the local Dutch townsfolk most of the time, Wu Chung was short of things to do, and so he enthusiastically took Sherlock under his wing.

Sailors began to drift back to the ship in ones and twos at midday on the third day. Sherlock assumed that some kind of message had gone out. There were some that Sherlock didn't recognize – it looked as if Mr Larchmont and the Captain had recruited some Dutchmen and Englishmen left there by a previous ship as replacements for the men who had died in the storm. By mid-afternoon they were fully crewed again, and after Mr Larchmont had signed off some paperwork on the quayside the *Gloria Scott* cast off the lines that were holding her against the dock and began to manoeuvre out into the clear waters of the harbour.

Next stop Shanghai, Sherlock thought.

There was a different feeling on board the ship on the last leg of their voyage from Sabang to Shanghai. The sailors seemed more eager, happier. They knew that they were close to their destination, which meant they were close to the point when the ship would turn around and head back to England, where most of them had families. The presence of the new sailors was a factor in this different feeling, of course, but they quickly integrated into the crew, as Sherlock had done.

And there was Mr Arrhenius, of course. He seemed to spend a lot of time on deck, staring at the distant horizon. Once or twice, when Sherlock passed him by, he nodded in greeting. The other sailors obviously avoided him, and Sherlock heard mutterings in the evening singalongs that he was not human but some kind of demon beneath the veil. The nervousness of the crew got to such a pitch that Mr Larchmont had to call a meeting of all the sailors and reassure them – in his usual gruff tones – that Mr Arrhenius was as human as the rest of them, and he merely suffered from a disease that had disfigured his skin.

Mr Arrhenius always had his meals in his cabin. Wu Chung took him a tray twice a day – usually something better than whatever the crew were having. The crew saw this as another thing to mutter about, but it seemed only fitting to Sherlock – after all, the man was a paying passenger.

Three days after leaving Sumatra, Wu Chung asked Sherlock to take some food to Mr Arrhenius's cabin. The tray had two plates on it, one of chicken stew and one of raw fish. Puzzled, Sherlock manoeuvred his way along the ship's corridors until he reached the cabin near the front where Arrhenius spent his time. He knocked with one hand, balancing the tray with the other, and waited until Arrhenius opened the door.

Sherlock's arrival appeared to have taken Arrhenius by surprise. He wasn't wearing his hat, or his veil. Sherlock saw that his face and scalp were hairless, but that wasn't the most disconcerting thing about him. No, the most disconcerting thing about him was the colour of his skin. It was a silvery-blue, and as the light from the oil lamps in the corridor shone on the man Sherlock saw that the whites of his eyes were also the same colour. It was as if he was a metal statue come to life, and Sherlock found himself taking an inadvertent step backwards.

'Yes?' His voice was as high and as piping as Sherlock remembered.

'I have some food for you, sir.'

Arrhenius just stared at him. 'You are the boy from the docks, yes?'

'Yes, sir.'

'The cook, the Chinaman, usually brings my food.'

'He's busy, sir. He asked me to bring it.'

'Very well.' Arrhenius seemed annoyed, although Sherlock couldn't work out why. The Dutchman reached for the tray.

'Would you like me to put it on a table for you?' Sherlock asked.

'No – just give it to me.'

Sherlock handed the tray through the doorway. He turned to leave, but as he did so he saw something moving out of the corner of my eye – a shape, about the size of a dog, rapidly slipping out of sight in the shadows behind Arrhenius's back. As the thing moved Sherlock could hear a clicking noise. He glanced at Arrhenius to ask him what it was, but the Dutchman was staring at him with an expression that clearly indicated that he wanted Sherlock to leave. Confused, Sherlock backed away. The door closed in his face.

Fiddler was walking past as Sherlock stood there, thinking. Sherlock caught him by the sleeve. 'Does our passenger have a pet of any kind?' he asked.

Fiddler scowled. 'What, that devil-creature?' He shook his head. 'Not to my knowledge,' he said. 'But if he does then it'll be some kind of familiar from the depths of hell!'

'Thanks,' Sherlock said. 'Very helpful.'

As he moved away his foot caught something and he accidentally kicked it towards the bulkhead. It made a rattling noise. Curious, Sherlock bent down to see what it was. For a moment he thought it was a tooth, fallen out of someone's mouth – a common thing with sailors,

51

he had found – but it glinted silver, like Mr Arrhenius's skin. He picked it up. It was a pointed cone, slightly curved, and it appeared to have a hole running through it. He didn't have a clue what it might be, so he slipped it into his pocket in order to examine it later. If someone had lost it, maybe he could give it back to them – and find out what it was into the bargain.

It was later that day when one of the crew spotted something on the horizon, and called an urgent warning out to Mr Larchmont.

'Sails!' he yelled from his position in the rigging. 'Sails on the horizon!'

Sherlock was working alongside Gittens at the time, pulling frayed ropes apart into fragments that they would then plug between the planks of the ship to help keep them watertight. He glanced over at the dark-faced lad. 'What's the problem?' he asked. 'There're all kinds of ships sailing across the ocean. We've never had a warning before.'

'We're in the South China Seas,' Gittens said grimly. 'There're Chinese pirates all across these waters. They plunder any ship they find, and they ransom the passengers if they look important.'

'What if they don't look important?'

'I heard a story, once,' Gittens confided. 'Old sailor. He'd been on a ship that got boarded by Chinese pirates.

They were ransacking the place and they believed the captain had hidden some jewels from them, so they tied him between the masts, a rope tied tight around his right thumb and a rope tied tight around his right toe, and they hauled him up between the foremast and the mizzenmast. Then they took turns riding on him like he was a swing.'

'Ah,' Sherlock said simply, but inside he was sickened at the casual brutality that Gittens had described.

Gittens grinned, revealing a mouthful of blackened teeth. 'They normally start with the youngest,' he said. 'That'll be you, then.'

'And you next,' Sherlock pointed out.

He glanced over to where Mr Larchmont was standing by the rail, telescope to his eye. Larchmont turned, and his expression was as black as the storm they had only recently escaped.

'Sails on the horizon,' he confirmed. 'It's pirates, lads, and we're in for a fight!'

CHAPTER THREE

Larchmont passed by and clicked his fingers at Sherlock and Gittens. 'You two,' he snapped. 'Look lively now, and break out the weapons from the armoury. Spread them among the crew.' He slipped a rusty key from around his neck, where it was hanging from a cord, and handed it to Gittens. 'Get on now – quickly. I'll send sailors down to collect them. When you run out of weapons, start issuing belaying pins. When you run out of belaying pins, issue hooks and chains.'

'Armoury?' Sherlock questioned as Larchmont stalked away to shout at another sailor. 'I didn't even know we *had* an armoury.'

Gittens laughed bitterly. 'Don't start getting ideas,' he said. 'It's not like this is a Naval warship. The armoury is just a cupboard near the Captain's cabin, and the weapons are things that've been collected on various voyages over the past couple of years. There're some swords, some knives, and a couple of muskets and rifles so rusted they'll probably explode in a man's hands as soon as the trigger is pulled. There're also the axes that we use to chop timber up an' splice ropes, and there're rumours that the Captain has an Army revolver that he picked up in a bazaar somewhere which he keeps under his pillow in case of mutiny.' He laughed again, but there was no humour in the sound. 'Oh, and I suppose we can count Wu Chung's cooking knives as well. Let's hope he's been sharpening them regular-like.'

'It's not a lot to fight off pirates,' Sherlock said anxiously. 'Don't we have any cannon, or anything like that?'

'This is a trading ship. We carry cargo. Cannon are heavy, and they take up space that could be used for stacking crates or sacks. No, our best chance is to pile on full sail, and hope we can outrun them.'

Sherlock frowned. 'But the hold is *full* of cargo. That's going to slow us down.' He looked around. 'Mr Larchmont needs to order the crew to throw the crates overboard! We need to be as light as possible – that's the only way we can get up enough speed!'

He made to move off towards where Larchmont was shouting at the sailors to unfurl all the sails and tighten all the ropes, but Gittens caught at his arm.

'Don't be stupid,' he hissed. 'We didn't sail halfway around the world so we could dump our cargo at the first sign of trouble. That's where the Captain makes his money. He'd rather order half the crew to jump in the sea than throw the cargo overboard. Sailors are ten a farthing. They can be picked up at any port. Losing cargo means losing money.' He glanced out towards the sea. 'An' based on what I've heard about Chinese pirates, I'd be first in line to jump. I'd rather take my chances with the sharks, I surely would.'

Gittens pulled Sherlock with him towards the nearest hatch. They made their way rapidly down into the inside of the ship, and Gittens led the way to an anonymous padlocked door halfway along a corridor. Sailors pushed past them, expressions of alarm on their faces. Some of them started forming a queue beside the armoury – presumably on Larchmont's orders. As Gittens managed to unlock the stiff padlock the sailors suddenly squeezed themselves to the sides of the corridor, and Sherlock saw Captain Tollaway striding down the centre. The expression on his face was thunderous, but Sherlock thought he could detect a grey tinge of concern beneath the dark gaze.

His revolver was swinging in his hand.

'Take courage, boys,' he said to nobody in particular as he passed. 'We're not going to let these barbarous savages get their hands on our cargo! We'll fight to the last man rather than let that happen! A shilling to any man who kills one of the pirates!'

The queue of sailors let out a ragged cheer as he passed, but Sherlock suspected they were all wondering who the last man was going to be.

Gittens pulled the cupboard door open. Inside Sherlock saw swords and knives hanging from hooks. Some of them were rusty. Gittens gestured to Sherlock to pull them out and start handing them to the sailors in the queue. Gittens himself pulled bundles of oiled cloth out from the back of the cupboard and unwrapped them to reveal some long and antiquated guns. Sherlock had seen the farmers in Farnham use more modern weapons to scare off birds.

This was not looking good. He could feel a knot of apprehension coiling and uncoiling in his stomach. Surely, having survived the storm, he couldn't now die here, in the middle of the ocean, thousands of miles from everything he held dear? There were things he needed to do back home. What about Virginia?

After the weapons had been distributed, Gittens closed and locked the cupboard. He had kept two knives for himself, and he tucked them into his belt. One of them was short and chunky, with a leather-wrapped handle. The other had a curved blade and an edge that was shaped like a wave – it wasn't an English knife, that was for sure.

Gittens made as if to head back to the ladder, then hesitated. He pulled the first knife from his belt and handed it to Sherlock.

57

'Here,' he said roughly. 'Keep this. It might help. If anything helps, apart from prayer.'

Before Sherlock could say anything, Gittens was racing off.

Up on deck the tension was so thick that it seemed to hang like a veil of smoke above the crew. Half the men were either up in the rigging or pulling at ropes on deck; the other half were armed and clustered along the side of the ship off which the sails had been seen. Sherlock moved across to join them, worming his way through the press of bodies until he was up against the rail.

The ship was cutting rapidly though the waves, and spray drifted back into Sherlock's face. Their pursuers might have been sails on the horizon twenty minutes before, but now they were appreciably closer. Sherlock craned his neck to get a look.

The pursuing vessel was unlike anything Sherlock had seen before. Its hull was curved so that the bows and the stern were projecting upwards, raised above the sea, and the middle section rode low in the waves. The sails were a reddish brown in colour, and corrugated like fans, and rather than being flat across the top, like the sails Sherlock was used to, they came to points. It was difficult to see the stern of the ship, but from what little Sherlock could tell the rudder was much bigger than the one on the *Gloria Scott*, and it took three or four men to move it. Whatever principles of design the designers of the ship had followed, they were different to those used in England.

Sherlock could make out figures clustered along the side of the pursuing ship. They were all holding swords, and they were waving the swords above their heads.

Sherlock's fingers clenched on the leather-covered handle of his knife. It wasn't much to defend his life with.

The wind that was blowing from the direction of the stern brought with it the sound of voices. The pirates were singing some kind of war chant.

As Sherlock and the rest of the crew watched, the chase played out. Despite every scrap of sail that the *Gloria Scott* possessed being called into use, despite every rope being tightened until it creaked, the pursuing ship gradually ate up the distance between them. Sherlock could see the faces of the Chinese pirates: tattooed and snarling. Half of them were bald, while the other half had long hair that was either falling wildly around their shoulders or was drawn back into a plait hanging down their backs.

Mr Larchmont's voice rose above the rushing of the wind and the chanting of the pirates. 'Hold fast, my laddies! We'll be laughing about this adventure and drinking in the taverns of Shanghai before you know it!'

59

But they wouldn't be. Sherlock was sure of it. The Chinese pirate ship was built for speed, while the *Gloria Scott* was weighed down by her cargo. The pirate ship raced like a greyhound across the sea while the *Gloria Scott* wallowed in the waves like a pregnant bulldog.

Sherlock realized that Wu Chung was standing beside him. The Chinese cook stared out impassively at the ship behind them.

'It is called a "junk" in your language,' he said quietly after a while, 'although that is not our word for it. Junks are faster and better equipped than any other ship on the seas. We have been sailing them for thousands of years – while your people were just looking at the oceans and wondering how to get across them.'

'What will they do to us if they catch us?' Sherlock asked.

'Steal our cargo, for sure,' Chung said. 'If we had lots of passengers then they might hold them for ransom from the authorities in Shanghai, but we only have one and I don't think he would fetch very much money. These pirates are superstitious fellows. One look at his face and they would throw him overboard.'

'And what about the rest of us?'

'If we are lucky they will leave us locked up in the hold, adrift, with our sails ripped and all our food taken.'

'And if we're unlucky?' Sherlock had to ask the

question, but he knew he wouldn't like the answer.

Wu Chung obviously felt the same way. 'Do not ask,' he said quietly. 'You may find out, soon enough.'

'But you speak Cantonese,' Sherlock pointed out. 'You are Chinese – like them. Can't you talk to them – reason with them? There must be something that we can offer them that would make them go away.'

Wu shook his head. 'I may speak the same language as them, but I am not *like* them. Perhaps my appearance will save my life, perhaps not. The fact that I am on this ship with you means that I will be treated like you. Worse, perhaps, as I have left my home and I am working with foreign devils. There is nothing I can offer them that they cannot take for themselves.'

Sherlock glanced down at Wu's hand. The cook was grasping a large carving knife. His knuckles were white and bloodless, he was holding the handle so tightly.

Wu saw that Sherlock was looking at the knife. 'I will fight with you,' he said calmly. 'And, if that is the will of the universe, I will die alongside you.'

Sherlock shivered. 'I'm really hoping it doesn't come to that,' he said.

Even while Sherlock and Wu had been talking, the junk had got closer. Sherlock could make out individual voices, and he could see the pirates' weapons clearly. Some of them were holding curved swords; some were holding long pikes with wickedly barbed blades on the end; some were holding strange metal shapes that resembled nothing so much as two swords tied together and covered with jutting metal thorns. The deck of the junk was a forest of sharp blades.

He had never felt so threatened, or so helpless, in his life. He could see the fierceness of the pirates' expressions and the wildness of their clothing. Many of them wore turbans made out of red or blue cloth. Some of them were bare-chested, others wore rough shirts or waistcoats. Most of them also had broad leather belts around their waists into which they had tucked an array of knives, swords and ancient pistols, and baggy trousers tucked into leather boots.

Sherlock noticed that a lot of them were wearing jewellery. That made sense. It wasn't as if they could place their treasure in a bank on shore, and hiding it somewhere on board their junk meant taking the risk that another pirate would steal it. The only safe solution was to carry as much of their personal wealth as they could.

Despite his terror, Sherlock spotted that one of the pirates was holding something. It was about the size and shape of a turnip, and he was hefting it as if he intended to throw it. Sherlock wondered exactly what he thought he was doing. Throwing rocks, or the nearest equivalent, wasn't exactly going to help the pirates take over the *Gloria Scott*, was it?

Then he realized that a lot of the pirates were holding similar objects.

The rest of the crew of the *Gloria Scott* were equally puzzled. Sherlock could hear fevered discussions all around him as his companions speculated wildly on what the pirates were planning.

They had their answer sooner than they wanted. As the two ships came within throwing range three of the pirates fiddled with the objects in their hands. It took a moment for Sherlock to work out what they had done, but when the pirates balanced themselves like cricketers and threw the turnip-sized objects towards the *Gloria Scott* Sherlock could see that they each trailed behind them a length of string that had been set alight.

A fuse.

'Watch out, lads!' Mr Larchmont's voice rose above the commotion. 'This is the devil's work!'

The objects arced overhead. One of them hit a mast and bounced off, falling back into the strip of ocean between the two ships. The other two hit the deck, bounced a couple of times, then rolled to a stop.

Before anyone could get to them, they exploded.

They were something like fireworks and something like small bombs. Scarlet and yellow flames spread rapidly over the deck as some kind of oily substance splattered across the wood and soaked in. Sparks scattered like swarms of fiery insects. Sailors rushed to throw buckets of seawater on to the burning oil. Steam rose up from the deck, but the flames just hissed and then kept on burning.

'Sand!' Larchmont bellowed from somewhere towards the back of the deck. Break out the sandbags! Spread sand on the flames if you value your lives!'

Five more fireballs burst on the deck, spilling oil and flames and sparks in all directions. A sailor running with a bucket of water slipped and fell into the conflagration. Sherlock saw him roll out again instantly, but his shirt was on fire. Without thinking, Sherlock ran over to him and tried to brush the flames out, but the oil had soaked into the cloth and it wouldn't extinguish. Another sailor joined Sherlock, and together they managed to rip the shirt from the man's back and throw it overboard, singeing their fingers in the process.

Black smoke billowed across the deck, obscuring Sherlock's view. The smoke caught at the back of his throat and he choked. His eyes stung.

Panic engulfed the ship.

But only for a moment, and then discipline reasserted itself, bolstered by Mr Larchmont's shouted orders. A group of sailors ran forward with sandbags, dragged from somewhere inside the ship. They ripped the seams open with knives and scattered the sand across the burning oil. It smothered the flames instantly. Dark smoke drifted across the deck, but the hellish glow of the fire was gone. Discipline reasserted itself.

Either because they realized that the crew of the *Gloria Scott* were standing by with more sandbags, or because the pirates had run out of ammunition, no more fireballs sailed overhead from the junk. The tone of the pirates' shouts changed as well, from triumphant laughing to a darker collection of curses and threats.

Movement on the deck of the junk attracted his attention. He stared intently. Pirates were massing at the closest point to the *Gloria Scott*. They were carrying grappling hooks. Having softened the crew up with their fireballs, the pirates were preparing to board the *Gloria Scott*. Sherlock could swear that some of them were looking directly at him, and smiling with exposed teeth.

He felt an involuntary shiver run through him. His stomach churned, and there was an acidic, metallic taste at the back of his throat. Part of him desperately wanted the chase to be over, so that something would happen. As it was, all he could do was wait, and the waiting was unbearable. On the other hand, another part of him dreaded the inevitable battle and hoped the chase would continue until they hit land. All he had was a small knife

65

to offer up against swords, pikes and weapons the like of which he had never seen before. If it came to a fight he wouldn't last thirty seconds.

And then the first pirate threw the first grappling hook. It arced across the distance between the ships, trailing a rope behind it like a pencil line scrawled across the blue page of the sky. The distance was too great: the hook hit the side of the *Gloria Scott* and bounced off, but it was a signal that triggered the rest of the pirates into action. While the first one pulled his hook out of the water, ready to try again, the others swung their hooks around their heads and let them fly. The air was suddenly filled with sharp metal and wet rope. Most of the hooks fell short, but four or five of them cleared the *Gloria Scott*'s rail and hit the deck. A great shout went up from the pirates. The ropes were pulled sharply back before any of the *Gloria Scott*'s crew could get to them – pulled with enough force that the curved hooks embedded themselves in the railing that ran around the edge of the deck. The ropes pulled tight, forming precarious bridges over which the pirates could clamber like monkeys, but before any of them could get all the way across, the *Gloria Scott*'s crew started sawing through the ropes with swords and knives, or swinging at them with axes. Others tried to prise the hooks from the wooden rail by hand. None of those first ropes lasted longer than thirty seconds, sending the pirates who were climbing along them falling into the narrowing strip of water between the two ships, but by that time there were twenty more hooks embedding themselves in the *Gloria Scott*'s deck and rails and masts, or tangling themselves in the ship's rigging. Sherlock glanced around desperately.

Pretty soon there would be too many hooks and ropes for the crew to deal with.

'Look lively!' Mr Larchmont yelled. 'If you ever want to see your wives and girlfriends again, don't let these barbarians set one pox-ridden foot on this ship!'

Sherlock saw that as well as climbing along the ropes, the pirates were also hauling on them from the safety of their deck, trying to narrow the distance between the two vessels. It seemed to be working. The *Gloria Scott* and the pirate ship were nearly side by side now, and there was barely five yards between them.

A hook hit the deck next to Sherlock's foot. Before he could do anything the rope pulled taut, and the hook whipped away from him, catching in the wooden rim surrounding one of the hatches. Sherlock leaped towards it, desperately sawing at the fibres with his knife, but his blade was blunt and slipped off the wet surface. He grabbed at the hook and tried to pull it out of the wood. His fingers kept scrabbling for purchase.

He glanced up. There were pirates already on board,

fighting hand to hand with the crew! Ignoring them as best he could, he let his gaze trace the line of the rope to where it crossed the rail. A pirate with wild, shoulder-length hair and a massive scar down the side of his face was already halfway across!

Sherlock redoubled his efforts. The grappling hook shifted beneath his hands: the barbed tines hadn't penetrated very far into the sun-baked wood, and by straining every fibre of his muscles he could just about pull it clear.

Sherlock gave one last heave, and the grappling hook shifted so that only one tine was caught on the wooden hatch. He glanced up. The grinning pirate was almost at the rail now.

Sherlock kicked at the grappling hook, desperately trying to dislodge it.

Somewhere on the ship a gun fired, and fired again. The Captain?

Still kicking at the hook, Sherlock looked up again.

It was too late. The pirate had reached the deck of the *Gloria Scott*. He took a step towards Sherlock, raising his sword menacingly.

He had a dragon tattooed on his forearm: a beautiful, sinuous creature rippling over his muscle and coloured in iridescent blue. For a split second that seemed to last an eternity Sherlock found himself admiring the artistry.

The pirate's upper lip pulled back in a sneer of triumph. His teeth were mottled black with decay, and spaced like gravestones.

More in sheer frustration than in hope, Sherlock kicked the grappling hook one last time. It tore free of the hatch with a ripping of wood and a spray of splinters. At the same time a freak roll of the waves pulled the two ships apart by ten feet or so. The rope suddenly went taut and the hook hurtled back towards where it had come from. The sharp points caught the pirate in the shoulder. His face took on a look of pain and astonishment as the rope yanked tighter, dragging him off his feet and back towards the railing. His back hit the top of the rail with a sickening crunch and he vanished over the edge. Despite the sounds of clashing steel, shouts and gunfire that filled the air, Sherlock could swear that he heard a terrified scream cut short by a splash.

With the ships that close together, Sherlock didn't give the pirate much of a chance of climbing back up. If he didn't drown straight away then the hulls would probably squash him like an insect as they came together.

And good riddance too.

In a moment of relative calm, Sherlock glanced around, trying to orientate himself. His impression was that the battle was evenly matched. There seemed to be as many pirates as there were crew, fighting hand to hand, and a quick glance at the unoccupied web of ropes that now linked the two ships together suggested that all of the pirates who could come across had done so. The remainder were presumably needed to man the pirate ship, to steer it, and stop it from suddenly veering sideways and smashing into the *Gloria Scott*.

Off to one side he caught sight of Mr Arrhenius. The veiled man had emerged from his cabin to see what was going on. He was standing half hidden by the ship's middle mast. He raised his hand, and Sherlock saw that he was holding a pistol. Carefully he took aim and fired. A pirate across the other side of the deck suddenly jerked and fell down.

Arrhenius glanced at Sherlock and nodded. Sherlock raised a thumb in acknowledgement of the passenger's help.

As Sherlock turned away a movement caught his eye. One pirate had broken off from the fight and was slipping along the raised deck towards the rear of the ship, aiming for the doorway in the middle – the doorway that led back towards the cabins. He was small, and what little hair he had was pulled back into a waxed pigtail. It was the surreptitious way he was moving that attracted Sherlock's attention. In the midst of a chaos of wildly waving weapons and grappling figures, this man moved as if he didn't want to be noticed.

Amyus Crowe often told Sherlock to look for the things that stick out, the things that don't belong. Those are things that have a story to tell. Those are things that need to be explained.

So Sherlock followed.

By the time he got to the doorway the pirate had vanished into the shadows of the corridor. Sherlock hung back for a moment, in case the man was going to turn around and come straight out, but after a few seconds he went in after him.

The clamour of the fight outside died away quickly. Sherlock paused while his eyes got used to the relative darkness. The pirate had gone directly to the door of Mr Arrhenius's cabin. But Arrhenius was out on deck, fighting – Sherlock had seen him. What on earth was the pirate looking for?

The door was open a crack, and Sherlock moved quietly closer. He looked inside.

The pirate was a dark shape illuminated only by the meagre light shining through the portholes, but Sherlock could see him bending over a table. He seemed to be gazing intently at something.

Sherlock wished he could see what it was. As if fate had heard him, the ship suddenly pitched sideways, and Sherlock found himself falling against the cabin door. It swung open and he staggered into the room.

The pirate's head snapped up. His gaze skewered Sherlock. His fingers, which had been holding a set of papers on the table, let go, allowing them to roll up, but Sherlock had time to see that the thing the pirate had been looking at was a set of diagrams that looked like spider's webs of lines.

What was going on?

The pirate grabbed at the papers and came around the desk towards Sherlock. He snarled something in Chinese, and it took Sherlock a moment to translate it. 'Out of my way, boy, or I will cut your heart out and eat it.' At least, that's what Sherlock *thought* he said.

Sherlock straightened up. 'Put that back,' he found himself saying.

The pirate sneered. He stepped towards Sherlock, holding the bundle of papers in his left hand. He raised his right hand, and Sherlock saw with no surprise that he was holding a knife. He lunged, aiming the knife at Sherlock's chest.

Without thinking, Sherlock blocked the lunging knife with a sweep of his outstretched left hand, then thrust his right hand out, hitting the pirate's right arm with the heel of his palm. The impact temporarily paralysed the pirate's muscles. His fingers spasmed, and he dropped the knife. Sherlock realized with amazement that he had performed a classic *T'ai chi ch'uan* move, but faster than ever before.

The pirate took a step backwards. Still holding the papers, he twisted around and lashed out with his right foot, raising it high enough that if it connected it would break Sherlock's nose. His body leaned backwards to maintain balance. Anticipating what was going to happen, Sherlock dropped to his hands and bent left leg, and scythed his right leg around parallel to the floor, knocking the pirate's own right leg from beneath him. The pirate fell, sprawling clumsily. The papers flew out of his hand and landed beneath the table.

Sherlock was amazed. It was as if his body already knew what to do without his brain having to tell it. Thank heaven for Wu Chung's gentle instruction.

The pirate scrabbled across the deck, heading for the papers. Whatever they were, he wanted them badly. And Sherlock wanted to stop him just as much. He grabbed hold of the pirate's right foot and pulled him back. The man's fingers clutched at the carpet, but when it became obvious that he couldn't stop himself moving he rolled over and kicked out viciously. The heel of his boot caught Sherlock on his cheekbone. A lightning bolt of red-hot agony shot through his head, blurring all of his senses and all of his thoughts.

Hands grabbed him around the throat and started to squeeze.

CHAPTER FOUR

Spikes of pain shot up Sherlock's neck and down into his chest. His heart was pounding but his blurry vision was narrowing into a dark-edged tunnel.

He brought his hands up between the pirate's forearms and then, with all his remaining strength, knocked them apart. The grip on his neck loosened. He sucked in huge gulps of air until the pirate's hands snaked back around his neck and began to squeeze again.

Sherlock's vision was restricted to a spot the size of a coin held at arm's length. His skin and his muscles tingled as though someone was poking needles and pins into every square inch of it. He could hardly raise his hands, they felt so heavy.

Desperately, blindly, Sherlock reached out for the pirate's face. He clamped his fingers on either side of the man's head, and put his thumbs where he thought his eyes were. When he felt his opponent's eyelids, squeezed shut beneath the pads of his thumbs, he pushed as hard as he could.

The pirate screamed. His hands vanished from around Sherlock's throat. He pulled away, leaving Sherlock to fall backwards. Dimly Sherlock was aware of a scuttling, a blundering, as if the pirate had tried to get to his feet and run out of the cabin but had run into the wall and the door frame on the way. Sherlock rolled over and got to his hands and knees, then pushed himself up until he was standing. His vision was coming back now. The cabin was deserted. He put a shaking hand on the table and leaned there for a few moments until he thought his legs could take his weight without crumpling.

The roll of papers was beneath the table. The pirate hadn't taken it when he left the cabin.

When he felt strong enough he bent down and picked the papers up. He was about to put them back on the table and take a closer look when he noticed a box in the corner. It was the one he'd seen loaded on to the ship with Mr Arrhenius's belongings. There was something in it, scuttling around. Before he could investigate, he heard a voice from the doorway.

'What do you think you are doing?'

Mr Arrhenius was standing in the doorway. He was holding a gun, and frowning.

'One of the pirates got in here,' Sherlock said, feeling a painful rasp in his throat. 'I followed him in. We had a fight. He ran off. I don't know where he went.'

'I saw him stagger out on to the deck,' Arrhenius said.

He raised his gun and tapped it against his forehead, beneath his veil. 'I . . . stopped him, then I came in to see what he had been doing here.'

'He was trying to take this,' Sherlock said, holding the roll of papers up.

'Was he now?' Arrhenius said. There was something strange about his voice, and he was looking oddly at Sherlock.

'What is it?' Sherlock asked, feeling bolder now that he had got his breath back.

'Nothing for you to concern yourself with.'

Arrhenius extended his hand for the papers. Sherlock handed them over. He still desperately wanted to know what they were, but he knew that the strange passenger wasn't going to tell him.

'What's happening on deck?' he asked.

'Captain Tollaway and the rest of the crew are turning the tide,' Arrhenius declared. 'It seems to me that they are going to repel the boarders. You should go and join them.' He glanced around the cabin. 'I must see if anything else is missing.'

Sherlock headed out on to the deck. A crumpled body lay to one side. It was the pirate who had attacked Sherlock in the cabin. Sherlock looked at him for a moment, then turned away. He didn't feel any grief, or remorse, or fear. In fact, apart from the pain in his throat and the pounding of his head he didn't feel anything.

Mr Arrhenius was right – the crew seemed to be beating back the pirates. A handful of bodies were scattered around the deck, contorted in various positions, and a few of the pirates appeared to be withdrawing, injured.

'Avast!' Larchmont's voice yelled from the other side of the ship. 'Withdraw to me, laddies!'

Sherlock watched in confusion as the crew of the *Gloria Scott* disengaged from their individual fights and backed across the deck towards Larchmont. They were winning. Why disengage from the fight now?

The crew shifted, and a path momentarily opened up between Sherlock and Mr Larchmont, and Sherlock suddenly realized what was happening. Larchmont was standing by the rail, and he was holding a strange contraption. It was a metal tube about the length of a man's arm, sealed at one end and open at the other. It was pivoting on a metal knob which was attached to the rail. The knob somehow fitted into a recess in the tube. Sherlock had seen the metal knob before, while he'd been working on deck, and he had wondered what it was for. Now he knew. Gittens had said they had no cannon on board, but he had been wrong. There was one – a small one – and Larchmont was holding it. He was pointing it at the pirates.

'Light it up,' he said grimly. A hand holding a lit taper

emerged from the throng of crewmen. The taper touched a hole at the sealed end of the cannon.

Mayhem ripped across the deck.

Whatever was in the cannon, it wasn't a cannonball. Sherlock guessed it was probably a length of metal chain, along with nails and bits of scrap.

Those pirates who, miraculously, were not hit by the blizzard of metal turned and ran. The others . . . well, Sherlock didn't even want to look. There would be a lot of clearing up to do later.

The crew let out a ragged cheer.

'Well done, lads!' Larchmont shouted. 'Extra rum for everyone! Now make sure the motherless sons of the devil have really gone!'

Sherlock joined in as the majority of the crew crossed to the other side of the deck. They clustered against the rail, watching in disbelief. It was true – the pirates were casting off the lines that bound them to the *Gloria Scott*, and their ship was pulling away. The pirates on deck were shouting curses at the crew of the *Gloria Scott* and shaking their fists, but they were a lot more subdued than they had been earlier. There were fewer of them as well.

Sherlock felt sick, and his legs were suddenly weak. He leaned on the side of the ship and fixed his gaze on the distant horizon, waiting for the sensation to subside.

Why was he feeling like this? It wasn't as if he hadn't

78

been in danger before. In the past couple of years he'd been chased, knocked unconscious, drugged, locked up in a lunatic asylum and attacked variously by men, dogs, mountain lions, lizards, falcons and bears. It had been an eventful few years. So why was he reacting this way now?

Because, the logical side of his brain told him, he was a long way from home. Nobody was going to leap in at the last moment to save him – not Matty, not Mycroft, not Amyus Crowe and not Virginia. He had never relied on their help before, but in the back of his mind he'd always known that if his intelligence and strength weren't enough to carry the day then one of them would be there for him. But not now. Not here. And not for a long time to come.

The full weight of loneliness descended on him like a leaden cloud, and he found his eyes stinging with hot tears. If he died out here, on board the *Gloria Scott*, thousands of miles from England, then nobody would ever know. Even the other sailors would forget about him within a few weeks.

'Dangerous situation,' a voice said beside him. 'I am gratified that you came through it alive.'

Wu Chung was standing there, gazing out across the water with a faint, enigmatic smile on his face. He had a scratch on his shoulder which had bled on to his cook's apron, and there were scratches on his face.

'Are you all right?' Sherlock asked.

Wu Chung nodded. 'There was a fight,' he said. 'I won.'

'*T'ai chi ch'uan?*' Sherlock asked, imagining Wu Chung in full combat, fighting off an opponent with subtle movements of his hands and feet.

Wu shook his head. 'No – I used a frying pan. Unarmed combat is all very well, but if the universe in its infinite wisdom provides a weapon to hand then it would be rude not to use it.'

'I was in a fight as well,' Sherlock said.

'I can see. Your neck looks like someone has tenderized it with a meat hammer, and your voice is as hoarse as a man who has been smoking rough tobacco for many years.'

'I used the skills you taught me. They worked.'

'Of course they did,' Wu said, still gazing out across the sea. 'I am a good teacher, am I not?'

He turned away, still without glancing at Sherlock's face, and walked back across the deck. It was only then that Sherlock realized that he couldn't be sure whether they had been speaking in English or Cantonese.

Sherlock spent the rest of the day on activities that he hoped he wouldn't remember for very long – swabbing blood off the deck, throwing the bodies of pirates overboard, and sewing shrouds of sail canvas around the handful of sailors from the *Gloria Scott* who had perished in the battle. By the time the sun touched the horizon the deck was clear and there was little sign that anything untoward had happened, apart from the row of canvas-wrapped bodies lined up on the deck. Captain Tollaway read from a Bible, and the bodies were consigned to the ocean. The shrouds were weighted so that they would sink.

The sailors were in the mood for singing that night. Captain Tollaway had ordered the rum ration tripled, which made the sailors more than usually rambunctious, and they obviously wanted to blot out the memories of the pirate attack by any means they could. Sherlock found himself playing jig after jig on the cracked violin that Fiddler had lent him. He missed notes and sometimes segued from one tune to another without realizing, but the sailors didn't seem to notice. As long as there were rum and music they were happy.

Even while he was sawing away at the old violin, surrounded by drunken sailors singing at the tops of their voices, Sherlock's mind refused to stop thinking. He found himself trying to work out why the pirate who had raided the Arrhenius's cabin had made straight for the strange spider's-web diagrams. The implication was that he had known that they were there, and that he had some reason for wanting them. But that would imply either that the pirate had taken advantage of the completely accidental coincidence that his ship and the *Gloria Scott* were at the same point in the ocean at the same time, or that the whole attack had been deliberate – that the pirates had known in advance which ship they were going to attack. That suggested some kind of conspiracy above and beyond normal piracy. How could the pirates have known that the *Gloria Scott* was the ship they wanted to attack?

There was something very strange going on here. He wished he had somebody to discuss it with, but he didn't trust anybody on board any more than he had to.

What he wouldn't give to have Mycroft, or Amyus Crowe, or even Matty to hand.

A barely concealed sense of tension hung over the *Gloria Scott* for the remainder of the voyage. The crew kept casting worried glances at the distant horizon, keeping watch for more pirate ships, and both the Captain and Mr Larchmont spent considerably more time pacing up and down on deck than they had before the attack, trying to reassure the men by their presence. The crew were having to work harder as well. At the end of each extended shift, Sherlock climbed into his hammock exhausted, so tired that he slept dreamlessly until the bell was rung for his next shift.

During a break, a few days after the attack, he was

standing at the rail and looking out to sea when he realized that somebody was standing beside him. He turned his head, expecting it to be Wu Chung, or perhaps Fiddler. A shiver ran through him when he saw that it was Mr Arrhenius.

He was still wearing his black beekeeper's veil beneath his wide-brimmed hat. Sherlock could just make out the silhouette of his face beneath. His black leather gloves gripped hold of the rail. He seemed to be staring at the same point on the horizon as Sherlock.

'I believe we should be seeing land soon,' he said. 'According to the Captain, we have only a day or two until we arrive in Shanghai.'

'Landfall can't come soon enough,' Sherlock replied quietly. 'This voyage feels like it's gone on forever.'

Arrhenius nodded. 'It has certainly been eventful,' he admitted. He was silent for a while, then he said suddenly, 'I believe I owe you an explanation.'

'About what?' Sherlock hoped that it might be about the papers the pirate had been after.

'About my appearance. I understand that it shocked you, seeing me without my veil that time when you brought food to my cabin. I apologize.'

Sherlock shook his head. 'You don't owe me anything. I admit that I'm curious, but you don't have to tell me anything if you don't want to.'

'But still . . . I know how superstitious sailors get. Others have seen me, in unguarded moments, without my veil.' He laughed sadly. 'They probably think that I am some kind of supernatural creature – a demon, or a vampire perhaps. If I explain my condition to you, perhaps you can reassure them.'

'I doubt they would listen to me about anything,' Sherlock said dubiously. 'I'm still pretty much an outsider on this ship. But I'm happy to give it a try, if that's what you want.'

Arrhenius nodded. 'I would appreciate that. Thank you.' He paused, and Sherlock got the impression that he was searching for the right words. 'My skin has not always been this colour,' he said eventually. 'When I was younger, it was the same colour as yours.' He glanced sideways at Sherlock. 'Well, perhaps not as tanned. Anyway, business affairs meant that I did a lot of travelling to other countries – Africa, Egypt, South America . . . If you name a port in any country on the globe I can guarantee that I have been there.'

'I used to want to travel,' Sherlock said. 'Until I tried it. Now I can see why my brother prefers to stay at home.'

'Travel broadens the mind,' Arrhenius said, 'but it has its disadvantages. Hot countries in particular breed diseases more virulent than anything that exists in England, or in Holland. You may have heard about the terrible effects of cholera and typhoid and the bubonic plague, but the effects of the little known black Formosa corruption are horrible to observe, and as for Tapanuli fever . . .' He shuddered. 'Watching a man dying of Tapanuli fever is like watching a man whose skin is slowly melting away from his body. Truly a terrible way to go.'

'You've never . . . caught any of those diseases yourself?' Sherlock asked after a few moments' silence.

'Have you ever heard of silver being used to prevent disease?'

Sherlock shook his head.

'Silver has had some medicinal uses going back for centuries,' Arrhenius continued. 'Hippocrates, the Greek philosopher who is said to have been the father of medicine, wrote that silver could prevent illness and could help in the healing of wounds. The Phoenicians, who sailed the world long before either your country or mine had a navy, are supposed to have stored water, wine and vinegar in silver bottles to prevent them from spoiling. I have even heard of people putting silver coins in milk bottles to prevent the milk from going off, believe it or not.'

'And you've been treating *yourself* with silver?' Sherlock asked, fascinated.

'It seemed . . . logical,' Arrhenius said. 'It seemed to

me, based on everything that I researched, that it made sense. Silver prevents disease. So, every day for the past ten years I have taken a drink of colloidal silver – that is to say, of silver dust suspended in castor oil. In all of that time I have not been ill. Not one single time.'

'But . . .' Sherlock prompted.

'Yes, there is always a "but". In this case, over time the silver particles have collected in my tissues – most notably in my skin and my eyes. I am told, by the specialists that I have consulted, that the condition is called *argyria*. It is apparently quite rare.' He laughed abruptly. 'How ironic, that I should avoid so many other diseases only to fall prey to this one.'

'Does it hurt?' Sherlock asked.

Arrhenius shook his head. 'Not in the slightest. It is . . . what is the word? A disfigurement, nothing more. It does not hurt, and I suffer no ill-effects other than the change in the colour of my skin. To be frank with you, if I knew then what I know now, I would make the same decision. To look strange, as I do, is unfortunate, but to never suffer from any disease, not even a cold . . . that is truly something worth having.'

'What happens if you stop taking the silver? Will your skin recover?'

It looked as though Arrhenius was shaking his head, behind the veil. 'Sadly, no. The minute particles of silver have become embedded in my flesh. There is no going back. Not that I ever would.'

There didn't seem to be anything Sherlock could say to that, and the two of them stood there for a while in silence, looking out at the ocean. Eventually Arrhenius walked away, leaving Sherlock with his own thoughts.

Naively, Sherlock had expected there to be a moment when land was sighted as a dark smudge on the horizon, accompanied probably by a strong cheer from the crew and the breaking out of more rum. In fact, first a small island, barely larger than the ship, was seen in the distance. Then another. After a few hours there were ten or twenty islands on either side of the bows, and Mr Larchmont ordered the sails to be reduced to slow the *Gloria Scott* down and give him more control over the steering. They picked their way slowly among the islands. The mainland seemed to sneak up on them. For a while it looked like another, larger, island. By the time it became clear that it was more than that, distinct hills were visible in the hinterland behind the coves and harbours.

They had arrived at Shanghai. They had arrived in *China*.

Sherlock's feelings were mixed. Partly he was filled with

excitement at the idea of experiencing a new country, a new *culture*, where nothing would be the same as he was used to ('except,' he heard Amyus Crowe's voice in the back of his mind, 'human nature'). At the same time he was filled with sorrow, knowing that he was at the moment as far from home and as far from his friends as he was going to get. This was the end of the journey out. With luck, and perhaps a little careful planning, he could stay on the *Gloria Scott* and be part of the crew for the long journey home.

Would home still be the same when he got back?

Would *he*?

The temperature and the humidity had risen sharply as they approached land. The sea breezes that had been simultaneously pushing the ship along and cooling the crew down had died away, leaving a heavy stillness in the air. Sherlock could feel sweat breaking out across his shoulder blades every time he moved.

Fortunately, the riot of noise and colour and motion that was Shanghai harbour was enough to distract him from his thoughts and his discomfort. Boats and ships of unusual design were heading in every direction, usually at some speed, and everyone was shouting at everyone else. It reminded Sherlock of the times he had arrived on the train at Waterloo Station in London and seen people criss-crossing the concourse, somehow avoiding bumping into each other without apparently swerving or slowing down.

Sherlock noticed that several of the ships in the harbour were Chinese junks. He felt his skin crawl, remembering the pirate attack, but he told himself that the design was common to almost all Chinese ships. The pirates were sure to be a long way away by now.

Mr Larchmont ordered all of the sails to be taken down. Sherlock worked as the ship came to a gradual stop in a clear area of water out in the centre of the harbour. Mr Larchmont ordered the anchor to be weighed. For a while they just waited, but Sherlock became aware that a handful of small, flat-bottomed boats were heading their way. Presumably there had to be some kind of inspection, or at the very least a discussion with the local administrators, before they would be allowed to dock.

Sherlock gazed out at the harbour. A series of quays and jetties had been built along its curve, with watchtowers at either end of the crescent. Behind the quayside and the jetties Sherlock could make out a series of warehouses, all of which appeared to be built to the same design. Off to one side, and sprawling into the haze of the distance, was the town of Shanghai itself. It was surrounded by a wall that Sherlock estimated was about five times as high as Amyus Crowe. The presence of the wall and of the watchtowers suggested to Sherlock that the town had been subject to many attacks through its history, but the wall was crumbling in places, and the watchtowers were weather-beaten and almost falling down. Whatever bad things had happened in the past, Shanghai now seemed to be safe and perhaps even complacent, like an old and sleepy ginger tomcat with scars on its face and a torn nose.

As well as the Chinese junks there were a smattering of ships that looked more like the *Gloria Scott* in the harbour. Western traders were obviously welcomed by the Chinese. One ship in particular caught his eye. It was long, and low in the water, and painted white – or at least it had probably started out white, but was now a kind of creamy grey. It had two masts – one fore and one aft – but between them was a funnel and beside the funnel, in a kind of cage that protruded out sideways from the deck, was a large paddle wheel. It reminded Sherlock of the ship he had travelled to America on a year or so ago. That had used a coal-powered steam engine to power a pair of paddle wheels. The idea was that if the wind dropped then the engine could be fired up and the ship moved by the rotation of the paddle wheels in the water.

The funnel looked newer than the rest of the ship. He wondered if there had been some kind of accident. Maybe the ship had been damaged, and the funnel had been repaired and repainted.

His thoughts were interrupted by a commotion behind him. Captain Tollaway had appeared on the deck, with Mr Larchmont standing one pace behind him. He was wearing a fresh uniform and was even trying to smile.

Crewmen near Sherlock were helping three men on board. They had climbed up a rope ladder from their flat-bottomed boat. Two of them wore baggy robes of patterned silk which wrapped around their bodies, and padded slippers. The third man wore a similar robe, but with a loose black jacket over the top. All three of them had black caps on their heads. The caps had straight sides, flat tops and no brims. The overall effect was a strange mix of ostentation and reserve. They greeted the Captain effusively, bowing repeatedly. The Captain bowed back, looking uncomfortable.

The man with the black jacket seemed to be a translator. When the two administrators spoke in Cantonese he listened, then repeated the message back to the Captain in heavily accented English. When the Captain replied he did the same in reverse.

Whatever discussion or negotiation was going on, it was completed to the satisfaction of both parties. The meeting broke up with a lot more bowing, and the three men were escorted off the *Gloria Scott* again.

Mr Larchmont spoke with the Captain, then turned

to the attentive crew. 'We'll be docking in Shanghai shortly,' he announced. 'The Captain's intention is to be here for a week while we sell off our cargo, barter for a new one and reprovision for the voyage home. I'll be handin' out your wages, in cash, down in the crew room over the next hour. If you want your hard-earned money, you need to come an' get it from me, otherwise I'll spend it on dresses and jewels for my missus back in Lambeth.' He smiled at the chuckles and whistles that followed his comment. 'That's my story, lads, an' I'm stickin' to it. Now, I'll be pinning up a roster of shore leave, an' I want every man-jack of you to read it and follow it. This ship has to have a skeleton crew aboard at all times, and there have to be enough additional men to shift cargo in an' out.' He paused. 'It's been a hard voyage, an' we've lost some mates. You deserve a good time, but keep a hand on your wallets an' an eye on the local law. If you find yourselves in clink then I ain't guaranteeing that I'll be able to afford to get you out!'

It took most of the rest of the afternoon for the *Gloria Scott* to be towed to a vacant section of quayside by a flotilla of smaller boats. By the time the ship was fastened to the quay by thick ropes and a gangway laid from the deck down to the dock, the sun was dipping beneath the hills.

Within half an hour of having docked, the ship was

nearly deserted. Any crew member who wasn't required to stay behind had left. Even Mr Arrhenius, dressed in his beekeeper's veil and black leather gloves, had left the ship. He had nodded at Sherlock as he walked towards the gangway. Perhaps he smiled slightly, but the veil made it difficult to tell. The sailors gave him a wide berth as he walked past, and none of them would walk on to the gangway while he was standing on it.

Eventually, as the sky turned from blue to red, Sherlock stood at the top of the gangway, looking towards the town. He wanted to explore, but he was nervous. He didn't know anything about local customs. He might get into trouble.

A large hand touched his shoulder. 'You can come with me,' Wu Chung said in a kindly voice from behind him. He was speaking Cantonese, and Sherlock could understand him pretty well. 'You should meet my family. They will cook oysters, and crab, and jellyfish for you. It will be a feast like you've never seen before.'

Sherlock smiled, but shook his head. 'No, this is your time,' he replied. 'Go and see them again. Catch up on all the gossip. Tell them about your adventures. I don't want them distracted by having a foreigner there, and having to be hospitable.'

'You are a wise man,' Wu said. He squeezed Sherlock's shoulder. 'Any time you want to come and see me, make your way to Renmin Dong Lu, and ask for the Wu family. Everyone knows where we live. You are welcome, always.'

He took his hand off Sherlock's shoulder, but he still stayed where he was for a few moments. He seemed reluctant to leave. Sherlock turned to look at him. The big cook was staring wistfully out at the town.

'I wonder if they will remember me,' he said softly.

Before Sherlock could say anything, Wu Chung set off down the gangway. Watching him go, Sherlock considered how much he'd learned from the cook. Not only how to defend himself using the movements of *T'ai chi ch'uan*, but also how to communicate with the locals in Cantonese. He had been lucky in the teachers he had met over the past two years – Amyus Crowe, Rufus Stone and Wu Chung. And Mycroft, of course, although his brother rarely gave the impression that he was teaching Sherlock anything, despite the fact that everything he said contained a lesson of some kind.

He wondered with a slight and sudden flutter of his heart where his friends and family thought he was.

As he was about to disembark he heard a voice behind him say, 'I always wanted a crewman who could take orders without complaining, work hard without shirking and then walk off the ship without being paid. People told me I was mad, but I said to them, "You wait – one day I'll find a crewman just like that." And here you are, laddie. Here you are.'

Sherlock turned. He had already recognized the voice. It was Mr Larchmont, and he was gazing at Sherlock with a bemused expression on his face. He held up an envelope – rough brown manila, stained by many sets of fingerprints. 'Do you want your pay, or shall I donate it to the Jim Larchmont Charity for Distressed Ship's Masters?'

'Sorry,' Sherlock said, reaching out for the envelope. 'I nearly forgot.'

'You're a good sailor, laddie,' Larchmont said as he handed it over. 'I keep forgetting you started out as a stowaway. You deserve pay – more than some of those other wastes of victuals I was forced to employ.' He paused. 'You're coming back, I hope? Not stopping off here to make your fortune, or see more of the world?'

'I'm coming back,' Sherlock confirmed. 'I want to get home to England.'

Larchmont stared at him for a few moments. 'There're ships in dock that are leaving sooner than we are, and heading back for Blighty,' he said softly. 'If you want, I could have a word with one of the captains for you. Get you a berth.'

'Thanks,' Sherlock said, 'but I'd rather wait a few days and leave with the *Gloria Scott*.' He shrugged. 'I never

95

thought I'd say this, but the ship feels like home.'

'Aye,' Larchmont murmured. 'That she does.' He paused, and then in a louder voice said, 'You be off now before the sun goes down and the rats come out of their holes. Stay away from card games, strong spirits and any woman that tries to speak to you before you've spoken to her.'

'Aye aye, sir!' Sherlock saluted, and then turned and headed for the gangway. As he went he slipped the envelope that Mr Larchmont had given him into a pocket of his jacket. Before he could pull his fingers out, they encountered something else – a smooth, curved piece of metal. He pulled it out, curious as to what it was. It took a moment before he recognized it as the object he had picked up off the deck outside Mr Arrhenius's cabin a few days before. He stared at it, bemused.

'Fifteen seconds, laddie, then you have to stay and prise the barnacles off the hull!' Mr Larchmont shouted.

'Aye aye, sir!' Sherlock called back. He slipped the metal object back into his pocket next to the envelope of cash and sprinted down the gangway towards the Shanghai quayside.

CHAPTER FIVE

Standing on the quayside, Sherlock was impressed by the city wall looming over everything. The stonework was in obvious disrepair, but he could also see scars that looked like they might have been the result of cannonballs striking the walls and bouncing off. The scars looked fresh – the stone beneath was still bright, not darkened with age and not covered with moss. It looked as if there had been some kind of fighting around the city in the not too distant past. He wondered what had happened – and whether it was likely to happen again while he was there.

Off to the right was a city gate. Guards in flared metal helmets and brightly coloured uniforms were stopping everyone who wanted to enter the town – questioning them and checking their papers. Again, it was evidence that there was unrest in this country. He hoped things would be quiet while he was here. The locals could have whatever wars and battles they wanted, as long as they waited until the *Gloria Scott* had left.

He watched as various people walked past him. The Chinese were mostly dressed in variations on the baggy wraparound robes that he'd seen earlier on the ship, although some had a combination of loose trousers with a round-collared shirt. The materials were all embroidered, patterned or dyed in bright colours. It was very different from the browns, greys and blacks that he was used to in England, but he found that some things were still the same. He could tell various trades by the signs that they left behind. One man, coming towards him, was in his thirties but had hands that looked as though they belonged to someone much older – wrinkled and white. He probably ran a laundry, and spent most of his working day with his hands in hot soapy water. Another man had a tanned face and arms, but his hands were dead white. He was probably a baker, and the whiteness was caused by flour coating his skin. Several cooks passed by – they, like Wu Chung, had hands covered with tiny cuts. Numerous passers-by had wrinkles and patches of mud on their trousers, and Sherlock tentatively classified them as farmers who spent a lot of time kneeling down and either planting or pulling up vegetables.

Remembering the envelope that Mr Larchmont had given him, he pulled it from the pocket that he'd stashed it in and examined the contents. It was a loose collection of copper coins of various kinds. They weren't British currency. Most of them had square holes in them and odd symbols around the edges. He presumed that they were Chinese. He supposed that made sense – there was no point in paying the crew in pounds sterling if the local businesses only took local currency. He had no way of knowing what value the coins were, or whether they added up to a fair wage for the many weeks he'd spent on board the *Gloria Scott*, but he found that he didn't particularly care. Money had never been that important to him. Matty had never understood that about him.

Before he could decide what to do next, two things happened at the same time: a hand grabbed the envelope, and something struck him hard in the small of his back, sending him sprawling forward. He managed to twist as he fell so that it was his back that hit the ground rather than his chest. He could feel stones digging into his skin.

Three dark-haired boys were grouped together where he had been standing. They were all about his size. Despite their obvious youth the one who had taken his envelope had a thin moustache and the boy on his right had a straggly beard. The third boy was clean-shaven but his hair was long and greasy.

Around them, people walked past as if nothing untoward was happening. It was as if they were in their own little bubble, separate from the rest of the world.

'You don't need this, do you?' the one holding the envelope said in Cantonese. He held the envelope up, smiling. 'Just say if you want it back.'

The three boys laughed.

'Yes, I want it back,' Sherlock said, also in Cantonese, as he climbed to his feet and brushed the dust from his clothes.

The boys stared at him, surprised. 'You speak *Yue*?' the greasy-haired one exclaimed. 'I didn't think white barbarians could learn our language!'

'I can do more than speak your language,' Sherlock said darkly. 'Give that back.'

'Or what?' the bearded youth sneered.

He found his hands and feet naturally assuming *T'ai chi ch'uan* defensive positions. 'Or I'll take it back.'

The boy glanced at his friends. 'One against three? Hardly fair. One of us could defeat three of you, little boy.'

'Numbers aren't important. I want it back more than you want to keep it.'

'And besides,' another voice said in accented Cantonese from one side, 'it's not one against three – it's two against three. The two of us can take the three of you easily.'

The boys all turned their heads to see who was speaking. Sherlock took the opportunity to step forward and snatch his pay from the boy who had taken it. The boy's head spun back, and he grabbed for the envelope, but Sherlock stepped out of the way.

On the other side of the boys stood a Western youth of about Sherlock's age and about Sherlock's height. He was thin and he wore metal-rimmed spectacles. His hair was blond, almost white: it was swept back from his forehead and it was long enough to fall over his ears and collar. His clothes were Chinese, but somehow newer and cleaner than the ones that everyone else was wearing.

The youth with the moustache stepped forward and reached for Sherlock's envelope at the same time that his friends decided to remove the newcomer from the equation. One of them – the bearded one – reached out to push the blond boy's shoulder while the other one – the one with greasy hair – tried to step past him and put a foot behind his leg so that if he moved backwards to avoid the shove he would trip over.

Sherlock grabbed the approaching wrist with his right hand and then twisted his whole body underneath it. The boy jerked forward, forced over by the pressure on his arm. Sherlock glanced at the newcomer. The blond boy easily deflected the hand moving towards his shoulder. He stepped forward rather than backwards, throwing the boy with the greasy hair off balance. His right hand shot out, fingers curled so that the heel of the hand slammed into the bearded youth's ribcage. The youth doubled up in pain. Before the one with greasy hair could react, the blond newcomer lashed out with

101

his elbow, catching him in the face. Greasy Hair jerked back, blood streaming from his nose.

Sherlock felt the boy whose arm he was twisting trying to pull away. He twisted harder. The boy lashed backwards with a foot, but Sherlock had anticipated the movement and sidestepped him. He released the boy's wrist, but before the boy could turn around Sherlock kicked him hard in the buttocks. The boy sprawled forward, into the dust.

'Best leave now,' the blond boy said in English. He pulled Sherlock into a run. 'Bravado is all very well, but there *are* three of them, and they've been studying martial arts since they were five years old.'

'We didn't do too badly.'

'We were lucky. We caught them by surprise.' He looked around. 'And they have friends nearby. I know what they're like. Despite the fact that they spend their lives talking about honourable behaviour, they have no honour themselves when it comes to foreigners. One shout and we could find ourselves up against a crowd.'

'Good point,' Sherlock conceded.

Together they ran through the crowd, twisting and turning in case the Chinese boys were following. The blond boy changed direction several times. Eventually he led Sherlock behind a stall selling dishes of fish in some kind of sauce. A group of crates had been left on the grass, and he gestured to Sherlock to sit down.

'Thanks for rescuing me,' Sherlock said. 'I appreciate the assistance.'

'No problem,' the boy said. He slipped his glasses off and polished them with a handkerchief he took from his pocket. 'My name is Cameron. Cameron Mackenzie.'

'Sherlock,' Sherlock replied. 'Sherlock Scott Holmes.'

'You're off the ship that's just come in,' Cameron said. He wasn't asking a question – he seemed to already know. 'But you're not like an ordinary sailor. You're younger than most of them, and you didn't head straight for the taverns like they do.' He laughed – a quick *huff* of air, gone as soon as Sherlock heard it. 'They get their money when they leave the ships and they've usually spent it by the time they get to the city gates – not that the guards would let them in. Shanghai is still a town in isolation.' He spoke in English, although there was an accent in his voice that Sherlock thought was familiar.

'You obviously live here,' Sherlock said in return. 'Your Cantonese is excellent. But you're originally American, aren't you? I recognize the accent.'

Cameron nodded. 'Well, my father is. We came here when I was five.' He mopped his forehead with the handkerchief, and slipped his glasses back on. 'My father is a local shipping agent. He buys cargoes from the ships that dock here and then sells them on to the Chinese

103

businessmen at a profit. That's how I knew your ship had arrived. I saw you come down the gangway later than everyone else. I also saw that you were about my age, so I thought I'd say hello. Then those apes tried to take your money, so I decided to lend a hand. I hope you don't mind.'

'Not at all,' Sherlock replied. 'I take it you spend a lot of time here at the quayside, watching the ships arriving and departing.'

Cameron nodded. He looked away, seemingly slightly embarrassed. 'I don't remember much about America,' he said eventually. 'In fact, I think that even the things I do remember are just dreams, or things I've invented or that I've read somewhere. I like to talk to people who have recently arrived to see if they've been to America, and if they can tell me about it.'

'I've been to New York,' Sherlock said. 'Only for a week or so, but I did get out into the countryside. Do you want to hear about it?'

Cameron nodded eagerly. 'My father is from Chicago,' he said. 'But New York will do. It's another big city.' He paused, thinking. 'I know – rather than sit here in the dark, do you want to come to my house? I'm sure Mother and Father won't mind you having dinner with us.'

'If you're certain that will be all right,' Sherlock said.

'I am.' Cameron glanced critically at Sherlock's sailor's clothes. 'Although, knowing Mother, she will insist that you change into some of my old clothes. She's a stickler for dressing properly for dinner.'

'We're about the same size,' Sherlock estimated.

'All right. Come on then.'

Cameron led the way back to the road, and then towards the city gates. Looking behind him, Sherlock noticed the long, low white ship that he had seen earlier, from the deck of the *Gloria Scott*.

'What's that ship?' he asked. 'You know all the arrivals.'

Cameron followed Sherlock's pointing finger with his gaze. 'That's an American warship. It's called the USS *Monocacy*. It docked yesterday.'

'A warship?' Sherlock asked, remembering the cannonball marks on the city walls. 'There's not going to be a war, is there?'

'Not right now. It's a goodwill visit. The Captain of the *Monocacy* is asking for permission to sail up the Yangtze River. He says that his orders are to prepare better maps of the region. He's already paid a courtesy call on my father, as the most important American in the area.'

'What happened to the funnel?' Sherlock asked.

'You spotted that? I heard the Captain tell my father

that they lost it in a storm, but that they put in for repairs in a port in Japan.'

Sherlock got nervous as they approached the town walls, remembering the guards that he had seen earlier, but the guards obviously recognized Cameron and waved him in. They ignored Sherlock entirely – presumably if he was with someone who was allowed in then he was allowed in too.

'This is the "Gate of the Leaping Dragon",' Cameron explained as they went through. 'There are fourteen gates in total.'

As they passed into the town, Cameron turned to Sherlock. 'The town has only been opened up to foreigners in the past few years. Before that we had to live in a special area outside the town walls, and if we wanted to do business then people had to come to us. We weren't allowed in to see them.'

'What changed?' Sherlock asked.

Cameron smiled. 'Great Britain went to war with China to force the country to open up and allow foreigners in.'

'We obviously won,' Sherlock conceded. 'I don't remember hearing about it, though.'

'You did win. My father will probably want to thank you in person.'

Sherlock thought of his brother, who had some kind

of important job in the British Government. 'I'll pass his thanks on,' he said.

Cameron laughed – the same quick snort that he had given before. 'Of course, even though the Chinese authorities have let us into the town, they still make sure that all the foreigners are clustered together in one area, and there are regular police patrols to make sure we don't wander too far. They don't like us dressing in Chinese clothes either. If they notice me they always tell me off.'

The buildings in the town were unlike anything Sherlock had seen before. Most of them were only one or two storeys tall, and rather than being set in gardens, as English buildings would be, they appeared to be built *around* gardens. The roofs of the houses were amazingly ornate, covered with coloured tiles and usually curling upwards at the corners, and many of the residences had small statues outside the door, usually of fat, self-contented bald men, but Sherlock guessed there was more to them than met the eye. On street corners, and in small open areas between the houses, there were also statues of what Sherlock assumed were mythical animals. They mostly looked like a cross between dogs and lions, but some of them had horns and others had wings.

'*Bixie*, *Qilin* and *Tianlu*,' Cameron said, noticing

his interest. Sherlock didn't recognize the words, and Cameron didn't elaborate.

The Mackenzie family residence wasn't far from the city gates. From the outside it looked like all the other houses. Cameron knocked on the front door. An elderly man in a dark suit opened it.

'Master Cameron – your mother was beginning to worry.' His voice was quiet and dry.

Cameron pushed past him. 'I'm fine, Harris. I'm always fine.' He turned and indicated Sherlock. 'This is a friend of mine. His name is Sherlock – Sherlock Holmes. He's going to be staying for dinner.'

'Very well.' Harris nodded his head slightly at Sherlock, and held the door open so that he could enter. 'I will notify Cook. I presume you will be notifying your parents?'

'I'll do that now.' Cameron indicated that Sherlock should follow him. 'Come on – I'll introduce you.'

Sherlock didn't know what the interior of a proper Chinese house would be like, but the interior of the Mackenzie house was surprisingly similar to that of his aunt and uncle's house. It had similar dark wood panelling, similar tiled flooring in the hall, similar deep carpets in the main rooms and a similarly random selection of art scattered around. The only difference was that the artworks in the Holmes household were landscapes and paintings of horses, whereas the artworks in the Mackenzie household were mainly small statuettes of dragons and paintings of elderly Chinese men with long white beards.

Sherlock felt out of place in his sailor's clothes. He shifted uneasily, but Cameron didn't seem to notice. He pulled Sherlock eagerly into a side room.

'Mother, Father – I've brought a friend for dinner. Is that all right?'

The room was obviously a sitting room – comfortable chairs, side tables and a relaxed feeling. There was a man in one of the chairs, reading a newspaper. He was probably in his mid-forties, Sherlock guessed, with short hair that was black on top but greying at the temples. He was smoking a pipe. A woman was sitting near him, sewing. She was wearing a dress that looked to Sherlock as if it was made locally – scarlet silk embroidered with green fronds. Her hair was copper-red, and Sherlock noticed that her eyes were green. She was dressing to complement her complexion. She glanced up with a smile as Cameron entered.

'Darling – we were wondering where you were. We don't mind you bringing friends back for dinner, but not one of those Chinese boys, and not without a little advance notice.' She caught sight of Sherlock. 'Oh. Hello.'

Sherlock bowed his head. It seemed like the polite thing to do. 'I'm sorry for intruding,' he said. 'I met Cameron earlier. He helped me out when I was in trouble. My name is Sherlock. Sherlock Holmes.'

Cameron's father stood up and put his newspaper to one side. He extended a hand to shake Sherlock's hand. 'Pleased to meet you. I'm Mr Mackenzie, and this is my wife. Welcome to our house. There aren't many Western boys around here for Cameron to make friends with, so we're more than pleased to have you here.' He gazed critically at Sherlock's clothes. 'Just off a ship, I presume. The *Gloria Scott*?'

Sherlock nodded, embarrassed. 'It's a long story—' he started to say, but Mrs Mackenzie *shush*ed him. 'Time for stories later. Cameron, take Sherlock upstairs and let him try on some of your clothes. You are going to need to dress for dinner as well. The Captain and the senior officers of the USS *Monocacy* are dining with us tonight.' She wrinkled her nose at Sherlock. 'Normally we wouldn't be quite so formal, but you know what ship's captains are like.

He thought back to Captain Tollaway. 'Ye-es,' he said carefully. 'Mr Mackenzie . . . Mrs Mackenzie . . . I wouldn't want to put you to any trouble. It would be wrong of me to intrude if you've got dinner guests coming. It's probably best if I go.'

He tried to ignore Cameron's face, which was almost comical in its combination of disbelief and disappointment.

Mr Mackenzie slapped Sherlock on the shoulder. 'Good manners,' he said. 'Exactly what I'd expect from a Brit. Don't worry about it, son – we've got enough food and enough chairs, and I guarantee you'll eat better here than anywhere else you might end up. The matter's settled.'

'Malcolm . . .' Mrs Mackenzie started. Her husband looked at her. She looked at Sherlock, then back at him. She was obviously trying to convey a message.

'Son – where are you staying?' Malcolm Mackenzie asked.

Sherlock opened his mouth to answer the question, then realized that he didn't really have an answer. 'I . . . I suppose I'm staying on the ship,' he replied hesitantly. 'On the *Gloria Scott*.'

Mrs Mackenzie kept staring at her husband. After a few seconds he said, 'Nonsense. You're staying here, with us, for as long as you're in port. Cameron obviously likes you, and that's a good thing. He doesn't often get on with other boys.'

'Apparently I'm too critical,' Cameron said quietly. 'Which means that I tell people what I think, rather than what they want to hear.'

'If you can cope with that,' Mr Mackenzie said, 'then you're welcome here.' He checked the watch that hung from a chain on his waistcoat. 'Dinner's in an hour. You two get upstairs, get scrubbed up and get dressed up. And be on your best behaviour – Captain Bryan is an important man.'

Cameron led Sherlock not upstairs – as far as Sherlock could tell there *was* no upstairs – but along a corridor and then out through a doorway into a square central area that was open to the sky. It was beautifully landscaped, with boulders and small trees, and benches where people could sit. Brightly coloured paper lanterns had been hung around the edges, casting a kaleidoscope of light across the skirting paths but leaving the middle in relative darkness. The occasional night bird swooped by with a rush of wings.

Cameron crossed to the other side. Cameron's room was filled with models of ships and pictures of what Sherlock assumed were American street scenes, complete with horses and carts.

The blond-haired boy threw open a wardrobe and gestured at the clothes hanging up inside. 'Find yourself something smart,' he said. 'Jacket and trousers. My father will be wearing evening dress, and Mother will wear a gown, but they won't expect us to be all dressed up like that. As long as we're smart, we'll be all right.'

Sherlock stared at the array of clothes in amazement. He had forgotten all about having more than one set of clothes, about the social graces, about dressing for dinner and using the right cutlery.

'I'll have the maid draw two baths for us,' Cameron said, interrupting his thoughts. 'Looking at you, I'd say you haven't had a hot bath for a while.'

After so long spent ploughing across the ocean, Sherlock wasn't sure that he wanted to see water again, but after a few moments staring at the free-standing bath and waiting for some kind of emotional reaction to occur, he slipped gingerly beneath the water. It was warm, and it seemed to envelop him and caress him as he lay there, feeling his muscles relax and the accreted layers of salt and grime that had built up since leaving England start to dissolve away.

When they were both dressed they headed back towards the rest of the house. Sherlock could hear voices raised in conversation.

Malcolm Mackenzie and his wife were welcoming their guests into the garden. Chinese servants were circulating with trays of drinks. The butler – Harris – was standing off to one side, watching to make sure all the guests were happy.

The guests from the USS *Monocacy* were wearing

uniforms: navy-blue frock coats with two rows of gilt buttons running from top to bottom, navy-blue trousers and white caps with gold chains around the peak. There were also one or two men in evening dress, whom Sherlock assumed were business acquaintances of Mr Mackenzie. Mrs Mackenzie was the only woman there, but she didn't seem at all embarrassed by the fact. On the contrary, she was moving easily among the guests, making sure that everyone had a drink and someone to talk with.

'I hate these parties,' Cameron said morosely. 'I always end up talking to the most boring person present. The problem is that I usually tell them so.'

'You're talking to me,' Sherlock pointed out.

'Yes, but tonight is different.' Cameron gestured to a passing servant, who came over with a tray containing glasses of champagne. Cameron took two glasses, and passed one to Sherlock. 'Here, this should make the evening pass quicker.'

Captain Bryan was easily recognizable. He was the oldest man there, and the amount of gold braid and the number of gold stars on his uniform made him difficult to miss. He also had the loudest voice, and Sherlock listened as he told the story of how the funnel of the *Monocacy* had been ripped off like tissue paper by a waterspout that had swept over the ship off the coast of Japan.

'I've been meaning to ask,' Mrs Mackenzie interrupted when it became clear that the Captain could talk all night without stopping, 'what is the significance of the name of your vessel? *Monocacy* sounds as if it should be a form of government where only one person can rule!'

'Ma'am, the Monocacy River is a tributary of the mighty Potomac River,' the Captain answered, changing conversational direction with graceful charm. 'The name comes from the original Shawnee Indian name for the river, *Monnockkesey*, which, I am told by those who know, translates as "river with many bends".' He glanced around his audience, and continued, 'The Battle of Monocacy Junction was fought during the War Between the States, six years ago now, and our fine ship was named in honour of that battle, lest otherwise it be forgotten . . .'

Mention of the War Between the States reminded Sherlock of his time in and around New York, and of his confrontation with the bizarre Duke Balthassar. The man had been on the Confederate side – the losing side – and he had planned to set up a new Confederate nation in Canada. Whatever had happened in America, it seemed that the scars ran deep.

'How very splendid,' Mrs Mackenzie said, breaking into his thoughts. 'I'm afraid we have been away from our home country for so long, and news arrives so late here, that we only had the sketchiest idea of what was happening with the Confederates and the Unionists.' She rested a hand on the Captain's forearm. 'Was it . . . very terrible?' she asked in a quieter voice.

He patted her hand reassuringly. 'Ma'am, it is never easy or pleasant when a country tries to rip itself apart, when father is pitted against son and brother is pitted against brother. But we must remember that America is a young country, and is made up of many different parts, most of which have some kind of disagreement with another part. Squabbles can be expected.'

'Not just young countries,' Malcolm Mackenzie said, joining the group. 'China is an ancient country, but there are rebellious elements within it even now, and fighting breaks out from time to time.'

Sherlock remembered the cannonball scars on the town's walls. That would explain what had happened – there had been some kind of fight for control of the town between different elements. He moved closer to hear more.

'The majority of the local population are known as "Han" Chinese,' Mackenzie went on, 'and they have been living here for hundreds, if not thousands of years. The trouble is that the rulers are the descendants of an invading force known as the "Manchus", who came from the north. The Qing dynasty that controls China is entirely made up of Manchu Chinese, and the Han are the ruled.'

'I presume that the Han aren't happy about that?' Captain Bryan asked.

'Actually, most of them don't care one way or another, as long as they get to live their lives in peace,' Mackenzie replied. 'But there has been a small and persistent rebellion by elements of the Han against the Qing over the past twenty years. It's locally known as the Taiping Rebellion because of where it started. Every now and then there is a fight somewhere, or a town is taken over by the rebels and then liberated. Shanghai itself fell to a group called "The Small Swords Society" in 1853, but it was retaken by the Qing within a few weeks. Between 1860 and 1862, the Taiping rebels twice attacked the town and destroyed its eastern and southern suburbs, but they failed to actually capture the place. Their aim is to get the Manchu invaders to leave, but the Qing dynasty don't consider themselves invaders any more, and the rebels have no clear plan to get them to leave. So it keeps fizzling on and on.'

Cameron tugged at Sherlock's sleeve. 'Come on – this is boring. Let's find somewhere in the garden where we can sit and talk about America.'

He turned to go, obviously certain that Sherlock was going to follow him, but he bumped into a man who

117

was passing behind him. The man was wearing evening dress, and the white of his collar and cuffs threw into sharp relief the silvery-blue colour of the skin on his face and hands.

It was Mr Arrhenius.

CHAPTER SIX

Cameron sprang back, shocked. Sherlock caught him before he could stumble and fall.

'Ah, young Seaman Holmes, isn't it?' The voice was as dry and whispery as Sherlock remembered. Arrhenius's gaze scanned Sherlock up and down. 'You are better-dressed than I recall from the ship. I am, I confess, surprised to see you here. I believed this to be a *soirée* for businessmen and those of the officer class. I did not realize that . . . mere crew members were invited.'

Sherlock took a deep breath. 'Mr Arrhenius,' he acknowledged. 'It's nice to see you again.' He indicated Cameron. 'I have been invited to stay with Mr and Mrs Mackenzie while the *Gloria Scott* is docked. This is Cameron – their son.'

Arrhenius's gaze switched across to Cameron, and Sherlock could sense the boy shrinking back. 'It's all right,' he said quietly. 'Mr Arrhenius suffers from a . . . a skin condition. It's not serious, and it's not catching.'

Now that he knew Mr Arrhenius was present at the dinner, Sherlock could see that the other guests were casting the occasional glance at the man with the blue skin. They weren't nervous, or worried, but they were certainly interested. It was as if there was something magnetic about the man that attracted their attention, but they were too polite to say anything, or point, or make a fuss. What interested Sherlock was that although they were fascinated, they weren't all clustering around Mr Arrhenius to ask him questions. Sherlock didn't really understand that – if he had a question then he usually asked it.

Cameron Mackenzie obviously had the same approach to life as Sherlock. 'Does it hurt?' he asked, moving closer and staring, fascinated, at Arrhenius's face. 'It looks as if it should.'

'No, it does not hurt, my young friend. In fact, quite the opposite. The colloidal silver that I have been consuming for years, and which gives my skin this . . . attractive sheen . . . protects me from disease. I have not had the slightest illness – not a sniffle, not a sore throat – for all of that time. Not only does it not hurt, it actually *prevents* me from hurting. Do you see?'

Cameron nodded. 'Yes, I see,' he said seriously. 'That must be really useful. Does that mean your skin is valuable? If it's silver, I mean. You're not afraid that someone might kidnap you and try to peel your skin off and sell it?'

Arrhenius laughed: a sound like leaves being rustled

by the wind. 'Sadly, no. The silver is held in the form of oxides and nitrates. It would take a very clever chemist to recover any real silver from my skin – hardly enough to make the effort worthwhile, I am afraid.'

There was something about the thought that suddenly intrigued Sherlock. Not skinning Mr Arrhenius and extracting the silver from his skin – that would be macabre and wrong – but the idea that silver could come in different forms, like nitrates, and oxides, and so on, and that someone who knew enough about chemistry could tell the difference between them, and maybe convert one to the other. It was, he thought, a bit like being able to play around with the building blocks from which everything, from stones to trees to people, was made.

He realized with a sudden shock that Mrs Mackenzie had joined them while he was distracted with his thoughts.

'Mr Arrhenius, isn't it?' she said, touching Arrhenius's sleeve. 'We are so pleased you could be here.'

Arrhenius nodded. 'And I am very grateful to be invited,' he said. 'I have found that my appearance can sometimes get in the way of social events. I have become used to eating alone on my travels.'

'Nonsense,' Mrs Mackenzie said with a smile. 'You should see the effects that some of the local potions and medicines have. My husband bought a local remedy for hair loss from a market trader a year ago. He didn't tell me, of course, but he rubbed it into his scalp every night in secret. One morning he work up, and his hair was bright green. Not only that, but he had a rash all over his scalp, and his face, and his hands. I spent the rest of the day pretending that I couldn't see anything wrong, and I told the servants to do the same. It was so amusing!'

'And do I amuse you in the same way?' Arrhenius asked. His lips were curled into a smile but there was no humour in his voice.

'Of course not,' Mrs Mackenzie said reassuringly, touching his sleeve again. 'We're very grateful that you're here with us, and we are looking forward to hearing about your travels. Now, come and meet my husband . . .'

She led Arrhenius away from the two boys, still chatting to him. Sherlock noticed several people watch him go.

'What a strange man,' Cameron said. 'I wonder if I could make my skin like armour if I ate iron every day.'

'You would probably just get stomach ache,' Sherlock replied. 'And that's if you are lucky.'

He watched as Arrhenius and Mrs Mackenzie approached Cameron's father. Mrs Mackenzie briefly introduced them, and then moved away to speak to someone else. Sherlock found his gaze fixed on Malcolm Mackenzie and Mr Arrhenius. They didn't look like men who had been introduced moments beforehand. They looked, in fact, like men who already knew each other – or, at least, already knew something about each other.

As Sherlock watched, Mr Arrhenius reached into his uniform jacket and took out a package. He passed it over to Mr Mackenzie, who immediately stowed it away in an inside pocket of his own jacket. It was a perfectly innocent transaction, but there was something about the way both men tried to minimize the time that the packet was visible, and the way they both looked around afterwards to see if anyone was watching, that made Sherlock wonder what exactly was in the packet.

The two men talked for a moment or two. There was wariness there, and Sherlock detected anger as well – especially in the way that Mr Arrhenius was standing. Mr Mackenzie seemed defensive, but Mr Arrhenius was definitely losing his temper.

'Come on,' Sherlock said abruptly. 'Show me the garden. I don't want to stand here much longer. Someone else might try to talk to us, just out of politeness, and I hate making small talk.'

Cameron nodded, and led the way along one of the paths that snaked across the well-manicured garden. Eventually he found a pair of large rocks set into a patch

123

of sand near each other. The sand had been carefully raked into a series of concentric circles rippling out from where the rocks sat. Regardless of the careful arrangement, which struck Sherlock as rather artistic but also rather pointless, Cameron walked across the sand and sat on one of the rocks. Being rather more careful, but still leaving footprints, Sherlock sat on the other.

'You were going to tell me about America,' Cameron said.

'I was,' Sherlock replied, 'but I wanted to ask you something first. You mentioned the war between Britain and China earlier on, and your father mentioned it again just now. What actually happened? I don't remember hearing anything about it at the time, or being taught about it at school, and school was usually very good at making us learn about wars.'

Cameron shrugged. 'There were actually two wars,' he said. 'Both of them quite short. The Chinese call them the Opium Wars.'

'Opium Wars?' Sherlock asked, feeling a slight chill. Opium was some kind of drug – he knew that from having been knocked out on several occasions by agents of the Paradol Chamber. They had used a solution of opium in alcohol that was called laudanum. It had made Sherlock unconscious in a few seconds, and given him some very strange dreams.

'Opium is something that is made from poppies,' Cameron said. 'It can be smoked in a pipe, apparently. It makes people feel peaceful, and makes them forget all their problems, at least for a while. You Brits were getting natives in India to grow the poppies and extract the opium, then your ships were bringing it to China and selling it in exchange for silks and other stuff.'

'But that's the definition of trade. You sell things and you buy things, and you try to make a profit.'

'Opium is addictive,' Cameron pointed out. 'Once you've tried it, you want to keep on trying it. You can't help yourself. From what I've heard, and from what I've seen, a lot of the local traders and farmers and even the civil servants spent more and more of their time smoking opium. Crops were left rotting in the fields, and there was less and less food available to buy in the markets. It got to the stage where the streets were empty most of the time, because people were in their houses smoking opium.'

'That's obviously a bad thing,' Sherlock observed.

'The Manchu rulers agreed. They passed a law forbidding the sale or the use of opium.'

'Ah,' Sherlock said as he realized the implications of what Cameron was saying. 'And then the bottom dropped out of the market for the British importers.

They were still bringing the opium over from India, but they couldn't sell it.'

Cameron nodded his head. 'From what my father says, the whole British economy was dependent on the income from the sale of opium.'

'A bit like the Chinese traders and farmers were dependent on smoking it.' Sherlock paused. 'So we went to war so that we could keep selling this drug in China, even though people were getting addicted to it and it was having a bad effect.'

Cameron shrugged. 'Wars don't just happen for good reasons,' he pointed out. 'They happen for bad reasons as well, although your government dressed it up as the Chinese Emperor trying to stifle free trade and the noble Brits doing their best to make sure that their traders could make a decent living. Not much mention of opium there.'

'But still – it's wrong! We shouldn't have been selling this drug, and we certainly shouldn't have gone to war so that we could keep on selling it!'

'I agree,' Cameron said. 'But what do I know? You won the war. Smoking opium isn't illegal in England, so the traders claimed that they weren't doing anything wrong in the first place, and the Emperor was overreacting.'

'Maybe we shouldn't have won the war,' Sherlock muttered darkly. He couldn't help but wonder how much his brother Mycroft knew about this. Mycroft worked for the Foreign Office, and had something to do with international relations. Had he been involved in these Opium Wars? Had he advised against them, or had he been in favour of them? Sherlock made a mental note to ask Mycroft the next time he saw him. Assuming he ever did see him again.

Thoughts of Mycroft and of opium made him think once more of the times he had been drugged by the Paradol Chamber, and that swimmy, weightless feeling that he had experienced. He shuddered. Horrible though it had been, there was something strangely and dangerously seductive about that feeling. He never wanted to experience it again, and yet a little bit of him missed the way it made him feel. The way it had made him forget about everything that was worrying him.

'So,' Cameron prompted. 'America?'

Sherlock started to tell him about his experiences of New York, and the train journey across the American wilderness, but it turned into more of an account of the adventures he, Matty and Virginia had had. Cameron listened, wide-eyed. Every now and then he would question a detail or make a comment, but mostly he let Sherlock talk.

After twenty minutes or so a gong sounded, letting everyone know that it was time for dinner. Cameron and Sherlock headed together to the dining room, where everyone was gathering. Fortunately, the two of them had been seated together, and even more fortunately, the guests sitting beside and across from them at the long table spent all their time talking to each other and ignoring the boys. When Sherlock had finished his story, and Cameron had finished asking questions, they moved on to other subjects – Cameron's experiences in China, and Sherlock's adventures back in England.

Every now and then Sherlock heard some fragment of the conversations going on around him – Captain Bryan or the other officers from the USS *Monocacy* talking about their voyages, Mr Mackenzie talking about China, or the other businessmen telling stories about the strange places they had been and the odd people they had traded with. At one point he heard Malcolm Mackenzie ask Captain Bryan, 'Will you be received by the Governor while you are here?'

Captain Bryan shrugged. 'I must admit,' he said, 'to being confused by the various ranks of the dignitaries in China. I had anticipated sending my credentials to the person who rules Shanghai, but my translator tells me that he is of low rank, and not worth dealing with.'

'That's true,' Mackenzie confirmed. 'Although Shanghai is a major town from our point of view, it is ruled by a Prefect. He is subservient to the Governor of

Jiangsu Province, whose palace is located at Nanjing – a little way inland.'

'Ah,' Captain Bryan said, 'I believe that we are meeting with the Governor of Jiangsu somewhere upriver, at a special ceremony.'

Sherlock's interest in the conversation – not high to begin with – waned as the food arrived. It was quite amazing: shreds of succulent duck served with a dipping sauce made out of plums, followed by slices of peppery lamb with a mixture of crunchy vegetables, and then topped off with steaming dumplings filled with fruit. The food was washed down with sweet white wine. Sherlock ate as much as he could. The tastes and textures put him in mind, strangely, of Wu Chung. He wondered how Wu's reunion with his family had gone, and he decided to go looking for the cook as soon as he could the next day.

When the last course had been cleared away, Mr Mackenzie suggested that the men withdraw for port and cigars. Mrs Mackenzie ushered the two boys from the dining room. 'They'll be talking for hours,' she said, 'and it won't be anything worth listening to. The room will be so filled with cigar smoke that you'd be able to cut the air with a knife. I suggest that you two head for bed. Sherlock – I've had the maid make up a separate bed in Cameron's room for you.' She yawned suddenly, and covered her mouth. 'Oh my. I think I'll turn in as well. It's been an exhausting day.'

By now Sherlock knew the way across the interior garden to Cameron's room. He led the way in silence along one of the paved paths that crossed the grass, past the bushes and past the sandy area where they had sat earlier. The sky above them was black and cloudless, speckled with stars. A thin sliver of moon cast a silvery light over everything, reminding Sherlock of Mr Arrhenius and his grey-blue skin.

A dark shape moved between two bushes. Sherlock stopped abruptly.

'What's the matter?' Cameron asked, nearly bumping into Sherlock's back.

'I thought I saw an animal.'

Cameron opened his mouth to say something, but Sherlock gestured at him to shut up. He stood motionless, trying to make out the sounds of movement, or breathing, but there was nothing.

He stepped towards the bush that the dark shape had made for. Was it an animal – a cat, or a dog perhaps? Presumably they had cats and dogs in China?

Another step. Still nothing. Had he been mistaken?

He took another step, ready to turn back and head for bed. He let out the breath that he hadn't even realized he was holding. He had probably mistaken a night bird for something more substantial. Tiredness, and the stress of being in a strange country, were making him nervous.

A stone flew out of the middle of the bush. If it hadn't glanced off a branch on the way out it would have hit him in the centre of his forehead. As it was it caught him on his cheek and ricocheted away. He flinched, shocked. He could feel something warm and wet on his skin: blood. The stone had cut him!

'Hey!' he shouted, outraged. Before Cameron could answer, Sherlock had launched himself at the bush, but another stone spun towards his right eye. He ducked, and the stone sailed overhead, brushing his hair as it passed.

Suddenly a dark shadow broke away from the bush and headed across the grass. The meagre light from the moon wasn't sufficient for Sherlock to make out any details – all he could see was something about half his size moving away from him fast. He wasn't even sure if it was running, floating, flying or rolling. Before he could focus on the shape, it had disappeared into the darkness.

Leaving Cameron standing, Sherlock gave chase. Branches clawed at his face as he ran through the bushes. Petals and leaves exploded away from him, littering the ground. He crashed into a clear area. Ahead of him he could make out the dark shape scrambling up the grey trunk of a tree that twisted from the ground like a plume

131

of smoke from a fire. Sherlock raced across the ground separating him from the tree, only realizing as he ran that he was leaving crater-like footprints in the smoothly raked sand of another rock garden. He leaped across a smooth boulder that blocked his path. The tree trunk was a few feet ahead of him now, and without slowing down he jumped, fingers clutching for the lowest branches with both hands while his feet scrabbled for purchase on the silvery-grey trunk. Seconds later he was pulling himself up the tree's slippery bark. It was like climbing the rigging of the *Gloria Scott*. Ahead of him he could see a black shadow wriggling through the higher branches. Leaves lashed at his face, catching at the cut left by the stone. Blood trickled down his cheek.

He emerged into clear moonlight, head above the foliage like a swimmer emerging from a rough ocean. Beyond the edge of the leaves he could see the roof of the Mackenzie house – red tiles sloping gently away from him. Some of the tiles were disturbed, knocked out of place. That was the only sign left by whatever it was he had been chasing. It had vanished over the rooftop and presumably jumped to the street. He would never catch it now.

He made his way back to the garden. His muscles were complaining at the unexpected action, and his cheek throbbed where the stone had hit it. He also suspected

132

that he had small cuts and grazes all over his face where twigs and leaves had caught the skin.

'You,' Cameron exclaimed when he saw Sherlock, 'look like you've been dragged through a hedge backwards.'

'Very funny,' Sherlock growled.

'What happened?'

'What did you see?'

Cameron shrugged. 'Some things came out of the bushes at you. I wasn't sure if they were birds, or what.'

'They weren't birds – they were stones.'

'All right – they were stones. You ran off. I followed, but by the time I got here you were halfway up the tree. Then you came down again. If this was some kind of game then I guess you won, but you need to tell me the rules for next time.'

'I think you had an uninvited guest,' Sherlock said, trying to keep his voice as calm and as level as possible. His heart, however, was still racing.

'What kind of uninvited guest? You mean a *burglar*?'

Sherlock shrugged. 'I couldn't see. It might have been an animal, or it might have been a person.' He frowned, trying to picture the thing that he had half glimpsed. 'A very small person, perhaps.'

'It threw two stones,' Cameron pointed out. 'According to you, anyway.'

Sherlock put a hand up to his cheek. It came away

sticky with blood, but the cut didn't seemed to be too bad. 'Maybe it was a monkey. They can throw stones. Do you have monkeys in China?'

'There're certainly plenty of them around Shanghai. The sailors bring them, and leave them here.'

'Let's see if there are any tracks,' Sherlock said.

He led the way back to the sand of the rock garden. If Sherlock was hoping for distinct claw-marks or shoe-prints then he was disappointed. His own footprints had completely obliterated whatever tracks the intruder had left.

'I should tell Father,' Cameron said after a while. He sounded uncertain. 'He might want to call the local constables.'

Sherlock shook his head. 'There's no point,' he said. 'I can't be sure exactly what I saw, and whatever it was it's gone now. We'd be breaking up the party for nothing. We'll tell him in the morning, over breakfast.'

Sherlock checked his cheek again. The bleeding had almost stopped. He followed Cameron across the rest of the garden, keeping an eye out for any movements in the bushes.

'You need to clean yourself up,' Cameron pointed out. 'I'll get some water and a cloth.'

After washing the blood off his face and the dirt from his hands, Sherlock undressed and climbed into the low

134

bed that had been set up for him. It took him a while to get to sleep, however. It wasn't just the lingering excitement and the tension of the chase. He had become used to a hammock slung between two hooks, rocking with the motion of the sea, and the sound of the waves slapping against the hull. A flat bed, a comfortable mattress and complete silence apart from the sound of Cameron's breathing were disturbing in a way that they wouldn't have been a few months ago. Eventually, though, he did fall asleep, and almost wished he hadn't. On board the *Gloria Scott* he had always gone to sleep too tired to dream, or at least so tired that he slept through his dreams and never remembered them in the morning. Here, in Cameron's bedroom, in the Mackenzie household, he found himself dreaming about Virginia Crowe. She was standing in a field, a few feet away from him, her red hair flaring in the light of the Farnham sun. Sherlock stepped towards her, but she seemed to drift backwards two steps for each step he took. She got further and further away from him, and the faster he moved the faster she drifted away. Her lips moved, but whatever she was saying, whatever message she was trying to convey, was so faint that he couldn't understand it. Eventually she was merely a dark spot against the lush green of the fields, and then she was gone.

Sherlock woke up with tears on his cheeks, but he

135

wasn't even sure what he was crying about.

The boys washed and dressed quickly. Cameron had some spare Chinese clothes which Sherlock put on. He liked the idea of blending in.

Breakfast was just like the ones he was used to in England – bacon, scrambled eggs, sausages and plentiful toast. The sausages had a strange, spicy taste, and the bacon was cooked so crisp that he could snap it in half with an audible *crack*, but it was the closest thing he'd had to the food he remembered for months. There was even coffee – strong and black, with lots of sugar. He had forgotten how good coffee tasted.

Mr Mackenzie was sitting at the head of the table reading a newspaper. It didn't look Chinese – Sherlock suspected that the USS *Monocacy* had brought a stack of newspapers from America, and that Cameron's father was catching up on the news of the past year or so. He seemed to be distracted. He kept turning the pages and then turning back, as if he had realized that he hadn't been taking the words in.

'We thought we saw a burglar last night,' Cameron announced suddenly.

Mr Mackenzie looked up. He stared at Cameron, frowning.

'What do you mean, a burglar?' Mrs Mackenzie asked, concerned, from the other side of the table.

'In the garden,' Cameron amplified. 'As we were going to bed. Sherlock thought he saw something in the bushes. He went to take a look, but whoever it was threw stones at him.'

'Or *what*ever,' Sherlock corrected. 'We don't know for sure it was a person.'

'Dogs don't throw stones,' Cameron pointed out. 'Neither do cats.'

'But monkeys might, and 1 don't know what other animals you have in China that could throw stones.'

'The chances are,' Mr Mackenzie said casually, 'that it was a local child. I seriously doubt that burglars would throw stones. They would be more likely to throw knives, or those metal stars with sharpened edges that I've seen them use. I think you're overdramatizing. It was a long evening. Perhaps the excitement got to you.'

He raised the newspaper again, hiding his face behind it, but Sherlock was concerned to see that his knuckles were white, as if he was clenching his fingers tightly on the paper. Something was worrying him.

After breakfast, Sherlock and Cameron asked if they could head into town and look around.

'Be careful,' Mrs Mackenzie said, 'and be back for lunch. Get me some oranges, if you can. Nice ones, not bruised.' She turned to her husband. 'What about you, Malcolm? I was hoping we could go over the details for

137

tomorrow's cocktail party. Cook is getting into a state about it already.'

Mr Mackenzie lowered the newspaper again. His expression was brooding, thoughtful. 'I'm afraid that I can't – not this morning. I'll be in my study – I have some . . . some documents to attend to.'

'Can't they wait?'

'No,' Mr Mackenzie said, so sharply that his wife flinched. 'I need to look at them today.'

For some reason, Sherlock remembered the package that Captain Tollaway had handed to Mr Mackenzie at the dinner party the night before. Was that the 'documents' he was referring to?

'Oh,' Mrs Mackenzie said in a small voice. 'Well – perhaps I could come in later with a cup of coffee and a plate of biscuits for you, and we can talk about it then.'

'I'll be locking my door,' Mr Mackenzie said. His voice was harsh. 'These documents are very sensitive. I can't allow anyone to see them. I don't mean to be rude, my dear,' he said in a calmer tone. 'When I've finished with them, I'll come and find you. We can talk then.'

'Whatever you think best,' Cameron's mother said in a neutral voice, but her lips were pursed and here cheeks were flushed.

Sherlock looked over at Cameron. His new friend

shrugged. He was frowning with concern. Obviously this was unusual behaviour for the breakfast table.

The rest of the meal was conducted in silence. Cameron's father seemed embarrassed by his outburst, and his mother seemed not to want to start another conversation in case she provoked more anger. Cameron spent most of the time looking nervously from one to the other, trying to work out what was going on. Sherlock was also trying to work out what was going on. In particular, he was interested in why Cameron's father wanted to explain away what had happened the night before. In Sherlock's experience, most home owners who might have played unwitting host to a burglar would be concerned about stopping it from happening again – not pretending that it hadn't happened in the first place.

After breakfast, the two boys headed out into the town. The sky was blue and cloudless, and although there was a cold nip in the air it promised to be a good day.

'What do you want to do?' Cameron asked.

Sherlock remembered his thoughts at the dinner table the night before. 'Actually,' he said, 'I want to go looking for a friend.'

'I didn't think you had any friends in Shanghai.'

'It's the cook from the *Gloria Scott*. He has family here.' Sherlock tried to remember the address that Wu Chung had given him before leaving the ship. 'He said I

139

could find him at Renmin Dong Lu. That's East Renmin Street, isn't it?'

Cameron nodded. 'I know where that is. Not the nicest area in Shanghai. Are you sure you want to go and see this guy?'

'I'd like to.' Sherlock paused. 'If you think it's safe.'

'If anything happens we can always fight, or run away.'

Together they walked through the streets of Shanghai. Like the day before, there were people everywhere: carrying baskets or pushing carts, leading horses or pushing sheep in front of them with long sticks. Many of them wore broad straw hats to protect themselves from the heat of the sun. Unlike the hats Sherlock was used to back in England, these were all brim and no crown: shallow cones that reminded Sherlock of the sloping roof of the Mackenzie house.

Cameron obviously knew the way. The route took them down narrow alleys and wide thoroughfares, around corners and past rows of shops and stalls.

A sudden booming sound, echoing across the town, made Sherlock stop dead in his tracks. Other people in the street had stopped as well, and were talking to each other in low voices. 'What's that?' he asked.

Cameron frowned. 'Sounds like a ship's horn,' he said. 'I reckon that's the USS *Monocacy* calling all its sailors back, ready to set out on its mission to map the twists and turns of the Yangtze River.'

Sherlock noticed that the other people in the street weren't looking too happy. 'I'm not sure that the locals approve,' he pointed out.

'It never got mentioned last night – at least, not while we were there – but you have to wonder why the American Government wants to have accurate maps of a Chinese river thousands of miles from American waters. I doubt that they're doing it out of the goodness of their hearts.' Cameron shrugged. 'The obvious suggestion is that they think they might need accurate maps at some time in the future, and there're only two reasons for that – possible military action or a whole load of American traders heading upriver.' He indicated the locals, who were still muttering to each other in low voices. 'They're debating which of the two options they would prefer.'

Eventually, as they turned a corner, Cameron slowed to a halt.

'This is East Renmin Street.'

Sherlock nodded. 'Then let's ask someone where the Wu family live.'

Cameron smiled at a toothless old woman who was selling fruit at the side of the road. He said something in a burst of Cantonese too fast for Sherlock to pick out the words. She said something in reply, and gestured to a particular house, no different from the rest, a little way

141

away. As with the others he had seen, it was plain and anonymous from the outside: walls of white plaster, roof of red tiles and a door painted green.

The two boys had taken a few steps towards the house when the front door opened and a woman ran out. She was crying.

'He's sick!' she screamed in Cantonese, looking around desperately for help. 'Someone help me! My husband – he's sick! I think he is dying!'

The woman's panic was obvious from her desperate expression. She clearly feared for her husband's life.

Other people in the street detoured around her as she tried to catch their attention. Sherlock stepped forward. Despite the fact that he was European, not Chinese, she moved towards him.

'My husband,' she said again. 'His name is Wu Chung. Please – can you help me?'

CHAPTER SEVEN

It felt to Sherlock as if his heart had suddenly frozen over, and that the slightest movement might cause it to shatter. 'He's sick?' Sherlock repeated. 'But – but he was fine yesterday. I saw him.' Despite the icy paralysis of his heart, he found that his mind was racing. Facts and memories were spinning past his mental gaze. Wu Chung hadn't seemed ill on the *Gloria Scott*. When he had walked down the gangway and stepped on to dry land he had been fine – happy at the prospect of seeing his family, if slightly nervous. If there was some disease that was striking down the sailors then surely it should have taken hold on board the ship while they were at sea – and Sherlock should have been ill as well. *All* the sailors should have been ill – they had been together at sea for weeks on end. No, if he was ill then it was more likely that the cook had caught some local disease the moment he had stepped on to the quayside. But could a disease act that quickly? Sherlock asked himself.

The woman plucked at his sleeve. 'Please, you must help!'

Cameron took a step backwards. 'Look, Sherlock, if

there's some illness here then we should stay away. I've seen diseases go from person to person so fast in this town you would have to run to keep up.'

Sherlock looked around desperately, hoping someone else would interrupt with an offer of assistance, perhaps a passing doctor, but all of the locals were ignoring what was going on. They wouldn't even make eye contact.

'Is anyone else ill?' Sherlock asked, ignoring Cameron's suggestion.

The woman shook her head. 'Nobody.' She stepped back, obviously hoping that Sherlock would follow her. 'Not me, not our son, and none of the neighbours in the street as far as I know.' She glanced around bitterly. 'Not that they are taking much notice now,' she said, louder. 'They're frightened that Wu Chung has brought back some strange disease from foreign places. Cowards!'

Sherlock turned to glance at Cameron. 'Look,' he said urgently to the American boy, 'Wu Chung is a friend of mine. Probably the best friend I've made for a while, apart from you. If he needs my help then I have to give it.'

'If you want to do something to help,' Cameron replied, shaking his head, 'then you should get one of the local healers to take a look at him. You can't do anything by yourself.'

Sherlock's gaze switched from Cameron's implacable

expression to the near-panic on the face of Wu Chung's wife, and back. 'Let's at least take a look. It might be something he ate.'

He gestured to the Chinese woman to lead the way into the house. She nodded, a flicker of gratitude momentarily displacing her worry.

'And you can tell the difference between a stomach ache and a contagious illness *how* exactly?' Cameron asked as Sherlock followed her into the darkened entrance.

Sherlock glanced over his shoulder. 'I don't know,' he admitted, 'but I have to do *something* to help. Even if it's just to reassure him. Or her.'

Cameron hesitated, shrugged, and followed Sherlock in. 'This is stupid,' he said quietly. 'This is *so* stupid. My mother would have kittens if she found out.'

The interior of the house was cool and shadowed. It smelt strange, like sweet smoke. The walls were made from rough plaster, and there were paintings hanging on them, not on canvas and framed as they would have been in England, but on scrolls with wooden batons top and bottom to stop them from curling up. In the corners of the rooms, and set in niches in the walls, were small wooden figurines – dragons and fat men with loincloths. There were no chairs, just cushions on the tiled floor, and the tables were set low to the ground so that people could kneel at them or sit cross-legged.

'You said you *know* my husband? We have never met, have we? You don't live in Shanghai?'

'I was on the ship with him,' Sherlock replied. 'The *Gloria Scott*. I said I would come and see him, once he had settled back at home.'

'Ah – then you are Sherlock! He told us about you.' She smiled briefly, before her face settled back into lines of concern. 'He said that he hoped you would join us for a meal, because he had some news for you – but then he suddenly collapsed.'

'Yes, I am Sherlock – and this is my friend Cameron.'

She nodded: a little bob of the head that seemed to involve her shoulders as well. 'I am Tsi Huen.'

She led them down a passageway to what was obviously a bedroom. The bed, like the tables in the first room, was set close to the floor. In contrast the windows were high up, well above the height of a man's head.

Wu Chung was lying on the bed. Sweat covered his pockmarked face, and he was shaking. As Sherlock got closer he could see that the cook's eyes were bloodshot.

'My friend Sherlock!' he exclaimed. He was obviously trying to sound hearty, but his voice was thin and strained.

'Wu Chung – what happened?'

He shook his head. 'I do not know. I went to sleep last night. I woke with a start early this morning, before the sun came up. I don't know what it was that woke me, but when I tried to get out of bed I found that my legs would not hold me. I collapsed, and I started to shake. It feels like fire is running through my veins! And my mouth is drier than a desert!'

A boy came in through the doorway. He was about the same age as Sherlock and Cameron: Chinese, of course, thinner than Wu Chung but with similar features and hair. Wu Chung's son, Sherlock assumed. He was carrying a pitcher of water which he held out towards his father. The expression on his face was like his mother's: panic, barely under control.

'Here, drink this. I got it for you from the well.'

Wu Chung grabbed at the pitcher and drained it in three great gulps. He wiped his hand across his damp mouth. 'That helps,' he said. 'Thank you.' He glanced up at Sherlock, and smiled. 'I was hoping that I would see you,' he said. He patted the bed beside him. 'Come, Sherlock, sit. There was something I wanted to tell you, and there is a message I need you to take for me.'

'What is it?' Sherlock asked.

'The thing I wanted to tell you was that I won't be on the *Gloria Scott* when she sails.'

'I know you don't feel like it,' Sherlock said, trying to

147

sound reassuring, 'but you're going to get through this. I promise.'

'No, I mean I was offered another job.'

'As a cook?' Sherlock asked, surprised.

'Yes. On board that big ship we saw in the harbour yesterday. The American one.'

'The USS *Monocacy*?' Sherlock shook his head, trying to imagine Wu Chung cooking for hundreds of American Navy personnel rather than a few tens of English sailors. 'How did that happen?'

Wu Chung glanced over at his wife, and smiled. 'Talking to Tsi Huen yesterday, when I arrived home, she persuaded me not to go away for such a long time again. She told me that I needed to be here for Wu Fung-Yi while he is growing up.' Wu coughed, blocking his lips with the back of his hand. 'I knew she was right, so while she cooked dinner I walked back to the harbour to see if anyone else was looking for a cook. In a bar near the wharf I found that the American warship was seeking an assistant cook. I signed up straight away.' He smiled. 'They desperately need a man who knows what he is doing. I have discovered that the new Head Cook has ordered far too many barrels of fresh water. Hundreds of them! The ship is heading up the Yangtze River – they will have all the fresh water they want! I told him it was too much, but he wouldn't listen to me.'

'Did you tell Captain Tollaway that you wouldn't be coming back?'

'I sent a message to Mr Larchmont. I know he and the Captain will understand.' He glanced up at his wife. 'I have spent too long away already. I have missed so much of their lives. The American ship is sailing up the Yangtze River for the next few weeks. I will be back before anyone misses me, and then I will look for other opportunities in Shanghai.'

'But when does it sail?' Sherlock asked. He felt saddened at the fact that he would not be sharing the voyage back to England with his friend.

'Tomorrow,' Wu said. His face was ashen. 'But I will not be able to make it. Not the way I am feeling now. And a cook who is ill is a cook that nobody wants preparing their food. I need you to take a message to the Captain of the *Monocacy*. Tell him that he will need to find another assistant cook.'

If he can, at such short notice, Sherlock thought, but he smiled reassuringly at Wu Chung. 'I'll take the message,' he said. 'I'm sure you can find another job locally without much trouble.'

Wu shook his head. 'Not the way I am feeling right now.'

'Have you eaten anything that might have caused this?' Sherlock asked.

149

'Nothing that my family haven't eaten as well.' His face spasmed, and he suddenly twisted sideways and brought up the water that he had drunk moments before on to the floor. Tsi Huen stepped forward to take his shoulders.

As he settled back into the bed, pale and shaking, Sherlock noticed something on his back. He only saw it for a moment, as Wu Chung's cotton shirt shifted, but it caught his attention.

'Lean forward,' he said.

'What?'

'Lean forward!'

Tsi Huen and her son glanced at each other, puzzled. Wu Chung stared at Sherlock for a moment, then he nodded. His wife and son helped him as he sat up in the bed and leaned forward. Sherlock peeled the damp cloth away from his shoulder.

There, below Wu Chung's neck and above his right shoulder blade, were two red marks. One was small and neat while the other was larger and had ragged edges. The two marks were about an inch apart, and the skin all around them was marked with a red rash.

Tsi Huen gasped. 'Snake bite!' she cried. She leaped back from the bed, staring horrified at the tiled floor. 'Fung-Yi – get back! It might be under the bed.'

Sherlock's body wanted to jump back as well, but his

mind was fascinated by the idea that there might be a venomous reptile underneath the low bed. With body and mind fighting, he froze in place. It took Cameron grabbing his shoulder and physically pulling him to make him move.

Wu Chung drew his knees up to his chest and glanced around nervously. 'I didn't feel any bite,' he said.

Safely five feet away from the darkness underneath the bed, Sherlock dropped to his knees and peered into the shadows, ready in case something lashed out at him. But there was nothing. The space beneath the bed was empty.

He stood up, shaking his head. 'If there was a snake there then, it's gone now.'

'Of course there was a snake!' Tsi Huen exclaimed. 'You saw those marks!' She wailed in anguish. 'How could this happen to us?'

Looking around the room, Sherlock wondered the same thing. 'The windows are so high that I can't see how a snake could climb up there,' he mused, 'and this bedroom is at the end of a corridor. The snake would have had to slither a long way to get here, and then slither a long way to get back. Why would it do something like that?'

'Maybe it got in through a hole,' Cameron suggested.

Sherlock looked around the room, at the line where

the walls met the tiled floor. 'Look at it,' he said. 'I can't see any holes.'

'There are no holes,' Wu Chung's son, Wu Fung-Yi, said proudly. 'Mother made me fill them all up with clay so that rats and mice can't get in. I check every week to make sure that no more holes have appeared.'

'Good boy,' Wu Chung said weakly, lying back down in the bed. His face was grey and sallow.

'When did you last check?' Sherlock asked.

'Yesterday,' the boy said.

Cameron looked around. He hefted his stick. 'I'll check the other rooms, in case it's still here.' He looked at Tsi Huen. 'If that's all right with you?'

She nodded. 'Be careful.'

'Look under all the furniture,' Sherlock cautioned.

Wu Chung's son stepped forward. 'I will help,' he announced. 'Two sets of eyes are better than one.' He nodded soberly at Cameron.

Tsi Huen seemed about to object, but a look from her husband made her close her mouth. 'Let him go,' Wu Chung said, voice weak. 'He is a brave boy, and I am very proud of him.'

Cameron and Wu Fung-Yi left the room, cautiously glancing around. Wu Chung gestured Sherlock and Tsi Huen closer to the bed.

'Best that he is not here,' he said. 'I do not want

him to see me like this.' He coughed, and Sherlock was shocked to see blood on his lips. 'Maybe it would have been better if I was ill. With a snake bite, there is no recovery. Do not let him back in. No child should have to watch his father die.'

Tsi Huen cried out, then stifled the cry with the back of her hand. Her eyes were wide and scared.

'You're not going to die,' Sherlock said with more firmness than he felt. Looking at Wu, he thought the man might be right, and he suddenly felt tears springing to his eyes. 'We need to get you a healer,' he said. 'Where can we find one?' He caught Tsi Huen's eye. 'Cameron and I will go and fetch the healer. We'll take Wu Fung-Yi with us.'

Tsi Huen nodded her gratitude, tears in her eyes. Sherlock could see that she knew what Sherlock was doing – giving her a chance to say goodbye to her husband, if indeed he was dying.

Cameron and Wu Fung-Yi came back into the bedroom. 'No snakes,' Wu's son announced proudly. 'We checked everywhere.' He glanced over at his father, and his eyes were suddenly sorrowful. He suspected what was happening as well.

'We're going for a healer,' Sherlock announced.

Tsi Huen wrote a quick note on a scrap of paper with an inked brush. 'Here,' she said, giving it to Cameron.

153

'This is the address, and a note for the healer. Be quick. Be as quick as you can.' She frowned at Cameron. 'You can read *hanzi*?'

He nodded, and scanned the note. 'I know where this is,' he confirmed.

Sherlock gazed over at Wu Chung. He nodded a farewell. The cook nodded back, smiling weakly.

'Come on,' he said. 'Let's go.'

The daylight outside was blinding, and it took a moment for their eyes to adjust. Cameron led the way quickly down the street. Wu Fung-Yi brought up the rear, glancing back at the house where his father lay ill. Possibly dying.

'Are there a lot of poisonous snakes in China?' Sherlock shouted to Cameron as they ran.

'Some,' Cameron called back over his shoulder. 'Usually out in the countryside. I've not heard of any coming into the towns. Not without ending up in a cooking pot, anyway.'

'The Chinese eat *snakes*?' Sherlock questioned.

Cameron nodded. 'The Chinese eat anything.'

At first Cameron led the way through the crowded streets, but Wu Fung-Yi kept trying to overtake him. 'I know where we are going!' he shouted.

Cameron jostled his way back to the leading position a couple of times, but eventually Sherlock caught him by the shoulder. 'Let him be at the front,' he said. 'He needs to feel like he's doing something to help his father.'

'I suppose so,' Cameron said, shrugging. 'I'd probably feel the same.'

Eventually they arrived at a small shack that was set apart from the other buildings in the area. Charms and trinkets hung on strings from the roof, gently swinging in the breeze. Sherlock noticed that the garden around it, front and back, contained plants that were different from the flowering shrubs that everyone else seemed to cultivate. These plants mostly didn't have flowers, or if they did then the flowers were dull and limp. They were thin, unimpressive things, more like weeds than anything that someone would want to keep around.

Wu Fung-Yi ran up to the doorway. There was no door: just a thin blanket that hung down over the opening. He banged on the door frame.

'Please!' he called. 'Honourable sir – we need your help!'

As Sherlock and Cameron joined Wu Fung-Yi, an elderly man pulled back the blanket. He was, perhaps, the oldest human being that Sherlock had ever seen. His skin was the texture of leather that had been crumpled up and left to dry out in the sun. His eyes were almost invisible behind a landscape of wrinkles that reminded Sherlock of cracks in the mud of a dried-up pond. He had a thin, white moustache that hung down on either side of his mouth to his collarbones. His head was almost bald apart from a white ponytail, barely larger than the strands of his moustache, which decorated the back of his head. When he opened his mouth to speak, Sherlock saw that he only had one tooth left, and his gums were black.

'Who are you, to disturb my sleep?' he grumbled in a high-pitched voice.

Wu Fung-Yi bowed quickly. 'My apologies, venerable healer. My father is ill. My mother sent me to beg for your help.'

The old man stared at Wu Fung-Yi for a long moment, his eyes mere glints of light in the dark folds of his eyelids. Stepping out into the garden, he moved his head to stare at Sherlock and Cameron. He was holding a wooden stick in his hand, and used it to support his weight. It was twisted, like a tree root. 'So, foreign devils as well,' he said casually. 'Interesting days. Interesting days indeed.'

Wu Fung-Yi turned to look at the two boys. 'They were visiting,' he said, half apologetically. 'They followed me here.'

Cameron seemed about to argue, so Sherlock poked him in the back. He shut his mouth, and handed over the scrap of paper that Tsi Huen had given him.

The old man unfolded it and read it. He nodded slowly. 'Snake bite, eh? Very serious. Very expensive to treat.'

Wu Fung-Yi bristled. 'We can pay!' he protested.

'If he can't I can,' Cameron said. He turned to look at Sherlock. 'Hey, I may think this whole thing is stupid but I'm not going to let your friend die if I can help it.'

'Thanks,' Sherlock said. 'I appreciate that.'

'Let me get the things I will need,' the old man said. Rather than turn back inside the shack, as Sherlock had expected him to do, he walked across to his garden. Bending over with the flexibility of a man a third his age, he took hold of various plants, checked their leaves and stems, and either pulled them out of the ground or left them and moved on. Eventually he had ten or so plants dangling from his hand.

'Medicine,' he said, waving the plants at the boys. 'Very good for snake bites and insects.'

The return journey was slower than the journey there. The old man walked faster than Sherlock had expected from the look of him, but he couldn't run. Or wouldn't run: Sherlock wasn't sure which. He even stopped once or twice to talk to people that he recognized on the way, and Wu Fung-Yi had to virtually drag him away from the conversation in order to get him going again.

When they got to East Renmin Street, Tsi Huen was

157

standing outside the door of the house. Her hands were fluttering like birds as she gazed along the street. When she caught sight of the three boys and the elderly healer her hands leaped up to her throat in relief.

'How is Father?' Wu Fung-Yi called as he got closer.

She winced. 'No better.' She placed her hands together and bowed to the ancient healer as he got to the doorstep. 'Thank you for coming. I am in your debt.'

He bowed his head to her. 'Let us see what can be done,' he replied. 'I make no promises.'

He entered the house, using his cane for support. Tsi Huen followed him, hands still fluttering. Wu Fung-Yi moved towards the door, but Sherlock put a hand on his shoulder. 'Wait here, with us,' he said. 'The healer needs to work, and you might distract him. Besides, your mother needs to worry about your father, not about you.'

Wu Fung-Yi turned to look at Sherlock. His eyes were shiny with tears. 'But . . . but he might die.'

Sherlock nodded. 'Yes, he might, and if he does you shouldn't be there. You should remember him the way he was.'

The time seemed to trickle past slowly. The three of them sat outside, waiting. At one point Cameron wandered off, and returned a few minutes later with a watermelon which he proceeded to cut up with a pocket

158

knife. The boys sucked the moisture out of the slices. There was little talking.

Tsi Huen came out of the house a short while after they had finished the watermelon. She looked tired, strained.

'How . . . ?' Wu Fung-Yi started to ask, but he couldn't finish the question.

Tsi Huen shrugged. 'He is very ill,' she said quietly. 'The healer is doing everything he can.'

She went back inside, and the boys went back to waiting.

After another hour or so, the healer came to the door. He gestured to Sherlock. 'You – foreign devil – you look intelligent. You remember where my house is?'

'Yes, sir,' Sherlock replied. 'I think so.'

'Very important – you need to go there now, quickly, and get a plant from the garden. It is a tall plant, up to your waist, with small blue flowers and leaves that are curled up. You understand?'

I understand,' Sherlock said. He nodded towards Wu Fung-Yi. 'But shouldn't he go? I mean, he knows the town better than I do. He won't get lost.'

The healer gazed at Wu Fung-Yi with an unreadable expression on his face. 'He needs to be here,' he said quietly. 'In case . . .'

'I understand.' Sherlock glanced at Cameron. 'But

even he knows the town better than I do.'

'Yes,' the healer said, 'but he does not look as intelligent as you do. He might bring back the wrong plant. Now go.'

'Yes, sir.'

Sherlock ran off, retracing the journey that he and the other two boys had made earlier. He ran as fast as he could, heart pounding in his chest and veins pumping in his neck and his temples. When he got to the old man's shack he stopped for a second, hands on knees as he sucked as much air into his burning lungs as he could. As soon as he was able to move again he ran into the garden and quickly sorted through the plants. Too tall . . . too short . . . flowers not blue . . . leaves not curly . . . yes! There was one plant, over near the fence, which matched the healer's description. Sherlock pulled it from the soil and ran back with it.

When he got to Wu Chung's house, Cameron and Wu Fung-Yi were standing outside with Tsi Huen. She was sitting on the front step, crying. Wu Fung-Yi's hand was resting on her shoulder. He was crying as well.

Cameron walked over to Sherlock.

'He's dead,' he said, and the sound of the two simple words was like stones dropping heavily to the ground.

CHAPTER EIGHT

'I'm too late!' Sherlock said. The full weight of the run to and from the shack suddenly descended on him: he felt weak and exhausted and defeated.

Cameron shook his head. 'It's not your fault,' he said sombrely. 'Wu Chung died about ten minutes after you left. The healer came out and told us that he had "joined his illustrious ancestors", which is what the Chinese people say when someone has died. You wouldn't even have been at the garden when it happened. There's nothing you could have done. You could have flown the entire way there and back and it still wouldn't have made a difference.'

Sherlock could hear Cameron speaking, but it sounded as if his friend's words were coming from a long way away, through thick cotton wool. He found that the enormity of the cook's death was more than he could deal with. He hadn't really prepared himself for the fact that it might actually happen. That Wu Chung might suddenly . . . not be there any more.

He felt strange. Disconnected. He felt as if he was floating slightly above the ground, and that the world was tilting gradually sideways.

He leaned over, put his hands on his knees and took slow breaths, trying to steady himself.

He had seen death before, of course. Even back when he had just left Deepdene School for Boys and moved to Farnham he had seen a dead body in the woods outside his aunt and uncle's manor house, and later he had seen men die on the Napoleonic fort that Baron Maupertuis was using as a base. He had seen Duke Balthassar die at the claws and teeth of his cougars, and also seen the stabbed body of a man at the Diogenes Club. There was the sailor who had fallen and broken his neck on the *Gloria Scott*, and the others that had been killed by the storm and by the pirates. But all of these had been people he didn't know – or, at least, hardly knew. He had never had to come to terms with the death of a friend.

It wasn't as if Wu Chung was a *close* friend, he tried to tell himself. He wasn't like Matty Arnatt, or Amyus Crowe – or even, he thought with a chill, Virginia Crowe. It wasn't as if he was a member of Sherlock's family, like Mycroft, or his sister Emma, and yet . . . Sherlock had been close to him. The Chinese man had taught him so much, and he had been an important part of Sherlock's life, and his absence would leave a hole that would be impossible to fill.

'How are Wu Fung-Yi and Tsi Huen dealing with

it?' Sherlock asked, and he could hear that his voice was hoarse – more of a whisper.

'His wife is pretty broken up,' Cameron said. 'It must be hard, having your husband away for so long, then losing him again the moment he comes back. The kid is trying to put a brave face on it. Frankly, I don't think he knows quite how to feel. He's kind of being guided by what his mother is doing.'

As Sherlock glanced over at the house, the healer emerged, still leaning on his stick. He walked past Tsi Huen and Wu Fung-Yi towards Sherlock and Cameron. He looked calmly at the plant that drooped from Sherlock's hand.

'I will take that back,' he called. 'I may be able to replant it. Maybe.'

'What happened?' Sherlock asked.

The healer looked at him in surprise. 'You know what happened. He was bitten by a snake. I did what I could, but it was no good. The poison had taken hold in his body. There was nothing I could do to help.'

'Are you sure it was a snake bite?' Sherlock heard himself asking. For a moment he was amazed at the words, until he realized that his mouth was expressing a thought that his brain was only just processing.

The healer nodded. 'There is a clear bite mark on his back.'

163

'But how did the snake get into the bedroom?' Sherlock asked. 'The only window was too high for any snake to slither up to, and if it had come in through the front door then it would have had to go through several other rooms, past several other people, before it got to Wu Chung.'

'Who can predict the actions of a snake?' the healer said, shrugging. 'There is no doubt in my mind – a snake bit him, and the poison killed him. I have seen this kind of thing before.'

'In town?' Sherlock pressed. 'In a bedroom?'

The healer raised a white, thin eyebrow. 'You have a better idea?'

'No,' Sherlock had to admit. 'No, I don't.'

The healer reached out and took the plant from Sherlock's hand. Sherlock watched as the old man walked slowly back to Tsi Huen. Still crying, she took some coins out of a purse and passed them to him. He bowed his head, thanking her, and walked away, the plant still dangling from his hand. Sherlock found himself hoping that the healer hadn't charged her for the plant that had arrived too late.

Wu Fung-Yi was standing to one side, staring at the house. Sherlock and Cameron walked over to join him.

'I'm sorry,' Cameron said awkwardly.

'Me too,' Sherlock said.

Wu Fung-Yi didn't say anything. He just stared into the distance.

'I wish I could see the body,' Sherlock said quietly to Cameron.

'What?'

'Wu Chung's body. I wish I could see it again.'

'That's a bit morbid, isn't it?'

Sherlock shrugged. 'Is it? He's dead – I'm sure he won't mind.'

'Maybe his wife and his son might.'

Sherlock glanced over at them. 'I suppose they don't need to know.'

'Why do you want to look at his body?'

'I want to check that bite. The one on his back.'

Cameron shuddered. 'Don't remind me.'

'Didn't it strike you that there was something odd about it?'

'Like what?'

Sherlock shook his head, trying to visualize the wound that he had seen on Wu Chung's back. Part of him knew that he was thinking about Wu Chung's death as if it was a puzzle so that he wouldn't have to deal with the emotion of it, but another part of him knew that there really *was* a puzzle there. 'I'm not sure,' he said. 'The fang marks, if that's what they were, seemed to be different sizes. One was bigger than the other – it looked torn.'

'So – the snake had a broken fang. What does that mean?'

'I don't know. But an old friend of mine once told me to look for things that were out of place. Those were the things that told you something interesting was happening, he said.'

'And a snake with a broken tooth is interesting?'

'That depends on what broke the tooth.' He looked over at where the boy and his mother were holding each other. 'Do you think if I asked her she would let me go in?'

Cameron looked over at Tsi Huen, then back at Sherlock. 'Her husband has died. I hate to think how I would feel if my father died suddenly. How would *you* feel?'

Unexpectedly, Sherlock found his thoughts suddenly pushed towards his own father, somewhere in India. Maybe he was dead. Maybe he had been killed in some British Army action against the natives, and the message hadn't even got to England yet. Or maybe it had got to England, and his mother, his sister and his brother already knew, but weren't able to tell him. He tried to analyse the feelings that welled up within him, but he couldn't. There was something there, some messy mixture of emotions, but he couldn't pull them apart.

'Sometimes,' he found himself saying, 'I wonder if my

father isn't already dead to me. I'm finding it increasingly difficult to remember his face, or his voice, or his laugh. I used to have memories of him – now I think that I just have memories of having memories.'

'That's awful,' Cameron whispered.

'Is it?' Sherlock stared at Wu Fung-Yi. 'Maybe the awful thing is caring too much.' He shook himself. 'Look, I made a promise,' he said. 'I told Wu Chung that I would tell the Captain of the USS *Monocacy* that he wouldn't make the voyage. I'd better go and do that.'

'I suppose I should go and tell my mother and father what has happened. I'm not sure how much use I can be here.'

Sherlock looked around. Nobody nearby seemed interested. 'I think,' he said, 'that being here is enough. Look, I'll be back within an hour, I promise.'

'All right.'

Sherlock left the house and headed downhill, towards the quay. His side ached from all the running, and he had to bend forward as he walked to keep the pain at bay. He hadn't noticed before, but there were places where the blue sweep of the bay was visible through gaps between the houses. He could even see the masts of ships sticking up above the roofs, and as he got closer to the waterside he could, every now and then, see the great wheel of the USS *Monocacy* looming above everything.

It was only as he was passing through the gate in the wall that ran around the town, past the uniformed guards, that he suddenly wondered how he was going to get back in. He shrugged the thought away. He would face that problem later, if necessary.

He made his way along the quay towards the long bulk of the American ship. There were still plenty of sailors and local Chinese people around. He kept an eye out for the gang of youths who had tried to steal his money the day before, but although there were plenty of people the right age around, he didn't recognize any of them. More importantly, perhaps, none of them recognized him.

Several gangways led up from the quay to the deck of the *Monocacy*. Each one was guarded by a pair of armed American sailors in dark blue uniforms. The sailors were all keeping a wary watch on the people walking past them.

Sherlock noticed that a lot of the Chinese locals were casting unpleasant glances at the ship, and at the sailors. Every now and then someone would shout an insult at the Americans. Sherlock understood the words – his Cantonese was getting better and better the more he heard – and he decided it was a good thing that the sailors couldn't. Some of the names they were being called were pretty nasty, and the sailors were armed, after all. Insults, tempers and guns didn't go very well together.

As he got near the gangway Sherlock saw with concern that a small group of locals was gathering a few feet away. One of them bent and picked up a rotten cabbage. He lobbed it through the air. It caught a uniformed American on the side of the head, exploding in shards of stinking vegetation and a spray of water. The sailor stumbled, then turned around and raised his gun towards the crowd. His face was twisted in anger and disgust. His companion caught his arm and knocked it down. The two of them argued for a moment while the crowd jeered.

Another vegetable flew out of the crowd and hit the ground between the two guards. They looked to Sherlock like they weren't sure whether to retreat up the gangway, take some action or pretend that nothing was happening.

The growing tension was broken when someone started walking down the gangway towards the quayside. It was the man Sherlock had seen the night before at the Mackenzies' dinner party – Captain Bryan. He was an impressive sight, in his full uniform and frock coat, and he was followed by two junior officers and a Chinese man in ornate robes – a translator, possibly. Sherlock thought he recognized the junior officers from the dinner party as well.

Even at that distance, Sherlock could see that Bryan's bright blue eyes were taking in everything that was

169

happening in front of him. He got to the bottom of the gangway and the two sailors snapped to attention. Without stopping, he strode directly across to the crowd.

'What is the meaning of this?' he snapped in English. The translator hastily translated.

The various members of the crowd looked at one another. Nobody seemed willing to speak for them.

'We are visitors here,' Captain Bryan continued. 'We are, I have been led to believe by your Governor, honoured guests.' He paused while the translator caught up. 'Word of the hospitality of the Chinese Empire has spread widely. I am disappointed to see that those words are apparently untrue.' Again he paused, and Sherlock noticed that some members of the crowd were looking ashamed of themselves. 'Wherever this ship has docked around the world, it has been met with the hand of friendship. Do not let this port be any different. Do not dishonour your ancestors and your Emperor with petty bullying.'

As the translator rushed to convey his words in the native language of the crowd, Captain Bryan let his gaze run across the various people standing there. None of them would look him in the eye. He waited for a few moments after the translator had finished, then abruptly turned and strode back towards the gangway, apparently disregarding the possibility that somebody might lob another cabbage at his back. His junior officers waited a few seconds, then turned and followed him. The translator had been looking nervously at the crowd. When he realized that he was alone he quickly scurried to join them.

Sherlock was impressed to see the crowd start to disperse. The locals looked as if the wind had been knocked out of their sails.

Sherlock suddenly realized that he was going to miss his chance if he didn't act quickly. He sprinted across towards Captain Bryan.

Hearing his footsteps, the two junior officers turned to face him. At the foot of the gangway the two armed sailors swung their rifles towards Sherlock, fearing that he was another local threat. He slowed to a fast walk and raised his hands in the air.

'I'm British,' he said. 'My name is Sherlock Holmes. I have a message for the Captain.'

'You were at the Mackenzie dinner party last night,' Captain Bryan said, turning around. 'I remember you. We never got a chance to talk.'

'You were far too busy and I was far too unimportant to bother you,' Sherlock said. 'But thank you for pretending that you might have wanted to talk to me.'

Bryan smiled. 'You're refreshingly honest, son. None of my officers dare say anything that sounds like it might

171

disagree with me, and this country seems to run on saying one thing to your face and another behind your back. Now, you say you have a message?'

'Yes, sir.' Sherlock took a breath. 'You've recently taken on an assistant cook. I'm sorry to tell you that he died today. Almost his last words to me were that he wanted you to know so that you didn't think he had forgotten, or got a better offer.'

Captain Bryan frowned. One of his junior officers leaned forward and whispered something in his ear. He nodded, and turned back to Sherlock.

'We cast off and sail up the Yangtze River within the hour,' he said. 'It's too late to get another assistant cook. We will have to manage without, I suppose, which is annoying given that we have only just replaced our Head Cook with a local man. But I appreciate the effort you went to in order to convey the message.'

He nodded, and turned towards the bulk of the USS *Monocacy*. After a moment he glanced back at Sherlock.

'You knew this man?'

'I did.'

'Was he a good man?'

Sherlock nodded. 'I was with him on the *Gloria Scott*.'

'Then my condolences. Good men are hard to find. Good cooks are even harder. How did he die?'

'He was bitten by a snake.'

Captain Bryan shook his head sadly. 'Snake bite, eh? Must be a lot of the beggars around. Our own Head Cook was bitten by a snake, and died, a few days ago. You wouldn't find rattlesnakes in the middle of an American town, I promise you that.'

As soon as Captain Bryan reboarded the ship, a whistle blew somewhere on deck. The pairs of armed sailors at the bottom of each gangway snapped to attention, then quickly scurried on board. As Sherlock watched, the gangplanks were pulled up to the deck of the ship by invisible hands. Within a few moments only guy ropes attached the ship to the land. It was now a separate world. An American world.

Sherlock waited for a while, but the ship didn't move. Presumably they were raising steam, or checking their charts, or otherwise getting ready.

Eventually he turned away and headed back towards the town wall.

As he approached the gate, and caught sight of the guards in their yellow and red uniforms and their metal bucket-like helmets, he suddenly remembered his earlier fears about getting back into the town. What was he going to do?

He looked down at his clothes. Fortunately, he had selected things from Cameron's closet that made him look at least passably like a Chinese youth. His face was

173

another thing. One look at his eyes and his skin would be enough to give him away.

His mind raced. He had to do something to disguise himself.

Glancing around, he saw an elderly beggar at the side of the road. He wore a wide straw hat to protect his face from the sun, and he stared at every passing person with a pleading expression on his face and his hand outstretched. Sherlock crossed the road to him. His eyes lit up when he saw Sherlock approach.

'A copper coin, young master?' he asked. 'A copper coin that I can use for a cup of tea and a bowl of noodles?'

'Two copper coins,' Sherlock said, 'for your hat.'

The beggar stared at Sherlock. 'Three,' he said.

'That's a lot of tea and noodles.'

The man smiled, revealing a mouth that had too many teeth for a proper beggar. 'I have a big appetite,' he said, patting his stomach.

Sherlock delved into his pockets and retrieved three copper coins, along with a strange piece of metal that he couldn't immediately identify. He threw the coins to the beggar. 'Here – try not to eat it all at once. You'll get indigestion.'

'Chance would be a fine thing,' he beggar grumbled. He took the hat from his head and threw it to Sherlock. 'Be careful with it.'

Sherlock paused for a moment, gazing at the metal object in his hand. It was the thing he'd picked up from the ship's deck outside Mr Arrhenius's cabin. He still didn't know what it was. For a few seconds he thought about throwing it away, but he hated a mystery, even one so small. He would keep it until he knew what it was.

Sherlock set the hat on his head and tipped it forward so that it shielded his face. Looking around, he saw an abandoned bamboo pole by the side of the road. Near it were two broken buckets. He picked them up, dusted the dirt off them and hung them from either end of the bamboo pole, then balanced the pole carefully on his right shoulder so that one bucket hung in front of him and the other one hung behind. Then, with a deep breath, he set off for the gate.

He managed to get in behind a group of workmen returning from somewhere in the dock area. They were grumbling, and shoving each other, and he found that if he stayed at the back and bowed his back to disguise his height then he was pretty effectively blocked from the sight of the guards.

'Hey, you!' one of the guards called. 'You with the buckets!'

Sherlock kept his head down. If he showed his face then they would know he was not Oriental. If he even opened his mouth to speak they would hear his strong accent.

One of the guards stepped into the road in front of the group of workmen.

Sherlock desperately tried to think of some convincing story that would explain why he was trying to sneak into the town disguised as a Chinese worker. He looked up, ready to say something, but the guard was hauling a Chinese woman out of the front of the group. She had two buckets balanced on a pole over her shoulder as well. They were filled with something that looked like milk. Maybe it *was* milk – Sherlock couldn't tell.

'We're thirsty,' one of the guards said. 'Give us some of that or we won't let you in!'

Sherlock breathed a sigh of relief. Although he felt sorry for the woman, he was glad that the guards had missed him. He walked past them, head bent, while they were drinking noisily from her buckets.

Once inside the town wall, he breathed a sigh of relief. Strange, he thought, how just yesterday the *Gloria Scott* had been home and Shanghai had been unfamiliar territory, but now Shanghai felt like home. The crowds, the smells, even the houses . . . maybe he had simply been immersed in it over the course of the day, but it did feel familiar.

176

And Farnham? That felt like another world now. Like a dream.

He quickly moved on. He wasn't sure what awaited him at . . . at Tsi Huen's house . . . but he felt an obligation to go back there. Cameron was expecting him, for a start, but he had got to like Wu Chung's son in the few hours he had spent in the boy's company. He had a quiet dignity about him, and Sherlock wanted to make sure he was going to be all right.

A Western face flashed past him, heading across his path, and Sherlock had to look twice before he recognized Cameron's father – Malcolm Mackenzie. The reason he was so difficult to recognize was that his face was twisted into what Sherlock first thought was a scowl, but then recognized as a frown of worry and concern.

Sherlock was about to shrug it off as a chance encounter and continue on his own way when he realized that Malcolm Mackenzie was being followed. Something was slipping through the crowd behind him.

CHAPTER NINE

Whatever it was that was following Malcolm Mackenzie, Sherlock couldn't make out its shape. He only had a rough idea of its size, which was about that of a large dog. Mainly he could just see movement, a blur as something passed in front of walls or vegetation. He shifted around, trying to get a better view, but it was impossible. Whatever was following Cameron's father seemed always to be behind a person or a tree or a cart. It had an amazing ability to stay hidden.

Sherlock suspected it was the same thing he had glimpsed in the garden of the Mackenzie house the night before. Maybe it hadn't been a burglar, but had been watching Malcolm Mackenzie for some reason, observing him from a distance. Or maybe it *was* a burglar and it was still targeting him as a victim.

Sherlock found himself torn. On the one hand he wanted to get back to Cameron, and to Wu Fung-Yi and his mother, but on the other hand he wanted to find out what this thing was and why it was following Malcolm Mackenzie. The latter won. Instead of going straight on, he diverted sideways, keeping Cameron's father in sight.

He knew that if he kept his eyes on Malcolm Mackenzie then all three of them would end up at the same place. Wherever that turned out to be.

Strangely, nobody really took any notice of this mysterious thing that was slipping past them. Some people turned around, confused for a moment, as it passed, but when they saw nothing there they scratched their heads and went back to what they had been doing.

Fortunately, Sherlock was able to keep following Mr Mackenzie without being seen himself. Partly this was because the follower was intent on its quarry while Malcolm Mackenzie was staring grimly ahead, jaw clenched hard, and partly it was because Sherlock was effectively in disguise. He thought about getting rid of the bamboo pole and the buckets, to make it easier to get through the crowd, but decided for the moment to retain them. He could always throw them away later, if he needed to.

Mackenzie was heading uphill. The closer he got to the top, the larger, more ornate and more colourful the buildings became. They were spaced further apart as well, so that each building had a cleared area of space around it. That made things more difficult for his tracker, as it had fewer and fewer areas of shadow to keep to. Twice Sherlock saw it dash across an area of open ground, but frustratingly he still couldn't make out what it was – only that it seemed to be running on two legs and crouching low to the ground.

Eventually there was only one building ahead – a massive, sprawling construction on the top of the hill with walls so white they dazzled the eye. Its roof was made of yellow tiles and it was surrounded by cherry trees. Guards, dressed similarly to those outside the city gate, stood beside the various doorways, and at the corners of the building. Sherlock decided that it had to be the residence of someone important – perhaps the Prefect that Captain Bryan had mentioned.

The crowd had thinned out as well, so that the only people around were those going to the building – the Residence, as Sherlock decided to think of it – and coming away from it.

From the top of the hill the whole of Shanghai spread out below Sherlock. He could see the twisty streets and the broad thoroughfares that crossed them. He could see the square houses with their hidden gardens forming splashes of green in their centre. He could see the walls of the town, holding everything inside in a tight embrace. Beyond the walls he could see the blue waters of the South China Seas glittering in the sunshine. Several ships were lined up along the quayside – including the *Gloria Scott*, which he recognized from the masts and the rigging with which he had become so familiar over the past few months. He could also see the long grey bulk of the USS *Monocacy*. Her steam-driven wheels were turning, and white steam was emerging from her funnels. She was preparing to leave the dock and head up the Yangtze River.

Turning his attention back to the buildings, Sherlock saw Mr Mackenzie heading directly for the Residence's main entrance, but whatever was following him seemed to have vanished. The main entrance was a formidable double-gate made of thick wood and studded with metal bolts. It had four guards standing on either side of it. A Chinese official stood directly in front of the gates. He wore a long embroidered robe with big sleeves, and a small black brimless hat on his head. People were going up to him and talking for a moment, and he would either let them in through the gates or send them away. Most people were sent away, with only a trickle heading in. Sherlock noticed that at least some of the people who got in handed across a purse of coins to the gatekeeper. The transactions were quick and well hidden by the official's long sleeves. Bribes? Perhaps.

As well as the arriving and departing townsfolk, some people had stalls from which they were selling drinks, snacks and hats to keep off the sun. Sherlock walked past the official in front of the main entrance and found a space near enough to listen to what was being said without being observed. He crouched down and kept his hat low over his face, hoping anyone who did notice him would take him for a beggar.

Malcolm Mackenzie was third from the front of the queue. He kept twitching and moving as if there was something bothering him.

Sherlock glanced around as surreptitiously as he could. He was looking for the mysterious follower. Surely it couldn't have disappeared? Eventually he saw it – or at least he saw something that he thought was it – in a cherry tree overlooking the Residence. Foliage and blossom concealed it, but Sherlock could see the branch bending under its weight, and while there were birds in all the other trees this one was empty of wildlife. They had obviously been scared off.

'My name is Malcolm Mackenzie,' Cameron's father said in Cantonese when he finally reached the official. 'I need to speak to Prefect Chen urgently.'

'Have you applied for an appointment?' the official asked calmly.

'No. As I said – this is urgent.'

'Ah.' The official took his hands from his sleeves and spread them wide in a shrug. 'All business is urgent to those who have it, but what is urgent to one man may be trivial to another.'

'I promise you, this is an emergency,' Mackenzie

said with obvious frustration.

'Nobody ever comes to the Prefect saying, "I have a small matter which has no real importance and can wait",' the official pointed out imperturbably.

Mackenzie looked ready to swear, but instead he pushed a hand into his pocket and came out with a handful of coins. 'Will this make my business more urgent?' he snapped, thrusting the coins under the official's nose.

The official looked pained. 'Regrettably,' he said, 'it will not.' Sherlock suspected it was the aggressiveness with which the bribe had been offered, rather than the size, that was the problem. Or perhaps only Chinese people could bribe Chinese officials.

'May I know when an appointment can be made?' Mackenzie asked through clenched teeth.

'For that, you will need to speak to the Prefect's appointments secretary.' The official inclined his head. 'He is at the Gate of Celestial Blessings, which is on the other side of the Residence.'

Mackenzie's hands were clenching and unclenching. 'Could I perhaps leave a message for the Prefect?'

'You may leave a message, and I will ensure that it is passed to the Prefect's correspondence secretary. If he decides that it is important enough then he will pass it on.'

'Do you,' Mackenzie said, 'have a brush, ink and paper?'

'There will undoubtedly be someone around here selling those items,' the official said smoothly. 'And for an additional sum he will surely be able to phrase the message in a way that will catch the Prefect's ear.'

Mackenzie nodded. 'Thank you,' he snapped, although it was clear that he would have liked to say something else.

Sherlock watched as Mackenzie turned away and looked for someone who could write a message for him, or provide the means with which he could write his own message. A stall near to the corner of the Residence seemed to have what he wanted. He headed for it. Unfortunately, few other people were down at that end of the wall, and Sherlock suspected that if he tried to follow he would be seen by Cameron's father, disguise or no disguise.

Sherlock turned his head to look at the cherry tree. The branch that had been bowed down earlier was now at its normal height, and there were birds perching on the higher twigs. The mysterious follower had moved tree, or had left altogether.

When Sherlock looked back towards the letter-writer's stall, the stallholder was rolling a paper up and sealing it shut with a blob of red wax. He handed it across to

Mackenzie with a flourish. Cameron's father snatched it away and virtually ran across to the official in front of the main gates, bypassing the queue of Chinese townspeople who were already there. He tried to hand the scroll to the man directly, but the official shook his head with a sorrowful expression on his face.

'Please – join the queue at the back,' he said. 'I will take it from you in due course.'

'This really is urgent!' Mackenzie protested.

'What is urgent today is of passing interest tomorrow,' the official said as if he was quoting something. 'Clouds pass in front of the sun and then are gone.'

Mackenzie stared at him for a long moment, then grudgingly went to the end of the queue, which by this time consisted of about ten people. Impatiently, he waited as they were dealt with one by one, tapping the scroll against his leg. Eventually he was in front of the official again.

'Yes?' the official asked.

Mackenzie looked at him in disbelief. 'I need the Prefect to see this,' he said. 'Is there a way to get it to him?'

The official took the scroll. 'I will pass it to the Prefect's correspondence secretary. After that, the matter is in the hands of the gods.' Slipping the scroll into one of his voluminous sleeves, he clapped his hands together

185

twice. A younger official, also in robes, ran through the gates from inside the Residence. The official passed the scroll to him with a flurry of instructions in a language that Sherlock didn't recognize. Was that the Mandarin language that he had heard about – the language reserved for officials and for the Manchu rulers? The younger man ran off, disappearing inside the Residence again.

'It is done,' the official said to Malcolm Mackenzie, bowing. 'May blessings rain down on you like blossom from the cherry tree.'

'And may your honour and wealth increase steadily, like a trickle that becomes a stream and then a river,' Mackenzie replied. It was obviously a rote response: something that was expected in conversation with high-class Chinese. He stared at the official for a long moment, obviously debating whether or not to add something else, but eventually he turned and walked away, hands clenched by his sides. Passing on the message obviously hadn't relieved his worries.

Sherlock gave him a few minutes' head start, then he gathered up his buckets and his bamboo pole and headed downhill. With the mysterious follower gone, or hidden, there was no point in hanging around, and Cameron's father was almost certainly heading back home, disappointed, so there was no point in following him.

His sense of direction had always been pretty good, and he quickly found his way back to a cross-street that he knew would take him back to the Wu family house on East Renmin Street.

Within ten minutes he was outside the house. The street was empty apart from a handful of passers-by. Leaving his bamboo pole and buckets at the side of the road, Sherlock gingerly walked up to the door and knocked on the door frame.

Cameron appeared in the opening. He looked tired, drained.

'What's been happening?' Sherlock asked him.

Rather than answer, Cameron slipped out of the house and joined Sherlock. 'Some friends and relatives have come round,' he said. 'They're speaking so fast I can hardly keep up. A Taoist priest is here, and the body is being prepared for burial.'

Sherlock nodded. 'How are Tsi Huen and Wu Fung-Yi?'

'What's the phrase? "As well as can be expected".' He shrugged. 'This is the tropics. People die all the time here. It's . . . expected. Or at least, it's not unusual.'

'This is,' Sherlock muttered.

'What do you mean?'

'I just don't believe that a snake could have made its way to Wu Chung's bedroom and out again without help

187

and without being seen. The distance was too far, and there were no windows, and Wu Fung-Yi was positive that he'd stopped up any holes in the walls or the floor.'

'What are you saying?' Cameron's face was a picture of curiosity.

Sherlock's voice was grim. 'I'm saying that the snake was introduced deliberately. I think Wu Chung was murdered!'

'But why?' Cameron asked, obviously stunned.

Sherlock shrugged. 'Maybe it was something to do with the fact that he'd just got back. Maybe there was someone here who hated him enough to kill him.' He paused, sorting through the possibilities. 'Or maybe people resented the fact that he'd got a job with the Americans and wanted to punish him. There's obviously a lot of local discontent.'

'Don't get me wrong, but he was a cook. An *assistant* cook.'

'He was a cook, yes, but with a job on an American military ship,' Sherlock said. The words suddenly triggered a memory. 'Captain Bryan told me that the Head Cook on the *Monocacy* had died after being bitten by a snake. That can't be a coincidence, can it?'

'It's an intriguing theory,' Cameron said, cocking his head to one side and staring at Sherlock. 'But there's no evidence. All you have is a story that fits the facts, but I could come up with a story just as plausible.'

'Like what?'

'Give me a minute and I'll think of one.'

Sherlock hesitated for a moment, wondering whether to say the next words or not. 'Look, Cameron – I saw your father earlier, when I was coming back from the quay. He was heading up to the Prefect's Residence, and he was in a hurry. He wanted an audience. He didn't get in, so he wrote a message and got an official to take it in for him. He stressed that it was urgent. Cameron – I think *he* knows what's going on. That thing from the garden last night – it was following him!'

'You followed my father,' Cameron said quietly. His tone was quiet and level. Sherlock couldn't tell whether he was angry, surprised or intrigued. Or perhaps he was a mixture of all three.

'Yes,' Sherlock replied. 'I did. You would have done the same thing if you had seen him.'

Cameron stared at Sherlock for a long moment. 'Actually, you're right,' he said eventually. 'I probably would have done.' He sighed, and looked away. 'He's been acting strangely recently: irritable, argumentative and easily distracted. You saw what he was like at breakfast this morning. Even Mother is worried about him. I think something is wrong.' His mouth twisted suddenly, and Sherlock realized with surprise how worried Cameron was about his father, and how hard he was trying to hide it.

'I really think he knows what's going on,' Sherlock repeated. 'Or at least, he has an idea.' He felt his pulse pounding as the excitement of putting facts together to form a brick wall of evidence started to get to him. 'Did you see, in the garden last night, Mr Arrhenius gave your father a package? I think I know what it was. I saw a set of pictures in his cabin, on the *Gloria Scott*. They looked like spider's webs. I think that's what Mr Arrhenius delivered to your father.' He suddenly remembered the pirate attack. 'And I think there are people trying to get hold of those pictures. Pirates attacked the *Gloria Scott* and one of them sneaked into Mr Arrhenius's cabin, looking for something. Then there's that thing from the garden last night – I think it might be looking for the pictures too.'

Cameron's eyes flickered with interest. 'What was it? Did you see?'

'It moved too quickly,' Sherlock said. 'And it kept hiding in shadows. I couldn't get a clear line of sight.'

'So what are we going to do?' Cameron sighed. 'We think there's some kind of plot afoot involving the USS *Monocacy* but we don't know what it is. We think my father is involved, but we don't know how. We think these spider pictures are important, but we don't know why. Is that a fair summary?'

'Pretty much.' Sherlock scratched his head. 'I suppose we could always ask your father what's going on. He might tell us.'

'Possible, but not likely. We might be better off trying to find those spider pictures you talked about. They might tell us more.'

'All right,' Sherlock said. 'Let's do it.'

The two boys stared at each other for a moment, each one hoping that the other one was going to move first. Eventually Cameron broke the stalemate.

'Come on then,' he said brusquely. 'Let's get this over with.'

As they walked away, Sherlock wondered if he would ever see Wu Fung-Yi or his mother again. Would he remember even their faces in a year or two, or would it be just their names? It seemed such a waste, to have fragments of memories like that floating around inside his head, disconnected from anything real or important. He wished that he could remember perfectly everything that he had ever seen, read or heard, or that he had the ability to erase memories that he didn't need any more. As it was, he still remembered the nicknames and faces of the boys he had studied with at Deepdene School, and he wasn't likely ever to need those memories again.

The two of them made their way back to the Mackenzie family home through the by-now familiar streets of Shanghai. It was mid-afternoon, and the sun was shining down from an enamel-blue sky. Cameron stopped abruptly at one point as they passed a stall selling noodles. He threw a few coins at the stallholder and came away with two woven bamboo baskets of noodles mixed in with fragments of meat and covered with a sauce. 'Here,' he said, handing one over. 'Eat this. It's been a long time since breakfast.'

'I suppose it has,' Sherlock said, suddenly realizing that he was ravenous. He took one bamboo container, which came with two wooden sticks, and he used the sticks to shovel noodles into his mouth as they walked. The sauce was sweet and spicy, and the whole thing tasted wonderful. Why was food in England so bland? he wondered.

By the time they reached Cameron's house they had finished the noodles. Cameron threw the baskets away. 'Mother doesn't like me eating in the street,' he said apologetically. 'She thinks I'll catch some terrible disease.'

'Maybe you're protecting yourself from disease, by eating the local food and playing with the local kids,' Sherlock suggested. 'Maybe the people who stay indoors all the time and isolate themselves from everything are the ones who catch the first disease they encounter, rather than shrug it off.'

Cameron stared at him. 'You know you think too much, don't you?'

When they went inside, there was nobody around. The door to Mr Mackenzie's study was closed – possibly he was inside, doing the important work that he had been talking about at breakfast. Did it involve those spider diagrams? Sherlock wondered. Mrs Mackenzie wasn't anywhere obvious in the house, but Cameron said that she would often go and lie down for a while.

Neither of the boys wanted to open the door to Malcolm Mackenzie's study so that they could try to find the spider diagrams. Instead they gravitated towards Cameron's room. While Cameron flung himself down on his bed and lay there, an arm across his eyes, Sherlock found a notebook and sketched what he could remember of the snake bite on Wu Chung's back. There was something about that snake bite that still bothered him. As best he could, he drew out the two different fang marks – the one that looked like an ordinary bite mark and the ragged one that looked as if it had been made by a broken fang. He also tried to get the spacing between the marks correct. He wasn't sure why it was important that he kept a record, but he wanted to make sure that he had it to hand if he needed it.

Just as he had got the sketch the way he wanted it, recording accurately the wound he had seen on Wu Chung's back, he suddenly heard a gong being rung somewhere outside.

'That's the signal for afternoon tea,' Cameron said, taking his arm off his face. 'I guess we missed our chance to go and search Father's study.'

'That was bravado talking,' Sherlock said. 'I don't think either of us really thought we were going to do it.'

Quickly they washed their faces and hands, and changed into fresh shirts. Cameron led the way across the rock and sand garden and towards the main areas of the house.

Mrs Mackenzie was already in the sitting room, where pots of tea and coffee, and a host of small cakes, had been set out. She smiled at the boys. 'Did you have a nice day?'

Cameron shrugged, but Sherlock smiled at her. He liked Mrs Mackenzie. 'Yes, thank you. Cameron's a great guide to the area.'

She reached out and ruffled Cameron's hair. He pulled away, embarrassed. 'Yes, he's great at so many things,' she said proudly. She glanced towards the door. 'Malcolm's going to miss out on all the cakes if he doesn't hurry up. Cameron – be a dear and fetch your father.'

Cameron grabbed a plate and a cake and, despite his

mother's disapproving look, walked out of the dining room holding the one and eating the other. Sherlock wandered across to the table. 'Would you like me to pour you a cup of tea?' he asked.

'That would be lovely,' Mrs Mackenzie said.

Outside, across the corridor, Sherlock heard Cameron knocking on the door.

'Father? You're missing out on cakes and tea!'

There was obviously no answer, because Cameron knocked again. 'Father? Are you in there?'

Sherlock became aware that Mrs Mackenzie was sitting perfectly still, listening to what was going on with a concerned expression on her face.

'Father?' Cameron knocked again. Moments later, Sherlock heard the sound of a door being pushed open.

The next thing he heard was a cry of pure anguish – 'Father!' – and the sound of a plate smashing on the floor.

CHAPTER TEN

Sherlock and Mrs Mackenzie both looked at the doorway, startled, then glanced at each other. Mrs Mackenzie's face was anxious and surprised. Sherlock knew that his own face must have looked the same.

He rushed for the door. Mrs Mackenzie was only moments behind him, her hands already up over her heart as if trying to stop it from bursting out of her chest.

Malcolm Mackenzie's study was down the corridor and around a corner from the sitting room. As he hurtled around the corner Sherlock saw Cameron standing in the doorway. He seemed to be frozen in place. He was gripping the door frame so hard that Sherlock could see the bones of his knuckles shining white beneath the stretched skin. A smashed plate and a squashed cake lay on the floor by his feet.

Servants appeared at both ends of the corridors: Chinese and Western faces all sharing the same shocked expressions.

Sherlock got to his friend and skidded to a halt. He stared at Cameron's face for a moment, then his gaze followed Cameron's inside the room. The scene he saw there would remain with him for the rest of his life.

The study itself reminded him of his brother Mycroft's office. Bookshelves covered the walls, lined with leather-clad volumes in various colours. An ornate frame supported a large globe of the world in one corner. A desk sat towards the back of the room: a big slab of some dark native wood set on thick legs. Off to one side was a comfortably stuffed armchair with a small side table next to it. A book was opened, upside down, on the table. It sat beside a half-drunk glass of some amber-coloured liquid: probably whisky and soda, judging by the slight smoky odour that Sherlock could detect in the air.

Behind the desk was a wooden chair, and behind the chair was a wide window that looked out on to the interior garden. The window was closed and the glass was intact – no breath of air disturbed the curtains that hung in front of it.

In the chair behind the desk sat Malcolm Mackenzie. His hands were both in front of him on the desk, as if clawing at the papers that were scattered over it. His face was contorted into a mask of absolute horror: eyes wide and mouth open. His hair appeared to be sticking up in shock.

He wasn't moving. His eyes weren't looking at Sherlock, or Cameron, or anything in the study. They were focused on an empty area of space off to one side of

197

the door. Sherlock deliberately followed his gaze, trying to see what he was looking at, but nothing was there. Nothing at all.

Sherlock's heart already felt like it had moved too high in his chest and was in danger of blocking his throat and stopping him from breathing, but the next thing that he saw threatened to stop it beating entirely.

Malcolm Mackenzie's arms were extended so far to the desk that the sleeves of his shirt and jacket were pulled halfway up his forearms. On his right forearm was a mark that Sherlock thought for a moment was a tattoo, but as his eyes lingered on it he realized the horrible truth. It was a bite mark: two holes punched into the skin with a smear of blood across them.

'Father?' Cameron said again.

Sherlock pushed past him just as Mrs Mackenzie got to the door. She gasped, hand raised to her mouth. His paralysis broken, Cameron rushed to the desk. He and Sherlock got to Malcolm Mackenzie at the same time. Sherlock reached out to touch one of his hands while Cameron put out a hand towards his face. Mackenzie's skin was cold, and he did not react to the contact.

Sherlock slipped his fingers beneath Mr Mackenzie's wrist and raised it off the desk, checking for a pulse. There was nothing. No blood was flowing through his veins, and his arm was as unresponsive as the branch of

198

a tree. When Sherlock let it go, his hand landed with a dull *thud*.

'I'm afraid,' Sherlock said, his voice cracking, 'that he's dead.'

Mrs Mackenzie let out a cry. A few moments later Sherlock heard a second *thud* as she passed out and fell to the floor.

'Take her to somewhere comfortable to lie down,' Sherlock snapped at the servants who had begun to appear in the doorway. He saw the face of the butler, Harris, behind the others. He was looking white and shocked. 'Harris!' he called. 'Look after your mistress! Get the maids to take her to her room!' When the butler didn't move, Sherlock clicked his fingers loudly. 'Quickly! And send someone for a doctor. Not a local healer, but a real doctor – a European. There must be one somewhere in Shanghai!'

'There is,' Cameron muttered. 'Dr Forbes. He lives about five minutes away.'

Sherlock glared at the butler until the man suddenly seemed to get a grip on himself and started issuing orders to the staff. Sherlock patted Cameron on the shoulder, then crossed to the door and closed it. He knew that Malcolm Mackenzie was beyond any need for privacy now, but even so he felt that the man ought to be respected, and not gawped at. Besides, if the snake was

199

still in the room he didn't want to give it a chance to escape. He wanted it dead.

As the door closed he turned back to look at Cameron. His friend was staring at his father's twisted face. 'What happened, Sherlock? What *happened* to him?'

'He was bitten by a snake, by the looks of it,' Sherlock said. He moved closer and indicated the bite on Malcolm Mackenzie's arm. 'There's obviously a lot of it about.'

'But what are the chances of two snake bites happening in one day while we are around?' Cameron asked dazedly.

'A more interesting question,' Sherlock mused, gazing closer at the bite, 'is what are the chances of the *same* snake biting two different people in different places while we are around?'

Cameron frowned. 'What do you mean?'

Sherlock indicated the bite. 'Look — one of the fang marks is larger than the other.' He took from his pocket the sketch he had made earlier, based on his memories of the bite on Wu Chung's shoulder. He held the sketch beside the real bite. 'They're exactly the same size, exactly the same distance apart, but one of the marks looks like the fang that made it is broken.'

Cameron glanced around the room, his face twisted into a scowl. 'It might still be here, mightn't it?'

'The window is closed. Was the door closed when you got here?'

'It was.'

'And someone would have spotted a snake leaving in the past few minutes, there were so many people around. It *must* still be here.' Sherlock's eyes quickly catalogued all the shadowy hiding places around the room – beneath the furniture, on top of the books, hidden in the curtains. 'We're going to have to search for it.'

Cameron pulled open a drawer of his father's desk. From inside he removed a revolver. 'My father taught me to use this,' he said quietly.

Sherlock grabbed a walking stick that was propped up against the door frame, on the basis that it was better than nothing.

For the next ten minutes the boys made their way carefully around the room looking for the snake. Sherlock would use the walking stick to poke, prod and investigate any likely hiding place, while Cameron would stand back ready to shoot if anything lashed out. Sherlock had no idea how fast snakes might move. His only previous experience of reptiles was with the giant lizards that Duke Balthassar had kept as evil pets. They had been very slow and deliberate in their movements, but he suspected that snakes might be faster. Every time he came to somewhere dark and hidden – a gap between two books, or a cushion propped up on a chair with a space behind it – he was careful to stand well back when

201

he used his stick to poke around. His heart was racing and he could feel sweat breaking out over his chest. The thought that, at any second, a venomous snake might come hurtling through the air towards his face made him feel more scared than he had been in a long time.

Every once in a while he would glance over at Mr Mackenzie. The man just sat there as if he might suddenly turn around and ask them what they were doing, but Sherlock's heart ached when he remembered, each time, that Malcolm Mackenzie wasn't going to do anything any more. Sherlock had liked him. More than that, he had *respected* him. And Cameron had obviously loved him.

Eventually they had to accept that there was no snake in the room. All the possible hiding places had been investigated. Sherlock had even swept his stick along the top of the curtains in case the snake had somehow climbed up there, but nothing came falling down. It had gone.

Cameron was shaking with suppressed fury, and his face was white. He obviously wanted to take his revenge on the snake, and was feeling cheated. 'Where *is* it?' he kept on asking. 'Where *is* it?'

'It's gone to the same place it went in Wu Chung's house,' Sherlock said.

'Are you *sure* it's the same snake?'

'Oh, I'm sure. I just don't know whether *we* are following *it* around or *it* is following *us* around.'

Cameron glanced at him. 'How can either of those things be? Snakes are stupid. They can't think for themselves.'

'Indeed,' Sherlock murmured. 'Strange, isn't it?' He glanced up guiltily, aware that he was ignoring the tragedy of Malcolm Mackenzie's death and concentrating more on the interesting problem posed by the snake, but Cameron didn't seem to notice.

The door suddenly opened and Harris appeared. He ushered in a smaller man with a pointed white beard and a ruff of white hair around his otherwise bald head. 'Ah, young Cameron,' he said, spotting Sherlock's friend. 'A tragedy. A real tragedy. Your father – good man. Always thought so.' He cocked his head to one side and stared at Sherlock. 'I don't know you. Do I know you?'

'Sherlock Holmes – I'm a friend of Cameron.'

'Ah. Yes. Good.' He seemed to notice Malcolm Mackenzie for the first time, and he crossed to the body, checking it over carefully. 'You have, I presume, looked for the serpent? I would hate to find it lurking down a sleeve or something.'

'It's not in the room,' Sherlock confirmed. In fact, he had examined Cameron's father's body quickly while his friend had been distracted. The snake hadn't been

203

hiding in his lap, in his clothes or anywhere else around the body.

'How's Mother?' Cameron asked quietly as Dr Forbes took out a stethoscope and listened to Malcolm Mackenzie's chest for any trace of a heartbeat.

'Looked in on her briefly,' the doctor muttered. 'Strong woman. Needs a barbiturate to help her sleep. Obviously distraught.' He glanced at Cameron. 'What about you, young fellow. How're you feeling?'

'Shocked,' Cameron admitted. 'Confused. Scared.'

'All quite normal reactions.'

Sherlock indicated the body. 'I presume . . . ?'

Forbes shook his head. 'No trace of life, I'm afraid. Looking at the swelling and the redness around the wounds, I can tell it was a poisonous snake. Probably caused a heart attack straight away. Poor man.'

'That's not what happened to Wu Chung,' Sherlock mused. When he saw Dr Forbes raise an eyebrow he added, 'Another man was bitten earlier today – a local Chinese man. He died as well, but it took a lot longer.'

Forbes frowned. 'Might have been a different type of snake. Different venom.'

'On the contrary,' Sherlock said, 'we think not only was it the same type of snake, we think it was the same *actual* snake.'

'Then the venom should have worked in exactly the same way.'

'That's a good point,' Sherlock said. 'If it *was* the same snake then something changed between then and now. I wonder what it was.'

Dr Forbes stepped back from the desk. 'I'm afraid there is nothing I can do, young man,' he said. 'Your father has been dead for a while now. I will fill in the death certificate to say that he was bitten by a venomous snake. The local authorities will need to be alerted, and they may wish to make their own investigation . . . I can do that, if you wish.' He grimaced. 'So sorry. Tragic. Very tragic. Your father was a good man. I'll have the servants move the body to a bedroom, where it can lie peacefully until the funeral arrangements can be made.'

Forbes left the room. Sherlock and Cameron were silent for a few moments.

'I should be doing something,' Cameron said. 'I should be arranging the funeral, or comforting Mother, or organizing the servants. After all, I'm the man of the house now.' His face seemed to crumple, and he looked smaller: a vulnerable child. 'What's going to happen to us? With Father gone the business is finished.'

'Perhaps you could go back to America,' Sherlock suggested lamely. 'I'm sure your father has built up quite a bit of money from his business. Your mother might want to move back home, near her own family if she has any. And you've always wanted to see America.'

Cameron nodded slowly. 'Maybe.' He shook himself. 'I'll go and check on Mother, and I'll make sure that the local authorities know what's going on. I'll send a message to the local Catholic priest as well. I'm sure he can advise on what we need to do about a funeral.'

He walked out, leaving Sherlock behind.

Moments later Harris and two male Chinese servants entered the room. The servants were carrying a stretcher – a length of canvas with a bamboo pole running along each side – and Harris had a folded sheet in his hand.

Harris nodded his head to Sherlock. 'We were instructed to . . .'

'. . . take Mr Mackenzie's body to his bedroom,' Sherlock completed when the butler hesitated. 'That's all right. Do you need a hand?'

Harris shook his head. 'I believe we can manage, sir.' He indicated the stretcher. 'It's been in a store cupboard for years. Nobody can remember why it was there. Good thing we had it.'

As Sherlock watched, Harris and the two servants gently lifted Malcolm Mackenzie's body from the chair and laid it on the stretcher. Once it had been arranged, hands on chest, Harris carefully placed the sheet on top of the body, hiding it from view. Harris directed the two servants to take an end each. They picked up the stretcher with some effort, and Harris led the way out.

Sherlock watched them go, feeling strangely useless. Everyone seemed to be doing something, apart from him.

He glanced around the room, waiting to see if anything caught his eye. He was remembering Amyus Crowe's dictum about looking for things that stood out, things that were unusual.

Eventually Sherlock wandered across to the window, more out of boredom than for any other reason. He wanted to check that it really was closed, that nothing could have got in or out. He ran his hands around the edges of the frame, and pressed against the glass experimentally, but there was no looseness, no give. The window was completely sealed.

He looked around the room, letting his eyes flick across things without really taking them in, hoping that something would spring out at him. And something did. He suddenly noticed a smeared mark on the floor by the door. For a second he thought it was dirt tracked into the room by him, or Cameron, or Dr Forbes, but the smear was to the left of the door frame, close to the wall. He walked over and knelt down, taking a closer look. Now that he was nearer, he could see that the smear was in the shape of a footprint. He could clearly see the impression of the toes, and the ball of the foot. He would have assumed that it was a child's footprint except for some marks in the carpet in front of the toes. The marks looked like they had been left by claws – something sharp that had dug into the carpet and caught the fibres.

He rocked back on his heels, thinking. A child with claws? An animal of some kind that left footprints like a child? What exactly was he dealing with here?

He remembered the thing he had seen – or almost seen – in the garden and then following Cameron's father through Shanghai. Had it been in Malcolm Mackenzie's study? It seemed likely, but what was it, and what did it want?

He searched around, but there were no other marks that he could see anywhere across the carpet. Just here. There was no way of tracing the creature's comings and goings.

He straightened up and was about to leave the room when it occurred to him that the papers on the desk were in a mess. The rest of the room was neat, and he didn't want Cameron or Mrs Mackenzie to walk in at some later time, see the papers scattered everywhere and be reminded that they were the last thing that Malcolm Mackenzie had touched. If Sherlock just put them into a neat pile, at least that would be something. At least he would feel that he was contributing towards

208

helping the family at their time of crisis.

He walked back to the desk and scooped up a handful of papers. They were upside down. He turned them over, on the basis that he might be able to put them into some kind of order while he tidied them. He certainly didn't want to read them – they were probably something to do with Malcolm Mackenzie's business arrangements – but they might be numbered or something.

He glanced at the top sheet, and his heart skipped a beat.

It was one of the sheets that he had seen in Mr Arrhenius's cabin, on board the *Gloria Scott* – one of the diagrams that had looked like a spider's web. Quickly he riffled through the remaining sheets. They were all similar – all diagrams that looked like various combinations of lines and circles crossing and recrossing each other. He spread them out on the table, fascinated by them. What on earth did they mean?

Sherlock's keen gaze scanned across the diagrams, looking for common elements, trying to see how they were constructed. The sheets of paper themselves were large but the paper was thin – almost translucent. If he held one up to the window then it seemed to glow with the light shining through it.

Each sheet had a large number of small circles drawn on it in ink. The circles were about the size of a coin. Each circle had two straight lines coming out of it in different directions, and the lines criss-crossed their way across the paper, forming triangles, parallelograms, rectangles and other more exotic geometric shapes. Except . . . no: he suddenly saw that two of the circles only had one line coming out of them, and seeing that made him realize that the lines actually formed a *path*. If he put his forefinger on one of the two circles that only had one line coming out of it, then he could *follow* that line across the sheet to a second circle, then follow another line to a third circle, and so on until he finally ended up at the other circle that only had one line coming out of it – or, in this case, going into it. It was a journey, but what did it mean? What was it trying to tell him?

He glanced at all of the pages in turn. He held them up to the light in pairs, trying to see if any of them were the same, or even slightly similar, but they were all different. Although they all consisted of small circles and long lines, all the circles and lines were in different places.

These were definitely the diagrams that Mr Arrhenius had kept in his cabin – the ones the pirate had been looking for. Sherlock had been right when he'd told Cameron that they were what the Dutchman had delivered to Cameron's father the night before. But why? Sherlock racked his brains. Were they some kind of coded message that was meant for Malcolm Mackenzie to see – something that only he could decode, and that would look like gibberish to anyone who came across them by accident? Was decoding them the work that Malcolm Mackenzie had talked about over breakfast, when he had got so irritable and angry? If so, it indicated that whatever message was hidden inside the diagrams was important. So important that, when he had decoded it, Mackenzie had headed straight for the Shanghai Prefect's Residence to tell him.

And then he had died. By accident? Sherlock was beginning to think not.

'What are you doing?' It was Cameron, standing inside the door and staring at Sherlock.

'Are you all right?'

'Difficult to tell,' Cameron said. 'I feel like I'm just being moved around at the moment, although I'm not sure what's doing the moving. What about you?'

'I think I've found some kind of coded message,' Sherlock explained. He gestured to Cameron to come over, and quickly explained his reasoning.

Cameron gazed at the diagrams, frowning. 'They don't mean anything to me,' he said.

'Your father never received anything like this before?'

'Not that I saw.'

'Hmm.' Sherlock stared at the diagrams. 'There must

211

be some kind of key that we could use to decode them.'

'What do you mean?'

'Well, there are different types of code that people use. With some codes you substitute something for the letters in the message – replace every letter "a" with a number "1", maybe, every letter "b" with a number "2", and so on – except that would be too simple, because it would be obvious that there were no numbers bigger than 26, so people would work out pretty quickly what you had done. You could replace every "a" with a "b", every "b" with a "c" and so on, up to "z", which you would replace with "a". That one's harder to work out.' He tapped the top diagram on the pile. 'But this is different. Here there's no substitution. There're no different sets of symbols, or letters, or pictures.'

'It looks like it's some kind of journey,' Cameron pointed out. 'You see how the sheets are nearly transparent? If you could lay them over a page from a book, then the small circles might end up over certain letters. If you started at the beginning circle and then moved along the lines, maybe the letters beneath each circle on the path would spell out a message. Maybe the person who created the diagrams used a book that he owned, and he told my father which book it was.'

'That,' Sherlock said, 'is a very clever idea. Except for the fact that there aren't many books large enough for

212

these sheets to fit over, and there's no guarantee that your father would have the same book unless they had arranged it all in advance.' He thought for a moment. 'What kinds of books could you guarantee people will own? A Bible, I suppose, and a dictionary. Maybe the Complete Works of Shakespeare. That's about it.'

'Bibles are big,' Cameron pointed out. 'At least, the ones they read from in church every Sunday. Those things are *huge*.'

Sherlock looked around the room. 'I suppose we could go through all the shelves and make a pile of all the books big enough for one of these diagrams to cover the page, and then work through them all, page by page, one after the other . . .' He felt his fingers contracting into a fist in frustration. 'And that's the real problem – even if we knew which book to use, we don't know which pages to go to for each of these sheets. There's nothing on them to tell us.'

'Maybe there was a separate key that mentioned which book and which pages?' Cameron said. 'Maybe that key took a different route, and arrived a few days ago in the post.'

Something in Sherlock's brain was telling him that Cameron had said something important. Several important things. Odd phrases kept repeating themselves: 'It looks like it's some kind of journey.' 'Maybe the

213

letters beneath each circle on the path would spell out a message.' 'Maybe that key took a different route.'

Journey. Path. Route.

'What else do most people have in their possession?' Sherlock asked. 'Maps! Every family, every home, has a map of the world! And there are certain maps that are generally regarded as being better than any others – Ordnance Survey maps in England, and Admiralty maps for the world. Where does your father keep his maps?'

'Where *did* he keep his maps?' Cameron corrected softly.

Sherlock winced. 'Sorry, that was clumsy.'

Cameron shrugged. 'It's going to take time.' He pointed to a shelf with no books on, but which contained a number of rolled papers. 'They're over there.'

'Help me look.'

Quickly the two of them unrolled the papers, one after the other. They were all maps – some of China, some of the area local to Shanghai, but some of the entire world. Sherlock quickly focused on the most detailed and colourful map – one that also showed current directions and shallow areas of the ocean as well as land masses. The text at the top identified it as an Admiralty map.

'Right, let's get it on the desk.'

Sherlock spread the map out on the desk while Cameron retrieved some drawing pins from a drawer and pinned the corners down. Then Sherlock took the first sheet with the spider diagrams on and placed it over the map.

It was smaller.

'Where does it fit?' Cameron asked. 'We could slide it all over the place.'

Sherlock moved the sheet until its top left corner corresponded with the top left corner of the map. 'Let's try the simplest option.'

He quickly located one of the circles which only had one line coming out of it. 'Here, let's start with this one.'

'It's right over a town in Asia,' Cameron pointed out. 'Ulan Bator.'

'All right, let's follow the line to the next circle.'

'It's still in Asia.' Cameron didn't sound too impressed. 'It's another town – Singapore.'

'*U-S*,' Sherlock murmured. 'Difficult to tell if that's the beginning of a message or just a random pair of letters.'

'Scotland,' Cameron said, tracing his finger along the line to the third circle.

'*U-S-S*,' Sherlock said. 'I'm beginning to get an idea where this is going. Quick – write down what I say.' He scooted his finger across the map from circle to circle, reading out the names of the cities, towns, rivers, country names and oceans that were revealed inside the circles.

215

Sometimes they surrounded the initial letters, sometimes they were buried somewhere in the middle of the name. 'Right,' he said eventually. 'What have we got?'

Cameron didn't say anything. His face was grim, and his eyes were scared as he spoke: '*USS Monocacy to be blown up on Yangtze River!*'

CHAPTER ELEVEN

'Are you sure?'

'Oh yes. It's very clear.'

Sherlock quickly ran his fingers from circle to circle again. Cameron was right. 'Hand me another sheet.'

Cameron passed the next one over. Sherlock matched it to the top left-hand corner of the map, but this time the circles only occasionally overlapped with any letters in the place names. He frowned, thought for a moment, then he slid the sheet sideways until the top right-hand corner fitted the top right-hand corner of the map. Quickly he checked the circles. They all had letters inside.

'Clever,' he said. 'It's a way of working out the order of the sheets. Start top left, then top right, then presumably bottom right and bottom left.'

'What does the message say?'

Sherlock let his finger slide along the lines. Each time he got to a circle he called out the letter. He tried to hold them all in his mind, but after five or six he lost track.

As he got to the last circle, he called out, 'Right – what have we got?'

'Nothing that makes any sense.'

Sherlock considered for a moment. 'Reverse it,' he said. 'Maybe we accidentally started with the last circle, not the first one, this time.'

Cameron scribbled down a reversed version of the message beneath the one he had already written. '*Explosion is going to be blamed on innocent Taiping rebels*,' he read breathlessly.

'The Taiping rebels? Aren't they the Han Chinese? Didn't your father say that they wanted to overthrow the Manchu rulers?' Sherlock asked.

Cameron nodded. 'That's right – they make the occasional small attack on a town, or take over a village for a while. They're more of a nuisance than anything else. They don't have any real power.'

'But if people think that they have suddenly blown up an American military vessel, they will take them seriously,' Sherlock pointed out.

'But why would they want to blow up an American military vessel? I mean, why would people *believe* that they wanted to blow up an American military vessel when everyone knows that their aim is to drive the Manchus from the country?'

Sherlock shrugged. 'Maybe they so desperately want China to be for the Chinese that they resent any outside influence whatsoever. Maybe they think that the Manchu rulers are corruptly accepting bribes from the American

Government. But the reasons don't matter – the Taiping rebels are a convenient scapegoat for whoever is behind the attack. The Chinese Emperor would send the army in to hunt them down like dogs. He would have to.'

'Worse than that.' Cameron looked grim. 'I can't see the American Government standing for it. They'd send in the Navy.'

'It could lead to war!' Sherlock said, appalled.

'And where there's a war, there are trade opportunities.'

Sherlock stared at Cameron. 'What do you mean?'

'I mean that, as the ruling class, the Manchu officials have currently got a stranglehold on all the trade in China. It all flows through their hands – they can dictate prices, and they get to decide what is bought and sold. It makes my father furious. He wants there to be complete freedom for the Western traders to buy and sell anything, and to undercut each other if they want to, without having to pay bribes to the Manchu officials. A free market. But if there's a whole American fleet standing off the coast, and if the Emperor is kow-towing to the American ambassador to stop a war starting, then the American traders have got the upper hand. America will end up annexing this whole area and turning it into a thirty-eighth state.'

'Are the trade opportunities that important?' Sherlock asked, hardly able to believe what he was hearing.

'The silk and the silver that come out of China could make every Western trader a millionaire,' Cameron said sombrely. 'And every Chinese peasant is a potential customer for Western goods – you Brits found that out with the opium trade. The US wants as big a part of that as possible.'

Sherlock looked at the remaining two spider diagrams. 'We need to find out what those last two messages are,' he said grimly.

By now the two boys had the process off pat. It only took a few minutes to decode the third message. It read: '*Explosion will take place at Snake Bite Hill on Yangtze River. Avoid area at all costs. Do not travel on USS* Monocacy *if invited.*'

Cameron stared at Sherlock. 'Whoever sent this message to my father is talking about mass murder as if it's another tactic for making money,' he breathed. 'He doesn't seem to care that people are going to die! They're talking about sacrificing the entire crew of the *Monocacy* and any Chinese who get caught in the blast too.'

Sherlock nodded. 'I guess they think it's a small price to pay for the trade benefits that will follow. The only thing that will cause the US Navy to blockade Chinese ports and go to war with the Emperor would be the death of a group of Americans.'

'What do you think is in the last message?' Cameron asked.

'I think I can guess,' Sherlock muttered.

This one took even less time: '*Prepare to take advantage of political and economic chaos to make best deals you can, for benefit of US companies. We are relying on you.*'

'I can't believe my father was involved in this,' Cameron whispered. His face had drained of colour and his voice was hoarse.

'If it's any consolation, I don't think he wanted to go along with it,' Sherlock pointed out. 'I don't think he *was* going along with it.'

'What makes you think that?'

'Well, we know he was expecting the message, but judging by the way he acted at breakfast this morning he really didn't like the contents. We know that he went to the Prefect's Residence with an urgent message. I think he decided that he couldn't go through with it, and wanted to warn the authorities.'

'And then he died.' Cameron glanced up at Sherlock, and his eyes were red with sorrow – and anger. 'Was his death an accident, Sherlock?'

Sherlock shook his head. 'It would be a huge coincidence if it was. No, I think he was killed so that he wouldn't be able to warn anyone.' He reached out and squeezed Cameron's arm. 'I'm . . . sorry.'

'But he'd already warned the Prefect,' Cameron wailed. 'There was no point in killing him!'

Sherlock shook his head. 'I think the message was intercepted by that . . . thing . . . that was following him, whatever it was. I think it saw the message being taken in by the official and so it somehow got into the Residence and retrieved it. I know it stopped following your father as soon as he passed that message on. The chances are it stopped following him and started following the message instead.'

'The message could have been taken and hidden by someone inside the Residence – someone who had been bribed.'

'A friend of mine once told me that the simplest explanation is usually the best. In this case, we already know that something was following your father. It makes more sense to assume that the thing then got hold of the message rather than invent a bribed official to do the same job.'

'But how do we know the message was actually intercepted before it got to the Prefect?'

'Because,' Sherlock said grimly, 'if it had got to the Prefect, you would have a house full of Chinese officials right now – and, of course, there would have been no point in killing your father.'

'So – so you think my father was trying to do the right thing?'

'I do. More than that – I think he was punished for it.'

'By whom?'

'That,' Sherlock said, 'is something we need to find out in a hurry.'

'But who was it that actually sent the messages?'

Sherlock shrugged. 'Who did your father work for?'

'He didn't work for anyone,' Cameron said. 'I mean, he had agreements with various companies back in the USA that he would represent their goods here in China, and take a commission on sales, but he didn't actually report to anyone.'

'I suspect that someone from one of those companies contacted him and told him that they had a plan that would increase the value of their goods a hundred times over. I suspect that they strung him along, not quite telling him what was going to happen. By the time he realized the truth, it was too late. He was in it up to his neck.'

Cameron suddenly looked confused. 'But what does this have to do with your cook friend – Wu Chung? Why was he killed?'

'I've been wondering about that. I still think it's because he accidentally got a job as a cook's assistant on

223

the USS *Monocacy*.' Sherlock thought for a moment. 'I think that Wu Chung found something out on board the ship that would have revealed their plans, and they had to kill him for it.'

'Do you remember what he said?' Cameron asked slowly. 'He said that he'd been on the *Monocacy* and he'd noticed that the Head Cook had over-ordered on barrels of water. He told them that the ship was going up a freshwater river, and they could get water any time they wanted, so why had they ordered so much?'

'You think there is something else in those barrels?' Sherlock frowned. 'You think there are *explosives* in those barrels?'

Cameron shrugged. 'It would take a lot of explosives to blow up a ship the size of the *Monocacy*. There were a lot of barrels. Wu Chung said so.'

'I suppose the conspirators could do something to the steam engines instead,' Sherlock mused. 'You know – increase the pressure or something until they blow up.'

'But there would be engineers and other people all around the engines. Getting to them, fiddling with the controls and then letting the pressure gradually increase would take a lot of time, and someone would have been bound to notice. No, the most obvious solution would be to bring a whole lot of explosives in.'

'Disguised as water barrels,' Sherlock agreed, nodding. 'It makes sense.'

'So what do we do about it?'

Sherlock gazed at Cameron. Cameron gazed back.

'We could tell the authorities here in Shanghai,' Sherlock suggested.

'But my father tried that, and clearly failed. Even if we *could* tell someone, they wouldn't believe two kids with a wild story like this.'

'We could get a message to the Captain of the USS *Monocacy*.'

'But we wouldn't know for sure whether the message ever got to him or not. Even if it did, why would he believe an anonymous message that told him his ship was going to explode? He'd just screw it up and throw it away.'

'So . . .'

'So . . . the only thing we can do,' Cameron said, 'is to head upriver after the *Monocacy*, get on board and somehow tell the Captain ourselves. You've met him, and he met my father. He would listen to us when he might not listen to someone he doesn't know.'

Sherlock nodded slowly. 'I can't see any other option. It has to be us.'

Cameron breathed out slowly. 'It's going to be an interesting journey. I've been up the Yangtze before, but not very far. My father took me fishing a couple of times.'

'How do we travel?' Sherlock asked. 'Horseback?'

'Too slow,' Cameron said, shaking his head. 'The ground is marshy along the banks of the river. To get to solid ground we would have to go a long way around. The *Monocacy* would make better time along the river than we would by road. No, the best thing would be boat. There are small sailboats that head up and down the river. They make pretty good speed. The *Monocacy* is limited by its weight. I think we can catch up with it.'

'Then we'd better start straight away.' Sherlock hesitated. 'What about your mother – what are you going to tell her?'

Cameron's gaze flickered towards Sherlock, then away. There was a sad expression on his face. 'The doctor has sedated her. He said she'll be asleep for hours. Days, maybe.' There was a glint of tears in his eyes. 'She loved my father desperately. Each time she wakes up and realizes once more that he's dead, the doctor says he may have to sedate her again . . .'

There was silence for a long time.

'And what about you?' Sherlock asked eventually. 'How long will it take for you to come to terms with it?'

'My father is dead. I know that, Sherlock. He's not coming back. Staying here isn't going to achieve

226

anything. I want to do something! I want to catch the people who killed him! I want to make a difference!'

'I understand,' Sherlock said.

'You don't,' Cameron replied softly. 'With the greatest respect, Sherlock, I'm not sure you ever will. You're not like ordinary people. You don't care in the same way. But thank you for being here anyway, and thank you for listening to me . . . Now, are we going to head up the Yangtze River and stop that ship from exploding, or are we going to stand here and talk?'

'There's one more thing we need,' Sherlock pointed out.

'What's that?'

'Wu Chung's son – Wu Fung-Yi.'

Cameron stared back at him blankly. 'What?'

'We need someone local, someone who knows the river. By the time we locate and hire a boatman or whatever, it will be too late. The only person we know who can help is Wu Fung-Yi.' Sherlock paused. 'And remember – they killed his father as well. He has as much of a vested interest as we do.'

'That's a point,' Cameron said. 'How exactly did they get a snake into my father's study and make it bite him? How did they get the same snake into Wu Chung's bedroom and make it bite him? That strikes me as a really chancy thing to do. There must be

227

better ways of murdering someone.'

'But they didn't want it to be obvious that your father was murdered,' Sherlock pointed out. 'And they certainly didn't want it to be obvious that Wu Chung was murdered. That would make people suspicious straight away, and there might have been an investigation. They had to make both murders look like accidents – and, from what I can gather, in a country like this, snake bites are a normal, everyday risk.' He frowned. 'I doubt that it was even a real snake. You're right – that would be too chancy. Snakes are unpredictable things, I believe. They couldn't guarantee that it would cooperate. No, the more I think about it, the more I suspect that someone used some kind of device that injected poison. They stuck it into Wu Chung's back while he was asleep, and they stuck it into your father's arm while he was distracted. It probably contained real venom that had been taken from a snake some time earlier, but it was a more manageable weapon. Like a hypodermic syringe or something.'

'That would explain how they got into the bedroom and the study,' Cameron said thoughtfully, 'but even so, it's a bit of a risk, isn't it? I mean, sneaking around people's houses?'

'That depends on who is doing the sneaking. If it's some hefty six-foot dock worker then yes, that might be noticed, but if it was someone smaller . . .'

'Like that thing you saw in the garden, and then you saw following my father?'

Sherlock nodded. 'Whatever that was, it was just the right size to slip into someone's house and inject them while they weren't looking.' He clenched his fist. 'If only I could work out what it is.'

'But what about the differences in the times it took Wu Chung and my father to die?' Cameron asked. 'If the same device was being used to inject poison, then it should have worked in the same way.'

'There could have been any number of differences. We don't know.' Sherlock shrugged. 'Maybe the poison they used on Wu Chung was an old batch, but they managed to get some newer poison to use on your father. Maybe it was a different snake with more powerful venom. We just don't know – not yet, anyway.'

'Are they going to try to stop us?' Cameron's face was determined. 'I hope they are. I want to meet them.'

'I think they're probably watching us,' Sherlock confirmed. 'So we need to be on our guard.'

Cameron hefted his father's revolver. 'I'm ready for them.'

'Let's be sure we've got the right people first.' Sherlock looked around the study. 'Let's take the messages and the map with us. We might need to use them to convince

229

Captain Bryan. Do you need to tell anyone where you're going?'

'I'll leave a message,' Cameron said. 'I'll say that I need some time to myself. People will understand. It will be chaos around here for a while, anyway. I'd be surprised if anyone noticed I had gone.'

Ten minutes later, the two boys were leaving the house. The evening sun was dipping down towards the horizon. Stallholders were beginning to pack up their wares ready to go home. Sherlock realized that he was hungry. He would have to make sure that he and Cameron got something to eat. He suspected that Cameron wasn't feeling hungry, but he had to keep his friend's energy up.

Cameron grabbed Sherlock's arm as they crossed the road. 'Wait,' he said. 'Look over there.'

Sherlock followed Cameron's pointing finger. Standing in plain sight a few yards away was the small, dark-haired figure of Wu Fung-Yi. He was watching them. Once he saw that they had seen him, he walked over. He nodded to Cameron. 'I heard your bad news,' he said sombrely. 'I am sorry for your loss.'

'Thanks. And . . . and I understand your loss now in a way that I didn't before.'

'Something is going on,' Wu Fung-Yi said, smiling sadly. 'Something strange. You already know about it.

230

My father knew it, and I know it now.'

'Is that why you're here?' Sherlock asked.

'I wondered who I could talk to.' Wu Fung-Yi shrugged awkwardly. 'Not my mother. She believes that my father was killed by a snake, but I remember the things you said about how difficult it would have been for a snake to get into the house. I know how hard I worked to fill up all the holes in the walls.' His gaze flickered from Sherlock to Cameron and back again. It was as if he wanted to trust them with something but he wasn't sure how to phrase it. 'I saw something, that night,' he said, more quietly. 'I didn't tell you earlier, because I thought that you might think I was mad. I didn't tell my mother either.' He took a deep breath, forcing himself to continue. 'I was sleeping, but I got woken up by a noise. I thought perhaps it was my father wandering around. I was not used to having him in the house – he snored, and turned over in his sleep, and made all kinds of new sounds. I remember looking over to the doorway of my room, and . . .' He hesitated. 'And there was something there. A shadow. It was too small to be my mother or my father, and too still to be a cat or a dog or a monkey. I couldn't see its eyes, but I knew it was watching me, so I kept very still. After a while, it was not there any more.' He shivered. 'There was something evil about it. I could feel its gaze on me, like hot coals. I

231

thought it might be an evil spirit, but now I know that it was the thing that killed my father.'

'We've seen it too,' Sherlock confirmed. 'We don't know what it is, but it has something to do with what's going on.' Sherlock glanced at Cameron, then back at Wu Fung-Yi. 'Let's talk while we move,' he suggested. 'We need to get hold of a boat, and we need to head upriver. Can you help?'

'Will it help explain my father's death?'

Sherlock nodded. 'It will.'

'Then talk.'

On the way through the town Sherlock and Cameron jointly explained to Wu Fung-Yi exactly what they thought was going on. As they walked, Sherlock realized that they were heading out of Shanghai in a direction that he hadn't been before.

'I thought we were going to the harbour,' he said. 'Isn't that where the Yangtze starts off? I mean, the river must flow into the sea, mustn't it?'

'That's true,' Wu Fung-Yi said over his shoulder. 'But the river widens out considerably there, and the currents are treacherous. If you want to head upriver then it makes more sense to cut across and meet it a little further up. Trust me, I know what I am doing.'

After a while Sherlock noticed that they were approaching the town wall. There was another gate here, but this one was guarded by only one soldier, and he was simply waving people in and out. Presumably the risk of foreigners being around this side of the city was less than at the harbourside.

'This is the "Gate of the Virtuous Phoenix",' Cameron said quietly as they approached. 'If we get separated for any reason we'll meet back here.'

They exited with no problems. Beyond the town a wide dirt road led away into the hilly Chinese countryside. The three boys started out towards the Yangtze River.

'What's the plan?' Sherlock asked as they walked.

'My uncle has several sailboats,' Wu Fung-Yi said. 'I'm sure he will lend one to us, if I ask.' He sighed. 'The news about my father will not have got to him yet. I will have to tell him.'

The landscape outside the town wall was hilly, making it difficult to see very far. The road meandered, but Sherlock detected that as they got further and further away from Shanghai it led gradually downhill. It was broad, and used by many people. Carts were heading in both directions – to the town and away from it. The carts were laden with hay, vegetables, wood and all manner of things, including some that Sherlock didn't recognize. There were other things on the road that took Sherlock by surprise. Some local farmers were pushing wheelbarrows, with a single wheel at the front, but at the back of the wheelbarrow a mast rose up into the air, and on the mast was a red canvas sail. The farmers were taking advantage of the strong breezes that blew across the countryside to help them push the wheelbarrows along. It was such an obvious idea that Sherlock couldn't figure out why nobody in England had done it.

As they walked, the ground underfoot became soggier. The fields that lined the roads were planted with large grasses that grew to the height of a man. The soil was waterlogged, and Sherlock could see arrangements of bamboo pipes bringing water from the river to the fields, and gates that could be opened and closed to flood them.

'What's growing here?' he asked Wu Fung-Yi.

'Rice,' the boy said. 'These are called "paddy fields". We keep them flooded and grow more rice than anything else. It is what we eat the most.'

'Like potatoes in England,' Sherlock murmured.

Finally the road then curved around the side of one last hill, and there before them was a wide expanse of blue water flecked with white wave crests.

'The Yangtze River,' Wu Fung-Yi said. 'Now the hard work *really* starts.'

234

CHAPTER TWELVE

Sherlock was amazed at how wide the Yangtze was, especially compared to the other rivers he had seen, like the Thames in London or the Hudson in New York. The far bank seemed miles away. Mist wreathed it, rising up from the paddy fields and making it look like some mystical fantasy land. Hills rose up on either side of the river, leaving it to wind through gradual, graceful curves which meant that it was impossible to see for more than a mile or so to either side.

'Third longest river in the world,' Cameron said proudly. 'It starts off in the Tibetan highlands and flows for six and a half thousand miles before it gets to the ocean.' He glanced sideways at Sherlock. 'What? I'm not supposed to be interested in the place where I live?'

Sherlock could see hundreds, maybe even thousands of boats on the river. Some of them were so small that they could take only one man with a paddle; others were so large that they had three or four fan-like sails and carried a full crew.

Along the banks were hundreds of flat-bottomed boats that seemed to have houses on board. Or at least shacks.

235

Sherlock realized these weren't boats for travelling: they were boats for living on. These were villages that had been built out into the river and then built up, bit by bit.

The boys scanned the river for the USS *Monocacy*, but there was no sign of it. Sherlock was sure that if it had been there then they would have spotted it.

'There!' Wu pointed off to their left, at a thin bamboo jetty that projected out into the river past the point where the boat village ended. Three boats were tied up to the jetty. 'That is where my uncle lives.'

'Then let's get down there,' Sherlock said.

The three of them headed downhill, the earth squishing underfoot. After a few minutes they passed the boat village and were at the jetty. Wu gestured them to stay by the bank and headed out to where three Chinese men were working on a boat. The biggest man, who had an extravagantly long black moustache, grabbed Wu as he came close and gave him a huge hug. He was grinning, obviously pleased to see his nephew.

Wu started to talk, and the men listened. Sherlock looked around. The riverbank plunged into the water pretty steeply just where he and Cameron were standing. Plants grew directly out of the water all the way along the riverbank, some looking like wild rice and some looking like bamboo. There were even flowers floating on the water, and when Sherlock looked closer he could see webs of stems supporting the flowers beneath the surface.

It all looked so beautiful, with the sun low in the sky and the misty hills across the other side of the river. It was difficult to reconcile the beauty with what Sherlock knew was going to happen soon. Somewhere upriver was an American ship crewed by a few hundred American sailors. If the bomb on board went off then they would probably all die, and that would only be the start of it. The US Government would send in the US Navy, there would be a blockade, the Chinese Emperor would probably order his ships to defend the country, and before anyone knew it America would be at war with China, just so some businessmen could get a better price for their imports, and pay less for their exports!

Sherlock hadn't given very much thought to his future when he got back to England. At some stage he would have to get a job, he supposed, but nothing really appealed to him. He didn't think he could do what his brother did – work for the Government. He wasn't diplomatic enough. Going into a business had been a possibility, but now, thinking about the callousness of these people who would start a war in order to make a profit, he promised himself that he would never work for any company that bought or sold goods.

Which didn't leave very much, he thought despondently.

Cameron must have been having his own dark thoughts about the USS *Monocacy*. He caught Sherlock's eye and said quietly, 'We have to try. At least we can get to the *Monocacy* by boat, and at least Captain Bryan knows us by sight. He might give us enough time to convince him.'

Wu waved at them from the jetty. Cameron and Sherlock walked out along the precarious wooden structure, feeling it creaking beneath their weight. At the far end, Wu introduced them to his uncle and his uncle's two sons. 'He's promised that we can take one of his boats for a journey upriver,' Wu said excitedly. 'But first he wants to be sure that we know how to raise and lower the sails and steer it.'

Sherlock gazed at the nearest vessel. Quickly he traced the various ropes that held the sail back to their fastening points on the boat's sides. Using the knowledge he'd so painfully gained from the *Gloria Scott*, he calculated which ropes pulled the sail in which directions. Then, climbing into the boat, he quickly furled and unfurled the sail with precise, economic movements.

Wu's uncle nodded approvingly. 'Good work,' he said. 'You obviously know your way around a boat.'

'Which way are the winds going to be blowing tonight?'

'Upriver,' Wu's uncle said. 'Inland. You'll have a good steady night breeze pushing you along.'

'Can I ask you something? Have you seen a large ship with a big wheel on the side? Has it come upriver recently?'

Wu's uncle nodded. 'What a strange ship that was,' he said. 'We all remarked on it. Its funnel was damaged. Never seen anything like it before, not in all my days. Someone said it was built by foreign devils and powered by evil spirits.' He smiled. 'No offence intended.'

'None taken,' Sherlock said. 'It *was* built by foreign devils, but it's powered by steam engines.'

The three Chinese men glanced at each other. 'Told you – evil spirits,' one muttered.

'How long ago did you see it?' Sherlock asked.

Wu's uncle thought for a moment. 'Three hours?' he ventured. 'Maybe four.'

Sherlock cursed mentally. The *Monocacy* had a good head start on them.

Thinking back to the messages that he and Cameron had decoded, Sherlock asked, 'Do you know a place called Snake Bite Hill?'

Wu's uncle looked at his sons. They talked quietly for a moment, then the big sailor looked back at Sherlock and said, 'Only place we can think of is near Wushan.

239

It's about, what, thirty miles upriver? Something like that.'

'Thanks,' Sherlock said. He glanced at Cameron and Wu. 'That's where we need to get to,' he said quietly. 'That's where it's going to happen.'

Within five minutes they were casting off and setting sail. The breeze pushed them away from the jetty across rippling water. Sherlock manned the sail while Cameron took the rudder and Wu sat at the front, looking out for sunken tree trunks or other obstructions in the water.

It didn't take long before they were out in the river itself, and Cameron was adjusting their course to take them in the direction they needed to go. The central channel of the river was congested, but between them they managed to stay on the outside of the channel, making good speed. There didn't seem to be any particular rules – sailors headed for wherever they wanted to go, and dared everyone else to get out of their way.

As night fell something splashed in the water a few feet off the hull of the boat. Sherlock shuffled across the deck to take a look. In the moonlight, he could see a strange fish gazing up at him with eyes that seemed almost human. The fish's skin was a rubbery grey, and it had a long, thin mouth – almost a beak – that stuck out from its head. The mouth was full of very small but very sharp teeth, and was curled up in what looked like a

240

smile. It floated there, in the water, gazing up at Sherlock. Sherlock's mind flashed back to fish he had seen in the ocean, off the side of the *Gloria Scott*. Porpoises, someone had told him. Was this a porpoise too?

With a flip of its broad tail, it was gone.

'What was that?' Sherlock asked Wu, who was watching him from the front of the boat.

'We call them "Goddesses of the River". Seeing one is considered good luck. You should think yourself blessed.'

'I'll try.'

Being on water made sounds travel differently, Sherlock found. Every few moments he would hear a voice say, 'Watch out!' or 'Careful there, you fool!', and he would look around, expecting to see a boat heading directly towards them, only to find that the speaker was hundreds of yards away and talking to someone next to them.

A sudden *crash* and a jerking of their own boat snapped Sherlock's attention back to the present. A rough Chinese voice shouted, 'May the spirits of the river-deeps curse your descendants, you clumsy fools!' They had collided with another boat. The owner – an elderly Chinaman with a mass of white hair – was gesturing at Cameron and cursing. Sherlock grabbed a pole from the bottom of their boat and pushed the other one away, smiling in apology as he did so.

'What happened?' he said as the other boat pulled away, its owner still shaking his fist at them.

'Sorry,' Cameron said. He looked dazed. 'I think I dropped off to sleep for a moment.'

'Look, it's been a long day,' Wu Fung-Yi said. 'A lot's happened to all of us. If we keep on going like this we're going to have a serious accident.'

'We need to keep going,' Sherlock said. 'We have to catch up with the *Monocacy* before that bomb goes off!'

'If we hit something and sink, we're not going to do anybody any good,' Cameron pointed out. 'And has it occurred to you that the *Monocacy* will probably drop anchor and stop for the night? If they keep going in the darkness then they might plough right into another boat and sink it, or they might hit rocks by the riverbank and smash their own hull open. If they stop and we keep going we might go right past them without realizing, and then we'll never be able to warn them.'

Sherlock had to admit that their logic was compelling. In addition, he realized that he was exhausted. 'Fine,' he said reluctantly. 'Let's pull over to the side and get some sleep. But we start again at dawn.'

The other two nodded. 'Agreed,' said Wu.

Cameron used the rudder to steer them to the nearest bank while Wu watched the water depth and Sherlock prepared to take the sails down before they ran aground.

With the three of them working together, they managed to guide the boat in safely. Sherlock jumped for the riverbank with a rope and tied the boat up to a twisted tree that was growing at an angle.

Looking out into the darkness of the river, he noticed a boat with two lanterns – one green and one yellow. It seemed to be tacking towards the shore a little way ahead of them. Presumably whoever was in charge had decided to stop for the night as well.

Sherlock jumped back into the boat, feeling it rock beneath his weight. Cameron was fetching blankets out of the shack that was sat in the back of the boat, while Wu seemed to be unwrapping something from a bundle of cloth that had been stowed beneath a seat. He handed a package to Sherlock.

'Food. Uncle told me there was some here. He was saving it for himself for later, but he decided that we needed it more than he did.'

Sherlock looked at the parcel Wu had given him, while Wu handed another one to Cameron. It looked like a large leaf that had been wrapped around something sticky and tied up with string. 'What is it?' he asked.

'Lotus leaves filled with sticky rice and dried shrimp.'

Cameron had already unwrapped the lotus leaf and was stuffing rice and dried shrimp into his mouth with his fingers. 'It's lovely,' he said through the food.

243

Sherlock tried it. Although the rice was cold and sticky it was still tasty, and the salty, fishy flavour of the shrimp gave it an added boost. It really was very good.

After they had eaten, and washed their hands in the river, the three of them settled down to sleep, wrapped in blankets. Sherlock suddenly realized how exhausted he was.

'Something occurred to me.' Cameron's voice came out of the darkness. 'We haven't named our boat.'

'Naming of a boat is a serious business,' Wu Fung-Yi said. 'It has to be done properly, with appropriate ceremony. Besides, my uncle may already have named it.'

Cameron wasn't going to let it go. 'We could call it the *Hudson*,' he said, 'after the Hudson River in New York.'

'That is not a good name,' Wu said. There was silence for a few moments, then he added, 'What about you, Sherlock? Any ideas?'

'I think we should call it the *Virginia*,' he said quietly.

Nobody argued. After a few minutes Cameron started to snore, so Sherlock assumed that he had got the last word in.

Something went *splash* nearby. A fish? One of the 'Goddesses of the River', perhaps? Sherlock suddenly appreciated that he didn't know anything about the local wildlife. Was there anything dangerous? He raised himself up on one elbow to ask, but then lay down again without saying anything. Wu would have warned them if there was any danger. He should put his trust in the Chinese boy and get some rest.

He realized, as he lay there, how difficult that was. He had never really trusted anyone – not helped by Mycroft constantly warning him about the dangers of doing so. He always assumed that he knew best, but out here, in a country he wasn't familiar with, he was going to have to trust Wu Fung-Yi to get them where they needed to go.

It wasn't a particularly pleasant thought to go to sleep on.

Stars twinkled in the black night sky. Wisps of cloud scudded across them like cobwebs blown by the wind. For a while he tried to identify familiar constellations and particular stars, but everything looked different here. He wondered for a while if Virginia was staring at the same stars, but then he realized that she couldn't be. She was nearly on the other side of the world from him now. Whatever sky she was looking at was blue and sunny, not black and starlit.

He slipped into sleep so gradually that he didn't even know it, and his dreams were a confused mish-mash of memories and faces. Matty was in there somewhere, and so was Amyus Crowe, but they were cheering him on from the sidelines as he ran some kind of race: the problem was that he didn't know where the finishing line was, or which direction he was meant to be running in.

He woke up some time later. It was still dark. He wondered what exactly had woken him up – Cameron snoring, perhaps, or Wu talking in his sleep?

Something hit the side of the boat. It sounded like someone's hand, or foot, brushing against the wood.

Sherlock's every nerve was suddenly alert. The boat rocked as whatever it was clambered stealthily on board. Was it robbers – pirates, maybe? Local villagers deciding to see if they could get any food or money from the three boys? Was it an animal, sneaking on board? A snake, perhaps? His imagination ran wild, painting all kinds of pictures of terrible things. He sensed, rather than heard, whatever it was looming over him, watching him. He tried to breathe deeply, evenly, making it seem as if he was fast asleep. He could feel a gaze fixed on the back of his head like hot coals. It was the most bizarre feeling.

Eventually he heard the intruder moving away. He yawned loudly, and turned over, keeping his eyes firmly closed on the assumption that the intruder would be looking at him to see if he was waking up.

Silence for a few moments, and then the intruder started to move again. Sherlock gradually opened his eyes. For a moment everything was blurry and dark, but then he began to make out shapes – the mast, the edge of the hull, the shack at the back of the boat and the shape of the rudder.

And something that hadn't been on their boat earlier.

It looked like a person, but smaller. Sherlock could see shoulders, and a small head, silhouetted against the night sky.

It was bending over Cameron.

'Hey!' he yelled, sitting bolt upright.

Whatever it was turned suddenly to face him. The clouds chose that moment to move away from the face of the moon, and it was as if someone had suddenly turned a spotlight on to their deck.

It was a child, younger than any of the three of them; a girl. And she was holding something against Cameron's throat.

CHAPTER THIRTEEN

Sherlock stared at the girl in amazement. She stared back, eyes full of some boiling emotion that Sherlock couldn't quite identify – fury perhaps? Or maybe violent frustration at being discovered?

Her skin was ashen-grey. Sherlock wasn't sure why. Her hair and her eyes were grey too. Her arms and legs were thin, like sticks, and her body didn't have an inch of spare fat on it. Her clothes were the same colour as her flesh: a dusty grey. She looked like a little statue, standing there, poised to run. Only the flickering of her eyes as she looked around for a way to escape gave away her essential humanity.

Sherlock's attention shifted to the thing that the girl was holding. It was made of metal, but it looked a bit like a set of dentures – teeth and gums glinting in the moonlight, just like the girl's skin. There was some clockwork in there somewhere, and a spring, holding the two sides of the device apart. Sherlock could see something red and rubbery as well, hidden behind the teeth. What on earth was it?

The girl's eyes jerked sideways, to Cameron, and

Sherlock realized what she was going to do. 'Get back!' he yelled, and Cameron threw himself backwards as the girl slashed the metal teeth at his throat. The teeth passed a hair's breadth from his carotid artery, snapping like castanets as the girl squeezed them together against the strength of the spring.

From behind the girl, Wu Fung-Yi appeared. He looked confused, like he'd woken up and still found himself in the middle of a nightmare. He grabbed at her arm. She turned around and hissed at him. Surprised, he stumbled backwards and let go. She turned her attention back to Cameron and leaped at him, arms outstretched, the teeth of the metal device aimed right at his throat. Cameron scuttled back across the boat's deck, terrified.

Sherlock's paralysis broke. He ran across the deck and grabbed the girl around the waist, pulling her back just as she got to Cameron. She lashed out with a foot, catching Sherlock in the head. Her feet were bare, but her toenails were phenomenally hard and sharp. Sherlock felt them gouge at his skin, tearing the flesh away from his forehead in a raw strip of agony. It was like someone raking him with a garden fork. He let go, and she went tumbling forward, rolling across the deck. Her hand slammed on the wood and the thing she had been holding went skidding into the shadows. She hissed again, head jerking from side to side. Her tongue licked at her lips, but Sherlock was shocked to see that it was black, rather than pink. It looked like some hideous slug trying to crawl out of her mouth.

Sherlock grabbed for the thing that the girl had dropped. His fingers closed on something hard-edged and metallic. Quickly he scooped it up. She glanced at his hand, then at his face, and then she leaped for him.

Sherlock threw the metal object to Wu Fung-Yi and shouted, 'Get this out of the way!' as the girl reached him, arms outstretched. He grabbed at her wrists, stopping her fingers a fraction of an inch before they touched his face. Her fingernails were just like her toenails: hard and sharp. They hovered in front of Sherlock's eyes, glinting like needles. She strained against him, trying to get her claws – and they *were* claws, Sherlock decided – on his skin. He knew what would happen then. She would rip him to shreds.

He stared deep into her eyes as the two of them stood there, locked in a frozen struggle. He tried looking for some fragment of humanity, for some small trace of emotion. But there was nothing. Apart from her shape and the way her hair curled, there was nothing human about her.

Snarling, she suddenly threw her weight backwards rather than forwards. Taken by surprise, Sherlock found himself pulled towards her. She brought a foot up against his stomach. He could feel the hard claws of her toenails raking at his skin. She dropped down to the deck, still going backwards, and Sherlock felt his feet lifting off the deck. She pulled him over her head, rolling on her back, and then let go of his wrists. He cartwheeled through the air, seeing the deck below him replaced by the reed bed. Black water glittered. He hit the surface of the Yangtze, sending up a huge splash. The impact drove the breath from his body. Water closed over his head. He could taste mud, and he could feel grit between his lips and his teeth. Desperately he struck out, but he had lost his sense of direction in the fall and he couldn't tell which way he should be going. His arms thrashed wildly. There were weeds beneath the surface of the river: long, slimy, stringy things that wound around him and stopped him from floating back to the top. He desperately wanted to take in a breath. Despite the fire that burned in his lungs, he thrashed his arms and legs, trying to break the insidious grip of the weeds. More by luck than judgement his foot hit a rock on the bed of the river, and he pushed upward as hard as he could. The reeds holding him tore free of the riverbed. His foot slipped off the rock, but it didn't matter – he'd given himself enough upward momentum that his head broke the surface and he gulped down mouthfuls of air.

For a few moments he couldn't hear anything apart

251

from the water rushing in his ears and the straining of his lungs as he tried to breathe, but gradually he became aware of voices calling for him – 'Sherlock! *Sherlock!*' – and voices from other boats asking for a bit of peace and quiet.

Something hit the water near his head. He jerked away, thinking that the girl had dived in after him, but it was a pole from the boat. Wu Fung-Yi was holding it out for Sherlock to take.

Sherlock grabbed the pole and let Wu pull him towards the boat. His arms were too weak to climb back in, and he had to let Cameron and Wu clumsily manoeuvre him out of the water. By the time he slumped to the deck all three of them were waterlogged and exhausted.

'What the hell was that?' Cameron asked.

'A girl,' Sherlock panted.

Cameron raised his eyebrows. 'I've never had much to do with girls,' he said drily. 'Are they all like that?'

Wu and Sherlock just looked at him, and then they laughed.

'What happened to her?' Sherlock asked.

It was Wu who answered. 'After she threw you into the water she stood on the deck staring at the two of us. She kept glancing from Cameron to me and then back to Cameron. I think she was trying to work out which order she was going to attack us in. Then you broke the surface and started splashing. She seemed to realize that there were too many things going on, so she rushed for the side of the boat and jumped on to the bank. I saw her running into a bunch of reeds, then I lost track of her.'

'I think,' Sherlock said eventually, 'that we've finally met the thing that broke into your house, Wu – and your house, Cameron. The thing that killed both your fathers.'

'But – a *girl?*' Wu said disbelievingly. 'Why would she?'

'I doubt that it was her idea,' Sherlock replied. 'I think she was following instructions.'

'I only saw her briefly,' Cameron said, 'but her skin . . . It reminded me of something. Of some*one.*'

The same thought had occurred to Sherlock. 'She looked like Mr Arrhenius,' he said grimly.

'Who?' Wu asked, frowning.

'Mr Arrhenius. He was a passenger on the *Gloria Scott*. His skin was that same silvery-grey colour. He said it had happened because he drank some kind of silver-based liquid to stop him catching diseases. He said that silver somehow naturally forms a barrier against illness.' Sherlock frowned, thinking. 'Maybe she's his daughter. The chances of two people having skin like that and not being connected are pretty slim. And I did think there was something, or someone, in his cabin, back on the

253

ship. He brought it on board in his luggage – there was a box with holes in it for air. But . . . a daughter?'

'There *was* something inhuman about her,' Cameron said, shivering. 'Did you see her eyes?'

Sherlock nodded. 'I could see intelligence there,' he said, 'but it wasn't like looking into the eyes of another person.'

'Do you think she was born like that?' Wu asked.

'If her father was drinking liquid silver before she was born then it might have had an effect,' Sherlock mused. 'Maybe it changed her, before she was born. I've heard that women who drink too much gin give birth to babies that have . . . problems. Maybe this is a similar thing.'

'I wonder what happened to her mother,' Cameron said quietly. 'I wonder if she's still alive.'

The thought was enough to stop the three of them talking for the next few minutes.

'What was that thing she had in her hand?' Wu said eventually.

'I don't know.' Sherlock glanced at the Chinese boy. 'You were the last one to have it. What did you do with it?'

'I think I threw it somewhere safe,' Wu said. He got up and crossed to the shack in the middle of the deck. 'In here, I think.' He disappeared for a moment, then returned with something metal in his hand.

'Here!' he said, handing it to Sherlock.

He held the object in front of his face and stared at it as Cameron and Wu moved closer. It was as he had thought: a false mouth made of metal, with a lower and an upper jaw hinged together – but it wasn't a human mouth. It was too small, too pointed, and the teeth were too long and sharp. The two fangs at the front in particular were about the length of his little finger. The right-hand fang came to a sharp point, while the left-hand one seemed to have broken off a little way from the tip.

It was a snake's jaw, fabricated out of metal, and spring-loaded so that the lower and upper jaws could be closed together with some pressure.

He had a feeling that he'd seen the missing tip from that fang before. He had a feeling that he had picked it up on the *Gloria Scott* once, when he was outside Mr Arrhenius's cabin.

Looking at the fangs, Sherlock realized that they had narrow holes in them, drilled all the way from tip to base. Behind the fangs, in the roof of the mouth, was a bulb made of some rubbery material. Sherlock squeezed it experimentally, and watched in shock as two small beads of liquid formed, one on each fang.

'Is that what I think it is?' Cameron asked.

'It's poison,' Sherlock said, fascinated. 'Don't touch

it!' He gazed at the drops of liquid, amazed. 'Look – this is a fake snake skull, made by someone out of metal, with a working poison-delivery system. With this, you can bite someone and inject enough poison into their veins to kill them. No need to wait for a real snake to come along.'

He suddenly realized what he had said. He glanced up to see Cameron and Wu both staring at him.

'This is what killed your fathers,' he said. 'My God – I'm so sorry.'

It was Cameron who asked the obvious question. 'My father was killed by a *girl*? A girl younger than *me*?'

Wu Fung-Yi shook his head. 'I can't believe it,' he breathed. 'Why would a small girl *do* something like that?'

'You've already seen her,' Sherlock pointed out. 'There's something not *right* about her. Assuming that she is Arrhenius's daughter, I think all that silver in her father's body caused her to be born . . . different . . . from other people. She looks different, and she thinks differently. I think her father uses her, like you would use a tool, or a weapon.'

'So what happens now?' Wu asked. 'Do you think she'll come back for us?'

Sherlock shrugged. 'Who knows?' A thought flashed into his mind, and he examined it for a few moments. 'I remember, when we came into the riverbank earlier on, I saw another boat. Or at least, I saw its lights. It had been behind us on the river. I saw it head for the bank ahead of us. Maybe that's where she came from. If she is Mr Arrhenius's daughter then he might be sailing that boat, either following us up the river or trying to get to the USS *Monocacy* before us.' He glanced at Cameron and Wu. 'I think I need to go and take a look.'

'Chances are it's a coincidence. There were lots of boats on the river. There's no guarantee that it was actually following us.'

'Maybe not,' Sherlock agreed, 'but the girl had to come from somewhere. It's almost dawn. You get the boat ready to leave. I'll do some reconnaissance.'

The two boys looked at each other, then they nodded. 'All right,' Cameron said. 'Be back in half an hour. We have to get to the *Monocacy* and warn the Captain about the bomb. If you don't make it back, then we have to leave without you. We don't have a choice.'

'I know,' Sherlock said.

He glanced at the metal snake jaws in his hand. There must be a safety catch somewhere: a means to secure the jaws so that they weren't dangerous to carry around. Looking more closely, he could see that if the jaws were pressed carefully closed, then all of the teeth were protected in sockets, and there was a small catch that

257

could be flicked across to hold the jaws closed. Making them safe, he slipped them inside his pocket. 'Back soon,' he said, with more nonchalance than he actually felt.

He jumped over the side of the boat and felt his feet sink into the soft mud of the riverbank. A faint line of broken plants led up the bank. That was probably where the girl had gone. He followed her trail and soon came to drier ground.

A path led along the riverbank, lined by tall grasses. Sherlock moved at a fast walk, crouching so that he didn't make a silhouette against the sky. He made for the place where he had seen the boat with the green and yellow lanterns stop. Assuming there weren't fifteen boats all moored at the same place, he should be able to work out which one he wanted.

Something moved through the grasses ahead of him. His heart suddenly seemed to beat several times in quick succession, hammering in his chest. He paused, hardly daring to breathe, waiting to see what was moving and what it was going to do. Was it the girl, preparing herself to attack him again?

A few feet away from him the grasses parted and a head pushed through. It was warty and covered in hair, with a long snout and two tusks pointing straight up from the lower jaw. It was a pig of some kind, he realized with relief. Actually, more of a boar than a pig. It stared at him with beady black eyes, snorting in challenge, but when he didn't respond it pulled back and moved away through the tall grass. It was probably just defending its lair, he decided. Maybe it had babies. He supposed that if the boar had attacked then he might have been in trouble, but it had been put off by his size and his apparent lack of fear. A useful lesson for the future, he decided: if you looked like you weren't afraid, then animals, and maybe people, would treat you as if you actually *weren't* afraid.

He gave the boar a few seconds to get out of the way, then he moved on.

A few minutes later he found himself looking at a boat similar to the one he and the other boys had been using. It was roped to a tree stump on the riverbank. Two lanterns were attached to the mast, but they weren't lit and Sherlock couldn't tell what colours they were. Was this even the right boat? Was he wasting his time?

Something moved on deck, and he ducked down behind a clump of reeds so that he couldn't be seen. Cautiously he parted the reeds and peered through the gap.

A man emerged from a cabin towards the rear of the deck. It was Mr Arrhenius. He was wearing his pale linen suit and a panama hat. His skin seemed to glow silver in the ebbing moonlight, and his eyes glittered like twin

259

jewels. He stood there for a moment, looking around, and then whistled a single note, quietly.

A little way from where Sherlock hid, the reeds parted and a small figure slipped across the mud of the riverbank to the boat. Quickly it scurried up the rope that held the boat close to the bank. Like Mr Arrhenius, its skin seemed to glisten in the meagre light.

The girl paused as she got to the deck. Her head moved back and forth, elevated slightly, as if she was sniffing at the air.

Mr Arrhenius walked towards her, stopping a few feet away. 'Were you successful?' he asked softly, his voice barely carrying through the air to where Sherlock hid. 'Are those interfering adolescents actually dead?'

The girl stared at him, not giving any indication that she understood his words. Or perhaps she did understand but didn't care enough to answer.

'What's wrong?' Arrhenius asked. Sherlock couldn't see how, but somehow he had picked up on something in her manner, some uneasiness or hesitation. 'Were they not there? Was it the wrong boat?'

She continued to stare at him for a few moments, then looked away expressionlessly, gazing out at the darkened river.

'You failed,' he said, somehow picking up the truth of what had occurred. 'Three boys, three *children*, and you failed!' His voice grew louder and more angry. 'And yet you dare to come back here?' He stepped forward. Before she could move he slapped her, hard. Her head jerked around and she stumbled, falling to her knees. She stayed there, on the deck of the boat, head lowered.

Sherlock was stunned. His experience of the girl was not huge, but so far he'd seen her as fast, strong, implacable and dangerous, yet she wasn't even trying to defend herself. It was as if she couldn't use her fists against her own father.

Arrhenius looked at the girl's hands, which were limp on the deck by her knees. 'And what about the poison injector? Where is it? Did you drop it? Did you leave it behind where it can be found?'

Sherlock thought he could see something glinting in the girl's eyes, but it didn't look like silver. It looked like tears.

'You *lost* it, didn't you?'

She didn't seem to want to meet Arrhenius's gaze. He stepped closer to her and grabbed her jaw, lifting her head up so that she was forced to look at him.

'Pathetic,' he hissed. 'All the things I have done for you since your mother died, and you treat me this way. Pathetic! We are already racing against time because of your failure. If you had killed Malcolm Mackenzie when you were supposed to, then it wouldn't have

261

been necessary for you to follow him to the Prefect's Residence and steal his warning note, and I would be at the place of the explosion already, waiting to give the signal. Because of you I now have to try to get there in this . . . this undignified fashion.' He squeezed her jaw hard: Sherlock could see the white indentations of his fingers in her skin. 'You are a disappointment to me, girl. A great disappointment.'

Sherlock suddenly realized that the ground where he was crouching was moving. It reared up, opening to reveal a wet, red throat and rows of ragged teeth. Baggy, scaly flesh hung below the mouth, swaying as the creature lunged for him, jaws gaping.

CHAPTER FOURTEEN

Sherlock fell backwards, shocked, as the creature that had been hiding by his side levered itself up out of the mud of the riverbank on four short legs that ended in vicious claws.

Its eyes were small and slitted, and they stared at Sherlock without emotion, like fragments of stone. Behind the rear legs its body turned into a long, flat tail that took up fully half its length. There were razor-edged ridges running along both sides of that tail. The thing was a reptile of some kind. Its skin was marked by deep cracks, and hung beneath it in swags and folds. Its head was flat, like a spade. Two nostrils were set at the very front, and set high, so that it could breathe while lying in the water, Sherlock deduced. It was obviously a hunter, and one that lay in wait, in hiding. From the tip of its snout to the end of its tail it was about the same size as Sherlock, but it seemed to be mostly muscle.

All this detail Sherlock picked up in the fragment of a second that it took the creature to use its tail to propel itself towards him. He stretched out his arms, trying to catch the thing in mid-air. His hands grabbed at its snout and clamped its mouth shut. Half of the teeth seemed to still be outside the mouth, pointing in all directions. He could hear air hissing through its nostrils, and he could smell its breath – rotting meat and rotting fish. Its front claws ripped at his chest, drawing blood and stinging, while its rear claws scrabbled for purchase on the ground. Its muscular tail lashed against the mud in an attempt to push it closer to Sherlock. The razor-sharp ridges along the sides of the tail raked against the skin of his legs, ripping the flesh and leaving lines of burning agony in their wake.

Sherlock twisted, forcing the creature around so that it was beneath him. His hands were still clamping its jaws shut, and he forced it down into the mud, manoeuvring his body so that he had one knee on its snout, holding its jaws closed, and the other knee trapping its tail. It writhed and squirmed beneath him but he was fairly sure that he had it trapped. For a while, anyway.

He glanced down at the boat, panicked. Arrhenius and his daughter were staring up the bank. They had obviously heard something of the struggle, but not seen anything. The incredible thing was that the creature was making almost no sound apart from the hissing of its breath through its nostrils. Any other animal would have been barking or growling or screeching or something, but this creature, whatever it was, seemed either unable or unwilling to make any noise when it fought.

With one quick action Sherlock put all of his weight into the hardest punch he could manage, directed right at the back of the creature's neck. It bucked beneath him once, then was still. For one glorious moment he thought that he had killed it, but then he realized that he could still feel its sides moving as it breathed. He must have stunned it – or perhaps it was just playing dead, waiting for him to release it.

'Go and see what's making that noise.' Mr Arrhenius's voice floated up from the boat below. 'If it is one of those adolescents then kill him. Then I want you to go back to their boat and retrieve that venom injector. I can't afford to have that discovered. Then use it to kill the others. This time, do it properly.'

The girl ran for the edge of the boat. She moved like an animal – four-legged, hands and feet all making contact with the deck. She leaped, and when she hit the bank she was suddenly running on two legs, using her hands to push reeds out of the way. She seemed desperate to prove herself to her . . . her what? Her *father*? Sherlock still couldn't quite believe it.

Sherlock's gaze snapped between the approaching girl and the creature that was pinioned beneath him. He couldn't work out what to do for the best, how to escape.

He could hear the hissing sound of the reeds parting to

let the girl through. She would be on him in a moment, and even without the poison injector she would be able to rip his throat out with the hard nails on her fingers. And she would, as well – he had seen no more mercy in her eyes than he had in the eyes of the creature he was kneeling on. But if he stopped holding the reptilian creature down, ready to defend himself against the girl, then it would almost certainly turn on him and attack. He couldn't hold it with one hand either, which meant that he couldn't get the poison injector out of his pocket.

He did the only thing he could. In the back of his mind he heard Amyus Crowe's voice saying, 'If life gives you lemons, Sherlock, make lemonade. Use whatever you've got to hand to your advantage. Things that seem like problems might actually be solutions to other problems.'

Still holding the reptile by the snout, he slipped his other hand beneath it and grabbed its leg. He took his knee off its tail. Immediately it started to struggle. Before it could wriggle loose from his grasp, he used every ounce of his strength to hoist it into the air. It bucked and twisted, but he held on.

The reeds parted and the girl emerged. Her teeth were bared and her black tongue was extended. Her glittering eyes fixed themselves on Sherlock and she snarled.

So he threw the reptile at her.

It tried to turn in mid-air to bite him, but he had

thrown it too hard and too far for it to reach him. It hit the girl full in the face. Shocked, she fell backwards, hands grabbing at the reptile to contain it. Sensing something warm nearby, the creature turned and tried to bite her. She grabbed at its snout with one hand and its scrabbling claws with the other. From what Sherlock could see of her face she wasn't scared, or even surprised. She was completely focused on defeating this new threat.

The two of them – girl and reptile – disappeared into the reeds. Sherlock could hear the continued sounds of their struggle, growing fainter and fainter as they rolled down the riverbank towards the water. There was a splash, and then a lot of splashing. Then there was silence.

He stood up and stared down at the river. He couldn't see the girl, or the reptile, but he could see Mr Arrhenius. The man was casting off, preparing to sail. He turned and stared up at Sherlock.

'You and that river alligator appear to have solved a problem for me,' he called cheerfully. 'She was getting to be more of a liability than an asset.'

'What you're trying to do is madness!' Sherlock shouted. 'Don't you realize how many people will die?'

Arrhenius shrugged as the boat drifted into the river. 'I do not care. I am being well paid for this. My employers do not care either. After all, they run mines where people die all the time, and factories where people breathe in

267

poisons every day that shorten their lives. As long as they make a profit, death is merely an unfortunate by-product of their business.' He raised his hat. 'You have been an interesting adversary. I trust we will not meet again.'

'I'll stop you!' Sherlock yelled. 'I *will* stop you.'

'Beware the bite of the snake, young man,' Arrhenius warned. He placed his hat back on his head and turned to check the sail.

Wildly, Sherlock plunged down the slope to the river. If he got to Arrhenius, if he could somehow stop the man from leaving, then maybe the ship wouldn't blow up. Arrhenius had seemed to tell the girl that he had to get to the place where the explosion was going to happen – presumably the same place the Governor of the province was going to board the ship – and give a signal. Mud clung to his feet and he almost fell over twice as he made his way down, but he was too late. Arrhenius's boat was out on the river and moving fast. There was an early morning breeze blowing from the coast, and Arrhenius's sails were catching it and pushing him on.

He slammed his fist into his leg in frustration. So near and yet so far.

Hesitating for only a moment, he turned and climbed the bank again. When he got to the path at the top he sprinted back towards where he had left Cameron and Wu Fung-Yi. There was no sign of the girl. If she had survived the fight with the reptile then she must have run off, looking either for her father or for shelter.

Sherlock tried to feel guilty about what he had done – fighting a girl! – but he couldn't. There was something drastically wrong with her. She was more animal than girl, and she was probably better off without Arrhenius. Sherlock had a feeling that she would survive no matter what the circumstances.

He wondered what her name was. It seemed such a trivial thing, but it was hard to think of her as a person without actually knowing.

It took him only a few minutes to reach the boat. He skidded down the bank and leaped for the deck. The two boys were waiting for him.

'What happened?' Cameron asked.

'I'll tell you as we go, but we're in a race,' Sherlock said, gasping for breath. 'We need to cast off, raise sail and head upstream.'

'You're injured,' Cameron observed, looking at the bloody scratches on Sherlock's chest, face and legs.

'Worry about that later. We need to move.'

As Sherlock cast off, Cameron struggled to raise the sail and Wu Fung-Yi took the rudder. Sherlock gasped out as much of the story as he could. 'Arrhenius needs to give a signal to the fake cook on board the *Monocacy*,' Sherlock finished as their boat drifted out into the river and the sail caught the breeze. 'If he's not there the bomb doesn't go off.'

'Why does he need to give a signal in the first place?' Wu called from the rear of the boat. 'Why not just set the explosives off?'

Sherlock thought for a moment. 'The *Monocacy* is a big ship. We know the explosives are stored in the fake water barrels, and that means they're probably stored near the galley, deep inside the ship, where the Head Cook can keep an eye on them. He'll have to light a fuse in order to set off the explosion. He won't know, hidden inside the ship, when the Governor steps on board. He'll need someone off the ship to tell him when to light the fuse – which means he'll probably be looking through a porthole, waiting for that signal.'

'But why can't someone else do it?' Cameron asked, glancing over his shoulder at Sherlock. 'Why does it have to be Arrhenius?'

Sherlock shrugged. 'Maybe Arrhenius doesn't trust anyone else. Or maybe they want to restrict the number of people who are involved with the conspiracy – after all, the more people who know then the more chance that someone will give it away, and this particular plot needs to be kept very secret for it to work.'

'There's something I don't understand,' Cameron said. 'What was my father's role in this? Was he one of the conspirators, or did he find out about it some other way?'

Sherlock mused. 'He was obviously part of it, but he also obviously had a change of heart. Maybe it was supposed to be his job to travel upstream to where the *Monocacy* is moored and give the signal, but he changed his mind. I remember seeing him talking to Arrhenius at the dinner party at your house. Arrhenius seemed angry. Maybe that's when he said that he wasn't going to take part in the conspiracy. I think he decided that he couldn't stomach the loss of life that would result from the explosion. So Arrhenius had him killed, but then Arrhenius had to take his place and give the signal.'

'So he was a hero, in the end?' Cameron asked quietly. 'He tried to do the right thing?'

'Yes,' Sherlock said. 'He did.'

It was possible to see across the river now. The sun wasn't yet visible above the horizon, but the stars had vanished and the sky itself was dark blue rather than black. The river was already filling up with other boats as people took the opportunity to make an early start.

'Which boat belongs to Arrhenius?' Wu asked.

Sherlock and Cameron both scanned all the boats they could see.

'Impossible to tell,' Cameron called back. 'It's still too dark, and they're all too far away. If the plan is to try and

271

intercept him, then we'll probably never make it. He's got a head start on us, and we can't spot which boat is his.'

Sherlock felt his fists clench in frustration. Their only chance was to stop Arrhenius from sending the signal, but if they couldn't spot him, and couldn't catch up with him, then what chance did they have?

The USS *Monocacy* was going to blow up, and people were going to die, and he couldn't do anything to stop it. He felt so powerless.

Sherlock noticed one particular boat which was floating outside the main throng. It was long and thin, and made out of wood that had been painted a bright red. The edges of the boat were decorated with gold paint, and the front had been carved into the head of a dragon: all sharp teeth and flaring nostrils and, bizarrely, strands of beard hanging down beneath its jaw. Ten men were in the boat: eight of them held oars, one operated a rudder at the back while the tenth sat in the front facing backwards with a drum between his knees.

'What's that?' Sherlock asked, pointing.

Cameron looked over. 'It's called a Dragon Boat,' he said. 'Each village has one. They race against one another at festivals.'

'Fast?' Sherlock asked.

'Very,' Wu called from the back of the boat. 'Look

at the muscles on the rowers.'

Sherlock glanced at the Dragon Boat. The oarsmen's arms were thicker than his legs.

'What are they doing out here?' he called to Wu.

'Practice,' Wu replied. 'They practise every morning before they go to work in the fields. There's a big festival coming up.'

'Steer towards them. I want to talk.'

Wu adjusted the rudder to bring them towards the Dragon Boat, while Sherlock and Cameron furled their sail so they wouldn't be carried straight past. The oarsmen and the drummer in the front watched them curiously.

'We need your help,' Sherlock called. 'We need to get upriver quickly.'

The men stared at him.

'I can pay,' he said. He glanced at Cameron, who nodded. 'How much to take us?'

The men briefly conferred. The drummer called across: 'Five *cash*.'

'Agreed,' Sherlock said automatically, not sure how much that was in coins but knowing that he had to get their help.

'Each.'

Sherlock looked at Cameron again. 'Agreed,' he sighed.

'We can't just leave my uncle's boat drifting here!' Wu called from the rudder.

Sherlock nodded. 'We'll leave three of the oarsmen on board. They can take it to the bank. We'll retrieve it later. That'll create room for us to sit. We'll have to row, I'm afraid.'

Cameron shrugged. 'It's a new experience. My life at the moment seems to be full of new experiences.'

Within a few minutes the three of them had swapped with three of the oarsmen, and Wu's uncle's boat was heading for the bank. Other boats diverted around them.

Sherlock glanced at the paddle. It was broad at the base, with a long handle. He hefted it experimentally, then glanced at the drummer. The man was naked to the waist, and as muscular as the rowers. His black hair hung down his back in a plait.

'Whenever you're ready,' Sherlock said.

The drummer grinned at him, then deliberately brought a drumstick down on the drum. A deep *dumm!* vibrated through the boat. He hit it again, with the other stick – *dumm!* The oarsmen all held themselves ready. As the third *dumm!* shook Sherlock's bones all of the oarsmen leaned forward and pushed their oars into the water. Sherlock, Cameron and Wu joined in.

The boat shot forward, white spume splashing up from the bows.

The man holding the rudder steered them so that the boat was heading upriver. Sherlock was amazed at how quickly they picked up speed. Other boats flashed past them, and Sherlock caught momentary visions of faces frozen in various expressions ranging from annoyance to surprise. They were easily travelling three or four times as fast as the other boats. At first he tried to keep a watch out for Mr Arrhenius, but everything began to blur into a continuous stream of images from which it was difficult to pick out anything in particular. Sherlock quickly fell into an exhausting routine of rowing. The muscles in his arms and shoulders burned with the unexpected exercise. The torn flesh on his chest felt as if liquid fire was dripping out of it. Water splashed his face, and he kept licking his lips just to get some moisture into his body. The sound of the drums became the sound of his pulse throbbing in his ears: *dumm! dumm! dumm!*

He glanced over his shoulder to where Cameron sat behind him. Cameron's face was set, his jaw clenched, and his gaze seemed to pass across Sherlock without really recognizing him.

After a period of time that might have been minutes or might have been hours, he heard Wu Fung-Yi's voice calling his name. 'Sherlock! *Sherlock!*'

'What?' he called, shaking his head to clear the fog from it.

'What's that up ahead?'

Sherlock looked past the oarsmen in front of him.

275

Beyond the bows of the Dragon Boat and past the carved wooden head of the dragon itself he saw a great wheel rising from the water.

'It's the *Monocacy*!' His voice was hoarse. 'We've made it! Tell them to steer for the ship!'

The *Monocacy* was stationary, close in to the riverbank. It was moored to a wooden pier. Hills rose up sharply from the edge of the river. Across on the other side were the ruins of what looked like an old military fort. One tower and a few walls still stood, but the rest was rubble.

The Dragon Boat carved its way through the water, heading for the USS *Monocacy*. Sailors on board noticed its approach and guns were trained on the Dragon Boat.

Sherlock motioned to the drummer in the front of the boat to slow the pace down, and bring them to a halt a hundred yards or so away from the ship. He set his oar in the boat and stood up cautiously, feeling the boat rock beneath him. He tried hard to keep his footing: if he fell into the water now then he wasn't sure his arms had the strength to stop him from sinking.

'My name is Sherlock Holmes,' he shouted in English across the water to the sailors. 'I am a British subject. I need to speak to Captain Bryan urgently.'

'Do not approach!' a voice called back. 'If you do you will be fired upon!'

'It is imperative that I speak to Captain Bryan!'

The fact that he knew the Captain's name obviously impressed the sailors. They conferred among themselves, and then eventually someone of higher rank was called.

'My name is Lieutenant MacCrery. What is your message?' he shouted down from his position on the deck of the *Monocacy*.

'Explosives have been hidden on board!' Sherlock yelled.

'*What?*'

'There's a *bomb* on board your *ship!*'

More frantic conferring, then: 'Did you say there's a bomb on board this ship?'

'That's exactly what I said.'

'Come alongside the pier. Be aware: there are weapons trained on you. Any sign of trouble and we will fire!'

Sherlock gestured to the oarsmen to take the boat over to the pier. They obviously couldn't understand what had been said, but they knew that there were guns pointed at them and they were nervous. Sherlock could hear muted discussions behind him along the lines that they ought to have asked for more money.

The Dragon Boat moved closer to the pier. Sherlock waited until they were beside the wooden structure, then he grabbed for a ladder that had been fastened to the side. The USS *Monocacy* rose above him like a dirty white cliff.

'I'll warn Captain Bryan,' he called to Cameron and Wu. 'You two keep an eye out for Mr Arrhenius. He can't be that far behind us, and I'd hate him to give the signal while I was on board.'

'What do we do if we spot him?' Wu asked.

'Raise the alarm,' Sherlock suggested. 'And then go after him.'

'He killed my father,' Cameron pointed out grimly. 'And he killed your father as well. I can think of a whole set of things I want to say to him if I see him.'

'Don't do anything . . . final,' Sherlock suggested. 'We may need him alive to corroborate our story. If we can get him on board the ship then I doubt he'd either want or be able to send the signal to the man with the explosives.' He glanced up at the ship and the cluster of sailors who were waiting for him. 'Wish me luck. This might be the most important and difficult conversation of my life.'

'If Arrhenius is here and we can't find him,' Cameron said, 'it might also be the shortest.'

CHAPTER FIFTEEN

As Sherlock pulled himself up on to the pier he realized that he was more tired than he had ever been in his life. Every muscle in his body ached, and his chest and legs throbbed with pain from where the alligator had scratched him. What he really wanted was to lie down and rest for a while, but he knew that he couldn't.

A gangplank led up from the pier to the *Monocacy*. A group of uniformed sailors were at the top. One of them gestured to him to go up. For a moment he thought about asking them to come down – he wasn't sure his legs could manage the climb – but he needed their help, so it was best that he went to them.

By the time he was halfway up his legs were trembling. By the time he reached the top he had to pull himself forward with his hands.

A group of sailors with rifles stood on deck. The rifles weren't pointed at Sherlock, exactly, but they weren't pointed away either.

As Sherlock caught his breath he noticed Captain Bryan approaching. He was checking his watch and talking with one of his officers. He looked stressed.

Glancing around, Sherlock noticed that there were no Chinese people on deck. The Governor's party obviously hadn't arrived yet, but the way Captain Bryan was looking at his watch suggested that there wasn't long to go.

Bryan's first words seemed to confirm Sherlock's deduction. 'Be quick, young man. I am expecting important guests. You have something to say to me?' He frowned when he saw Sherlock's face clearly for the first time. 'I remember you. I saw you at the dinner party at the Mackenzie residence, and again on the quayside yesterday.'

'Yes, sir. Thank you for coming out to see me.' Sherlock took a deep breath. 'Malcolm Mackenzie is dead. He was murdered because he was going to warn the Prefect of Shanghai about a plot to blow up your ship.'

'Why would anyone want to blow up this ship?' Captain Bryan asked. He scowled. 'No, forget that question – I can think of several reasons. The United States of America is not best liked in this part of the world.'

'Someone wants to get the American Government to interfere militarily in this region,' Sherlock said. 'It's all about trade.'

'Isn't it always?' Bryan replied. He glanced down the gangplank to the pier, and checked his watch again.

'Blast it, the Governor of Jiangsu Province will be here any moment.'

'That's when the bomb will go off,' Sherlock said. 'A signal will be given from somewhere on shore to light the fuse.'

'Where is this bomb?' Bryan barked. One of his officers caught at his arm and muttered something in his ear. Bryan shook his head. 'Doesn't matter whether I believe the kid or not,' he snapped. 'If there's the slightest chance of a bomb on this ship then it needs to be searched. Besides – look at him. He's been through hell to get here. *He* obviously believes the story.'

'I think it's near the galley, disguised in barrels of water,' Sherlock admitted, 'but I might be wrong. It might have been hidden anywhere.'

'Who planted it?'

'Your new Head Cook,' Sherlock said.

Captain Bryan led the way into the body of the ship and down a ladder. For a man who was in overall charge of everything, Sherlock reflected, he was very involved in details. He seemed to want to do everything himself. Sherlock followed, and behind him came a gaggle of officers. They marched along a corridor, around a corner, down another ladder and along another corridor. Sherlock tried to work out where they were in relation to the deck and the pier, and decided that they were on the other side of the ship, near the hull.

Captain Bryan pushed open a door and entered a large room filled with ovens, sinks, work surfaces and hanging pots. It reminded Sherlock of Wu Chung's galley on the *Gloria Scott*, but magnified a hundred times.

The galley was deserted. Captain Bryan clicked his fingers at two of his officers. 'Search everywhere,' he snapped.

On the far side of the galley, a door led into a storage area. Bryan crossed to it, with Sherlock and the rest of the officers close behind. He opened the door and went through.

This was obviously a larder. It was shadowy, lit only by two hanging oil lamps. There were shelves everywhere, stacked with boxes of provisions. Fruit and vegetables hung from hooks, along with legs and sides of pork, lamb and beef. Along the far wall, barrels were lined up and stacked three-deep, except for a space at one end.

'Check those barrels,' Bryan said to the rest of the officers. 'See if they weigh too much or too little. Break them open if you have to.' He glanced around. 'Where's that damned cook? Off smoking his opium pipe or something, I'll be bound.'

Sherlock and Captain Bryan watched for the next five minutes as the officers moved the barrels, shaking them to see if their contents were liquid or solid. The tops had to be prised off some of them with the crowbars hanging from hooks on the wall. Eventually every barrel had been checked. An officer crossed over to where Bryan and Sherlock stood. 'Nothing,' he said, glancing sneeringly at Sherlock. 'The barrels contain water, or rum, or salted meat. That's all.'

Captain Bryan turned to Sherlock. 'Looks like you've been sold a pig in a poke, son,' he said, not unsympathetically.

Sherlock felt his heart sink. He *knew* that his deductions were correct, but he couldn't see how else the explosives had been hidden. But if he didn't find them soon, the signal would be given and the ship would be blown up!

'I don't suppose you would consider evacuating the ship?' he asked.

Two of the officers laughed out loud.

'Just on your say-so?' Captain Bryan asked. ''Fraid not, son. That would be an insult to the Governor, who should be here any moment. Nice try, though.'

Sherlock wished that he could see the far bank, in case Arrhenius was out there, ready to give the signal. Perhaps seeing the man, and recognizing him from the dinner party, would be enough to convince the Captain that *something* was going on. Then Sherlock realized that there was no porthole in the larder, despite the fact

283

that by his reckoning they were right by the hull.

'Does it strike you,' he said, 'that this larder is smaller than it should be?'

The officers and Captain Bryan looked around critically. They glanced at each other with puzzled expressions. 'Now that you come to mention it . . .' one of them said, and tailed off, confused.

Sherlock indicated the far wall, against which the barrels had been stacked. 'I think you'll find that's a false wall,' he said. 'I think the explosives are behind it.'

The officers stared at each other, then set to work with the crowbars.

Sherlock was right. It took less than a minute to pull it down.

Behind the fake wall was a space about six feet deep. It was filled with barrels, and this time Sherlock didn't think that the contents would be water, rum or salted meat. A cord led out of each barrel. The cords all joined together into a braid which ran to a space on one side. Crouching in the space, below a porthole that let in a blaze of light from outside, was a Chinese man in a chef's uniform. He had the braid of fuses in his hand and a frightened expression on his face. Next to him, on the floor, was a box of matches.

'Arrest that man!' Captain Bryan barked. 'And for heaven's sake pull the fuses from those barrels before something disastrous happens!'

The Chinese cook tried to run for the door, but two of the officers grabbed him. They carried him out of the larder. Another officer scooped up the box of matches while the remainder went from barrel to barrel pulling the fuses out.

'How did he get in there by himself?' Bryan mused in wonder. 'And how did he intend escaping once he had lit the fuses? Surely he wasn't going to sacrifice himself?'

'I doubt it,' Sherlock replied. He indicated the corner of the hidden area where the man had been hiding. 'I think there was a hidden door there. Remember, there was a space there with no barrels in it. I think he was waiting for a signal to light the fuse, then he was going to escape into the larder, close the hidden door, jump into the water and swim away.'

'And he built all this himself?' Bryan asked, gazing at the fake wall.

'It didn't have to be convincing,' Sherlock pointed out. 'It was covered with barrels. He probably brought it on in sections.'

'Son, I owe you a debt of gratitude. If not for you, this ship would be a pile of flaming wreckage and hundreds of men would be dead.'

'And a war would be about to start,' Sherlock said quietly. He crossed to the porthole and gazed out.

He could see all the way to the far side of the Yangtze River . . . where a boat with two lanterns on the mast was tied up to the bank, just next to the ruined fort.

'Captain,' he said quietly, 'do you have a small rowing boat I can borrow?'

Ten minutes later Sherlock was climbing down a ladder attached to the side of the *Monocacy* and stepping into a boat that had been lowered down on ropes. Captain Bryan had wanted to send someone with him, but the Governor of Jiangsu Province had just arrived with his retinue, and all hands were required on deck for an official inspection. So while an important visitor was coming up the gangplank, Sherlock was secretly slipping away on the other side of the ship.

His arms still ached, and he found that rowing across the river pulled at his muscles in a way that sent spikes of pain across his chest and back. He was heading at right angles to the normal flow of boats, and he had to keep on stopping to allow other vessels to go past. Even so, there were a lot of shouts and curses directed his way.

He kept looking out for Cameron and Wu Fung-Yi, but there was no sign of them. If they were still looking for Mr Arrhenius then they were looking in the wrong place.

Eventually Sherlock's boat hit the bank on the other side of the river. He climbed out and secured it.

Reluctantly he trudged up the muddy riverbank and stood in front of the stone ruins of the fort. He really didn't want to do this. Every muscle in his body felt like it was on the verge of giving up, and the gashes across his chest, where the blood had coagulated, had pulled apart and started bleeding again while he had been rowing. His head ached where the girl had kicked it, and he was getting a fluttery sensation at the edges of his vision. But he knew that he *had* to do this. If he didn't, then Arrhenius would get away, and that wasn't right. Not after the murders of Sherlock's friend Wu Chung and Cameron's father.

Sometimes, he thought, doing the right thing was much harder than doing the wrong thing. Sometimes, doing the right thing was the hardest thing in the world.

Not looking forward to what he was going to find, he trudged around the half-ruined wall of the fort until he came to an archway that led inside.

Grass was growing up between the stones. There was no roof, and the remnants of the walls were barely higher than Sherlock's head. There were gaps in many places, where time and weather had caused the mortar holding the stones together to crumble.

Two Chinese soldiers were lying on the ground in the first room he came to – a large, hall-like area. Sherlock crouched by them. They were both unconscious; both

287

had bleeding gashes in their scalps. He suspected that they were guards who were assigned to the ruins, or perhaps they were part of a team stationed along the riverbank in preparation for the arrival of the Governor. Whatever the reason for their presence, it was bad luck for them. Neither of them was armed, and that worried Sherlock. Presumably Arrhenius had taken their weapons after overpowering them.

Having made sure that the two unconscious soldiers were at least comfortable, he moved on through a doorway into another room.

This room was as large as the first one. Mr Arrhenius was there, standing by a glassless window that overlooked the river. He was holding a lamp, and he was patiently opening and closing its shutter in a regular sequence, sending flashes of light across the river to the USS *Monocacy*.

Where nothing was happening.

'I presume you have managed to alert the ship's crew to the presence of the explosives,' Arrhenius said in his high-pitched voice. He didn't turn his head. 'I presume also that the crew have discovered the location of the explosives, despite the meticulous way they were hidden, and apprehended the agent who was waiting to light the fuse. I presume all of this because of the obvious lack of any explosion, despite the fact that I can see the Governor's entourage on deck and I have been signalling the agent for the past five minutes.' He set the lantern on the stone sill of the window and turned to face Sherlock. 'The agent was told that the fuse burned for five minutes, giving him time to make his escape,' he continued. 'In fact, it only burns for thirty seconds. In five minutes, someone might have discovered it and put it out.'

'Not,' Sherlock said, 'a problem now, I am afraid.'

'Apparently not.' Arrhenius sighed. 'You really are an impressive young man. You would not believe the amount of time, effort and cold, hard cash that has been expended on this plan. Then you come along and sabotage it just by –' he shrugged – 'just by observation and deduction. Really very impressive.' He reached behind him, to where Sherlock saw something propped up against the wall. 'Impressive, and troublesome. I think I will save the world the bother of dealing with you in the future by eliminating you now. That way, I will at least have accomplished *something* today.'

He brought his hands out from behind his back. He was holding a long wooden staff, Sherlock saw, but it ended in a strangely shaped metal blade. It looked very sharp. He must have taken it from one of the unconscious soldiers.

'Please,' Arrhenius said, 'try to resist. Try to escape.

That will make this process much more entertaining for me.'

'What happened to the girl?' Sherlock asked, stepping to one side. Distracting Arrhenius, delaying him from attacking, was, he decided, his best option.

His best option among a small group of very unsatisfactory options, his mind couldn't help adding.

Arrhenius turned slowly to follow him, holding the bladed weapon in front of him like an executioner at rest. 'My daughter? Oh, I presume she is still out there, somewhere back along the river.'

'And you don't care?'

'The older she grew, the more wilful she became. I was beginning to lose control of her. It was only a matter of time before she left me. The only question in my mind was whether she would try to kill me first, or merely disappear. By abandoning her – at your instigation, of course – I merely anticipated and controlled an unavoidable outcome.'

Sherlock shook his head. 'But . . . your own *daughter*?'

Arrhenius shrugged. 'Oh, I have no fatherly feelings for the girl. Her mother died in childbirth. Her own development was affected by the large amounts of colloidal silver that I had consumed, and that I fed to her as she was growing up. She was never normal, never like other children. She would never have grown up happy,

I am afraid.' He stepped forward, swinging the blade at Sherlock's legs. 'Just as you will never grow up at all!'

Sherlock flung himself backwards on to the flagstones. The blade whistled through the air, missing him by an inch. He tried to struggle to his feet, pushing his body forward and upward on his elbows, but Arrhenius rushed at him again, bringing the blade swishing down towards Sherlock's head.

He rolled sideways. The blade slammed into the flagstone. Sparks and fragments of stone exploded upwards. Sherlock felt them pepper his face, drawing blood, as he rolled.

Arrhenius seemed momentarily shocked by the vibrations from the impact of the blade on the stone. His face twisted in pain. Sherlock took the chance to climb to his feet and stagger away.

Holding the staff like a spear, Arrhenius turned and lunged at Sherlock, with the blade aimed directly at the boy's heart. With only a moment to work out what to do, Sherlock decided that his best option was to dive at Arrhenius's feet, tucking himself into a ball as he did so. Arrhenius tried to jump over Sherlock, but tripped and fell over the boy's rolling body. Sherlock sprang to his feet before Arrhenius could react and scrambled away on hands and knees.

He was by the wall now, the wall with the hole in

291

it looking out on to the river. On the floor near where Arrhenius had been standing Sherlock could see a sword. Arrhenius must have taken it from the second unconscious soldier. Sherlock scooped it up, hefting it experimentally in his hand. The blade was strangely shaped compared to the European swords that he was used to, but things were desperate and he didn't have much choice.

Sword in hand, heart thumping, Sherlock stepped forward.

Arrhenius suddenly reversed the staff and jabbed several times at Sherlock's chest with the blunt end. Startled, Sherlock parried with his sword, carving chunks out of the wood, but one of the jabs hit him right on his breastbone. He thought his heart had stopped, the impact was so hard. He staggered backwards, desperately trying to catch his breath.

Abruptly Arrhenius swung the staff around, bringing the sharp blade down at Sherlock's forehead. Sherlock could hear the air hiss as the blade carved through it.

He brought the sword up, holding it two-handed, so that it intercepted the blade. The impact drove him to his knees.

Using every last ounce of his strength, he forced his way back to his feet, pushing Arrhenius's blade up. For a long moment they both stood there, frozen like statues.

Sherlock's muscles screamed at the exertion.

Gradually Arrhenius pushed his blade closer and closer to Sherlock's face. Sherlock could see the liquid gleam of light on the sharp edge. Arrhenius's face was contorted into a snarl: blackened lips pulled back over teeth that glittered like metal. His irises were so dark they were almost black.

'I think you've been driven mad by the silver you've drunk,' Sherlock grunted. 'I think it's clogged your mind, like some kind of metallic sludge. You don't think like a human being any more. You don't *care* about people, just like your daughter doesn't care.'

'I have news for you,' Arrhenius hissed. 'I never did. Emotion doesn't pay the bills. Only silver does that.'

He stepped back abruptly, pulling his staff away and then swinging it around low, chopping at Sherlock's knees. Sherlock parried. The *clang* as the blades met echoed back and forth between the stone walls of the fort.

Arrhenius took two steps backwards. He didn't seem to be breathing heavily – in fact his grey-black lips were twisted in something approximating a smile – but Sherlock's lungs were burning with the effort of taking in air.

'Give it up, child,' Arrhenius said calmly. 'You can struggle, and then I will kill you, or you can lay down

293

the sword now, and I will kill you. Either way you will be dead, but you can save yourself a lot of pain and stress on the journey.'

'You killed my friend,' Sherlock said through clenched teeth. 'And you killed my friend's father.'

'I didn't kill either of them, not directly, although I will grant you that I did *organize* their deaths.' He paused, considering. 'I do not think that I have ever killed anybody directly.' He smiled. 'Until now, that is. This will be my first. I must say that I am looking forward to it. It will be interesting to find out what it actually feels like – taking another life. Thank you for giving me the opportunity.'

'You're welcome,' Sherlock said. 'But don't expect it to be easy.'

'Nothing worthwhile ever is.' Arrhenius made a small motion with his bladed staff. 'Now, shall we finish this? With the failure of the plan to blow up the USS *Monocacy* I am short several hundred thousand dollars in payments. I will need to start building diplomatic bridges with my employers if I want to keep on working.'

Sherlock opened his mouth to say something meaningless to delay the inevitable, but Arrhenius abruptly swung his staff around, aiming the blade at Sherlock's face. Sherlock jerked his sword up, blocking the blow, but the impact knocked him sideways, twisting him around. His shoulder slammed into the wall. His sword dropped from numbed fingers, clattering on the floor.

'Goodbye, Master Holmes,' Arrhenius said. He kicked the sword away. It skittered across the flagstones. Arrhenius hefted his bladed staff like a spear. The point was aimed at Sherlock's heart. Sherlock felt stone, cold and hard against his back. It seemed to be sucking the warmth, even the life, from him.

Sherlock let his hands drop to his sides. This was it. The game was over.

His fingers brushed against something in his right-hand pocket: a hard-edged, metal object. He slipped his hand inside the pocket and closed his fingers over it, feeling the rough edges. Feeling a sudden flush of hope.

'Goodbye, Mr Arrhenius,' he said.

He pulled the object out and raised it up to his face. With a flick of his thumb, Sherlock operated the spring mechanism. The jaws snapped wide open. His thumb found the rubber bulb inside and jabbed it, hard.

A spray of snake venom arced across the few inches between Sherlock and Arrhenius. Droplets splattered into Arrhenius's eyes. He screamed, dropping his bladed staff and clutching his hands over his face. He staggered backwards, still screaming.

'For God's sake!' Arrhenius cried. 'The pain! The *pain*!

Kill me! *Kill me now!* I'm begging you – *kill me now!*

'Not in cold blood,' Sherlock said quietly. 'That's not the kind of person I am.'

Arrhenius collapsed to his knees and he writhed, and screamed, and cried, and fell forward, so that he was lying on his face on the stone slabs that made up the floor of the ruined fort. Eventually Arrhenius stopped moving. Only then did Sherlock turn and walk away.

CHAPTER SIXTEEN

Three days later, Sherlock was sitting on an empty crate on the quayside, looking at the *Gloria Scott*. European sailors and Chinese dock workers were scurrying all over her like ants, checking the rigging and the sails, and carrying barrels and crates up the gangplank.

'She'll be leaving tomorrow,' Cameron said from beside him.

'I know,' Sherlock replied.

'You're going to be on her?'

He nodded. 'I thought about staying,' he said. 'But there's too much waiting for me back home. My brother, my friends . . .'

'And that girl,' Wu Fung-Yi said from Sherlock's other side. 'The one you don't talk about.'

'Then how do you know there's a girl?' Sherlock asked.

'Because you're going back,' Wu said with unarguable logic.

Sherlock turned to look at Cameron. 'What about you?' he asked. 'Do you think you'll stay here in Shanghai?'

Cameron shrugged. 'I doubt it,' he said eventually.

297

'I think Mother wants to go back to America. I must admit, I would like to see the place. I want to see if it's as big as everyone says.'

'And you're staying?' Sherlock asked, turning to Wu.

The Chinese boy nodded. 'My mother needs me. I'm all she has left. So I'll stay. Maybe I'll learn to cook, like my father. Maybe I'll do something else. Mother wants me to take the examinations for the Civil Service, but that costs a lot of money and takes a lot of time.'

'But if you get in,' Cameron observed, 'then you're made for life. No more financial worries, ever.'

Wu smiled, and nodded. 'My father would be proud,' he said, 'if . . .'

'Yes,' Cameron said quietly. 'If.'

'Write to me,' Sherlock said. 'If you can. If you get the chance. I'll give you the address.'

The three boys sat there for a while in silence, each thinking his own thoughts.

'Anyone fancy lunch?' Cameron asked eventually. 'I'm getting hungry.'

'One of the fishing boats brought a catch of squid in earlier,' Wu said. 'Fried in ginger and soy sauce, it's wonderful. You can't beat it.'

'Better than bacon and eggs?'

'Far better.'

298

The two boys stood up. 'You coming?' Cameron asked Sherlock.

'I'll follow in a while,' he said. 'Save some squid for me.'

The two boys walked off, arguing and shoving, and Sherlock watched them go with a smile on his face. It had never occurred to him that he would find friends as good as Matty and Virginia, but he had. Maybe he always would, wherever he went.

He thought about what he would tell Matty and Virginia about his adventures when he got back to England. He thought about the voyage out, the storm and the pirate attack, and he thought about the experiences he'd been through in Shanghai, and along the Yangtze River. So much to tell.

The pirate attack. Something still bothered him about that. It was the way he'd found that pirate searching Mr Arrhenius's cabin, apparently looking for the coded message intended for Malcolm Mackenzie. The pirate had known it was there, which suggested that the entire pirate attack had been mounted just so they could get hold of that message. But who had the reach and influence to organize Chinese pirates to attack a trading ship so they could get hold of a coded message?

The Paradol Chamber, of course.

They had abducted Sherlock in the first place, and put

him on the *Gloria Scott*. Sherlock had been assuming all this time that they had done it for revenge, to punish him for the way he had interfered with their plans, but maybe there was more to it than that. Maybe the Paradol Chamber had found out about the plot to blow up an American ship and wanted to stop it. Maybe a war between America and China didn't suit their plans, and they decided to interfere.

Was that the real reason the Paradol Chamber had placed Sherlock on the *Gloria Scott*? Had he inadvertently been working for them all this time? But surely with a reach like theirs, they could have stopped it in some other way? They didn't need a boy from England or some Chinese pirates to do it?

He smiled. It didn't matter, not really. He and Cameron and Wu had saved lives and prevented a war. It didn't matter whose idea it had been. They had done the right thing.

''Scuse me.'

He glanced up. A man was standing in front of him. He was wearing typical sailor's clothes, and judging by their sun-bleached, salt-caked look, and the tanned look of his skin, he had recently disembarked from a ship. Sherlock looked him up and down, and quickly characterized him, based on what he could see. Born in Yorkshire, but living in London. Married. Five

300

children. Mother alive but father died recently.

'Yes?' he said politely.

'Is your name Holmes? *Sherlock* Holmes?'

He straightened up. 'Yes. Yes it is.'

The man held out an envelope. It had been folded and refolded many times, and there was dirt in the creases of the folds, as well as water stains and candle wax on the thick brown paper. 'This is for you. I brought it all the way from England. I was given it.'

Sherlock's mouth was suddenly dry, and his heart was beating faster than it had when he had fought Mr Arrhenius. 'Thanks . . .' he said, reaching out to take it. His other hand delved into his pocket. 'Here, look, I should—'

The man shook his head. 'Don't worry. I've been paid well to deliver it. I've been working for your brother for several years now, travelling around the world for him. He told me not to take any money from you. He said, "Tell the young man that he needs to conserve his money if he is to have any hope of getting home in one piece."'

Sherlock laughed. The sailor's impression of his brother Mycroft was spot-on. 'Thanks,' he said. 'I appreciate it.'

The sailor looked around. 'You've been here a while,' he said. 'Any tips?'

'Apparently,' Sherlock said, 'the squid is very good.'

The sailor frowned, then nodded and walked off. Sherlock noticed that his legs were still not used to dry land.

With hands that trembled a little bit more than he would have liked, Sherlock opened the envelope. From it he pulled out a letter, and a smaller envelope. Putting the smaller envelope to one side he began to read the letter.

My dear Sherlock,

This is one of several letters that I have sent by various hands to many different destinations along your route, in the hope that at least one will reach you. If you receive more than one then please waste no effort in reading the others — they all say the same things. And before you ask, yes I did write all of these letters myself, rather than have them copied out by a secretary. It was a great deal of effort, but I felt that I should at least do something in acknowledgement of the harsh experiences that you have undoubtedly been through.

Your tutor, Mr Crowe, your aunt and uncle, and your friends Matthew

and Virginia have all enjoined me to pass on their best regards to you. Virginia in particular has asked me to enclose a letter with mine specifically from her. I do feel that I ought to prepare you for its contents. You have been gone for some time now — perhaps longer than you realize — and things have changed. Amyus Crowe has been forced to take on other pupils in order to earn a living, and Virginia has become particularly close to one of them — the son of an American businessman working in Guildford. His name is Aaron Wilson Jr, and he has asked Virginia to marry him. I am sorry to tell you that she has agreed . . .

Sherlock lowered the letter. His hand was trembling. He picked up the second envelope. The writing on the front was delicate, feminine. One minute ago, knowing that it was a message from Virginia, nothing could have prevented him from reading it. Now, having seen Mycroft's message, the last thing in the world he wanted to do was to open it.

But it was too late. The message had been conveyed. The genie had been released from the bottle.

He swallowed, and stared at the *Gloria Scott*, as it was being readied for the voyage home.

How could a few words change his world so completely?

How could his heart be broken so quickly by someone so far away?

Slowly he crumpled the half-read letter from Mycroft, and the unopened envelope from Virginia, as he stared blindly out at the bustling activity on the quayside.

AUTHOR'S NOTE

Five books. I never thought I'd make it to five books about Sherlock Holmes as a teenager, but I have, and there are more to go. At least *one* more and (Macmillan Children's Books willing) possibly another three or more on top of that. I've got to get Sherlock back from China in one piece, which might take some time, and then I've got to somehow resolve the issue of the Paradol Chamber. And, of course, there's what's happened with Virginia – how will that affect Sherlock's character? (Those of you who have read some or all of the Conan Doyle stories will, of course, know the answer to that one.)

Arthur Conan Doyle, who wrote the original Sherlock Holmes stories, told us that Sherlock was (by his mid-twenties) an expert swordsman, boxer, martial arts fighter, chemist, actor and violinist. I've managed, in the five books I've written about Sherlock's early life so far, to lay the groundwork for his boxing, his acting, his martial arts and his violin playing. I still have to do some work on his swordsmanship and his love of chemistry, and that's two different books right there.

As usual, I've tried to make the book as accurate as

possible, so rather than rely on what I thought China in the 1860s was like (based largely on an old Japanese TV series set in China and called *The Water Margin* that was shown, badly dubbed, in the UK when I was growing up) I have read an awful lot of books about the subject in an attempt to get the feeling right. Some of these are modern books looking back at China over a hundred years ago, while others were written by people who travelled in the Far East at about the right time.

The most useful of the modern-day books were, just for your interest:

The Opium War: Drugs, Dreams and the Making of China by Julia Lovell (Picador, 2011). An absolutely brilliantly written and exhaustively researched book about the hypocrisy and disgraceful double-dealing that characterized Britain's relationship with China. Sadly, she does have an unjustified pop at the fictional character of Fu Manchu in the last chapters – I always loved Fu Manchu – but apart from that it's immaculate.

The Scramble for China: Foreign Devils in the Qing Empire, 1832–1914 by Robert Bickers (Allen Lane, 2011). This is a good, albeit idiosyncratically written history of Western relationships with China.

Chinese Characters by Sarah Lloyd (HarperCollins, 1987). This brilliant book is, on the face of it, a travelogue of Sarah Lloyd's time in China, but it's also a meditation on Chinese people, Chinese history, the Chinese character and all kinds of things, and all written in clear but poetic prose. I read it because a lot of China now, especially the fields and farms, is not that different from the way it was in Sherlock's time. Well worth reading.

The most useful period book was:

A Lady's Captivity Among Chinese Pirates by Fanny Loviot (National Maritime Museum, 2008) – a supposedly true account of a Victorian lady who travelled from England to America and then to China, and was allegedly captured by pirates. How true the events actually are is a matter for debate . . .

Believe it or not, the disfiguring disease suffered by Mr Arrhenius is real. I wouldn't dare make up something that bizarre. It's called *argyria*, and you can look it up on the internet and even see pictures of people who suffer from it. More and more people nowadays are taking silver to try and ward off diseases, so *argyria* might well be something that's on the increase.

The USS *Monocacy* was a real American warship that was stationed in the Far East in the late 1860s and early 1870s. It did travel up the Yangtze River on a mapping expedition at around the time that I've set this book (actually, I may have fudged it by a year or two, for the sake of the plot). The ship was built in 1864, and remained in service until 1903, when she was sold to a Japanese businessman. Henry Francis Bryan was her captain for a few years. He went on to become the Governor of Samoa.

What else? The animals that Sherlock comes across during his adventures on the Yangtze River are real ones – the Yangtze River Dolphin (or *Baiji*) and the Yangtze River Alligator. The *Baiji* is in terminal decline at the moment, thanks to fishing and to pollution in the river. It may even be extinct. Oh, and a note for true Sherlockians here – the *Gloria Scott* in this story is not the same one as mentioned in the Arthur Conan Doyle story 'The Adventure of the *Gloria Scott*'. That boat was sunk in 1855 on its way to Australia. No, this is a different *Gloria Scott*. Why is it a different *Gloria Scott*? The simple answer is because I wanted to call it by the name of another ship mentioned in Conan Doyle's stories – the *Matilda Briggs* – but I remembered the wrong name, and by the time I noticed that I had remembered the wrong name it was too late to change it. It's as simple (and as stupid) as that.

A note on Chinese pronunciation, while I'm here. And Chinese names as well. In Sherlock's time, the way that Chinese sounds were converted to English was known as the Wade-Giles system (the Chinese language has sounds in it which don't occur in English). It was developed by Thomas Francis Wade, a British ambassador to China who published the first Chinese textbook in English in 1867. The system was refined in 1912 by Herbert Allen Giles (hence Wade-Giles). The Wade-Giles system was replaced with the Pinyin system in the 1950s. The problem is that the two systems can give quite different results from the same Chinese word. For instance, the city known as Peking in the Wade-Giles system suddenly became Beijing in the Pinyin system (you can see that they sound similar, but they aren't the same). Similarly, Mao Tse-tung, who controlled China between 1949 and 1976, suddenly became Mao Zedong. I've largely used the Wade-Giles system in this book, rather than the Pinyin system, because it's the one Sherlock and Cameron Mackenzie would have been familiar with. This does, unfortunately, give some of the names of the Chinese characters (Wu Chung, Wu Fung-Yi) an old-fashioned sound (Wu Chung would be Wu Zhong in the Pinyin system, while Wu Fung-Yi would have been the rather similar Wu Feng-Yi). Chinese names have the surname first, by the way, so while Sherlock *Holmes* is the son of Siger *Holmes*, *Wu* Fung-Yi is the son of *Wu* Chung. (Chinese women of the time typically kept their own names, which is why Tsi Huen doesn't have a Wu anywhere.) All clear? (You might be tested on this later.)

In an earlier book I talked a little bit about money in Victorian England. In China of the late Imperial period (which is when this book is set) the Emperor maintained a silver and a copper currency system. The copper coins were called *cash* (although funnily enough that probably isn't where we get the word 'cash' from). The silver system had several coins: the *tael*, the *mace*, the *candareen* and the *li*. (If you ever find yourself in late Imperial China, remember that 1 *tael* = 10 *mace* = 100 *candareens* = 1,000 *li* – a decimal system.)

So, where does all this leave us? Well, Sherlock has to get home, of course. He will undoubtedly have all kinds of adventures on the way (I think he will probably end up in Japan for several months, and maybe India), but those stories may never be told – or not told by me, at any rate. I think that the next book – the sixth one – will take place back in England, and I think it will involve the Paradol Chamber again (and perhaps mark the reappearance of a particular villain from previous stories). One thing is for sure, though – when Sherlock gets home he will be older and wiser, and a lot sadder.